ALSO BY KATHE KOJA

The Cipher (1991)

Bad Brains (1992)

Skin (1993)

Strange Angels (1994)

KATHE KOJA

KINK

A NOVEL

HENRY HOLT AND COMPANY
NEW YORK

Henry Holt and Company, Inc.
Publishers since 1866
115 West 18th Street
New York, New York 10011

Henry Holt ® is a registered
trademark of Henry Holt and Company, Inc.

Published in Canada by Fitzhenry & Whiteside Ltd.,
195 Allstate Parkway, Markham, Ontario L3R 4T8.

Library of Congress Cataloging-in-Publication Data
Koja, Kathe.
Kink: a novel / Kathe Koja.
p.   cm.
I. Title.
PS3561.0376K56   1996   95-46874
813'.54—dc20   CIP

ISBN 0-8050-4391-8

Henry Holt books are available for special promotions and
premiums. For details contact: Director, Special Markets.

First Edition—1996

DESIGNED BY KELLY SOONG

Printed in the United States of America
All first editions are printed on acid-free paper. ∞

1 3 5 7 9 10 8 6 4 2

To and for

Rick and Aaron

Acknowledgments

I would like to thank Chris Koja and Doug Clegg,
for their encouragement, and Allen Peacock and
Rick Lieder, for vision of various kinds.

I hate the aesthetics of the world. I create the enclosure that becomes the world.

—JOEL-PETER WITKIN

1

SACRED JEST

$\mathcal{I}$n bed we hear them: half-laughter, voices, TV noise and their own beneath it, movements unseen but felt as vibration: feet across a floor, soft thud of fucking as we lie together, Sophie cramped and cradled, long bare legs canted high around my hips and: *thump*, *boom*, finding a rhythm, fucking harder past Sophie's silent laughter, rag-doll head nudging, digging, nestling like a fist beside my own and "Maybe they're finally using the vibrator," whisper and giggle, pink lips to my ear. "Swizzle stick," and making me laugh, cold tickling fingers beneath the blanket as above the neighbors unseen in frieze, maybe they're doing it dog-style, frog-style, butterfly fuck, they can't hear us listening, they don't know what we know and afterward maybe they'll sulk or call each other names or maybe say nothing, get up and get out, all movements in cadence, the mimic of ours as slow and wet, whisper and giggle, in and out we start to do it too: footsteps and rushing toilet, TV off and the sound of the closing door and already Sophie's coming, fingernail tinsnips pinching my back and sides, pinching to leave welts and bumps and bruises blunt as scars, and I'm coming too, my mouth over hers as if I'm breathing for her, of her, through her, slack lips and strong wet thighs in the sound of descent, stairway voices and someone walking in the hall, Sophie kicking light and soundless at the covers, layers of pink-and-black satin, pale and panting and damp below: and silent above, they're gone now but they'll be back and when they are we'll know because we'll hear.

Because we'll be listening. Listening is part of the game.

Sophie taught me the game, I taught her, we taught each other. Not a real game, a contest with rules or a way to lose or even a way to win because the whole point was instead a way of seeing, of being, of knowing that nothing was serious, everything was a game, *we* were the game and all of it a dare: known when? with Sophie curled beside me on a night too hot to move, fourth-floor walk-up sickly with the day's dead air and the air conditioner junked again, again and no money to escape, go somewhere cool, hide in the cool and the dark, even a movie was too expensive. So broke so much of the time, so much money just to live, keep eating, keep going and Sophie sullen, cheeks clown-pink and some kind of rash on her breasts, cosmetic sweat and "I'll get us a beer," I said, sitting up, sheets peeling like skin in the motion. "You want a beer?"

"There isn't any," Sophie said.

Refrigerator air against my body, cold the first second then damp, basement-feel and all I could find was mineral water, limp dried-up lemon, but I tried, long-stemmed glasses carried back to bed to find Sophie flung arms out, murder-victim front-page posture and her dry stare, no hand out to take the glass: "What's that?"

"Mineral water." Cloudy with lemon, it looked like soap and "I don't want that," big lips pulled down, clown face, child face and "I'm *sick* of this," she said, not moving, staring, staring at me as I put down the glasses, sat beside her, empty presence on the sheets. "Jess, I just, I don't want to live like this, nobody wants to live like this . . . look at this place, *look* at it," sitting up now, back-hinge bounce and how beautiful she was, rashed and speckled breasts, long legs like a teenager's and rising, tilting forward in half-crouch and something said I didn't hear, head bent and "Sophie," I said, my smile helpless, "Sophie, look at me."

In that crouch, sprung posture and: "What?" but not unwilling: only demanding: *what?* and my hands on her forearms, sweat to sweat and "Come on," I said, "get your drink, come on," and I took my own drink and went to the window, sat on the sill, slim square to stare outside at all the motion, who can rest in this heat? and Sophie now beside me, standing not sitting, stilled motion of her breast close to my face.

"Look down there," I said.

"Why?" but she sat, wine glass and lean damp thigh and "Look," I said, pointing with my own glass, trying to make magic for her, "pick someone down there, anyone. Pick anybody and tell me what they're like."

At once disappointment, her flat frown: "Oh, come on—"

"No, wait," pointing again, "just wait a minute, take a look, look at those two." A man and a woman, her cropped hair, his breezy stride and they were sharing a bottle of something, fat-bottomed green bottle, champagne? Drinking, and kissing, and drinking again and when he said something she laughed, big horse laugh to make Sophie smile and "Maybe they're lovers," I said, "maybe they just got married and now they—"

"Of course they're lovers, look at them," and Sophie's smile almost tender for these strangers, drinking without attention her own stale drink and I wanted champagne for her, for me, for both of us; the ignorance of desire, *I want* so go on, jump out of the window, naked grab for that bottle and up again, fire-escape monkey, how do you like me now, sweetheart? and Sophie's murmur, poking me, *Jess listen* and the woman was laughing again, big laugh as they passed beneath us and "Oh right," she was saying, mirth still but no kindness, rich accent from some other, hotter place, "oh right," as "I *told* him," the man drunk, loud, floundering in her contempt, "I told him, I *said* I was gonna—" and gone: "See?" Sophie sweet and wise, nudging me with one damp elbow. "I told you they were lovers."

Pick someone else then; and again scanning the street, loose knot of kids arguing, play fight and "*Fuck* you, man!" shoving their way to the corner and gone and a car passing, an empty cab, a guy with a dirty little dog on the end of a long, black leash and Sophie's swallow and sigh, stem between fingers and without warning she smashed the glass, one fierce motion to the floor and then up, crossing the room to the armoire, grandma's furniture in black and brass and reaching inside, pale sleeveless shift to yank down over her bare body and "Come on," kicking into sandals, brushing with both careless hands the tangle of her hair. "Come on, let's go."

Go where? but I didn't say it, said nothing and she barely waited for me to pull on a T-shirt, keys in pocket and down the stairs, as hot outside as in but on the street things were a little better, at least the illusion of breeze, air moving, something moving and "Here," tugging me with our linked hands, bright grimy deli, dull flies on the fruit salad and she bought a forty-ounce bottle of beer, Crystal Lager and mountain streams, nothing could be as nice as that label looked and we found a spot to sit, cracked bench and her knee to mine, bottle in both her hands the way a child might drink: stretched fingers on brown glass, big knuckles and big feet too, see in her sandals the long freakish elegance of those toes. No talk, just the beer back and forth and her head on my shoulder, moist leg against mine and without saying a word, saying nothing at all she took my hand and placed it very lightly, very gently in her lap, placed it so I could feel the heat there, the special and particular warmth and "Touch me," she said, voice sweet and soft and almost drowsy, *touch me* and so I did, beer in one hand and the other in motion, tight little circles, seashell whorl: her body in the dress grown more and more still, taut flesh stretched from one pleasure to the next and everyone was looking—midnight kids yelling one to another, people passing in cabs and on foot and we there with our beer and her head on my shoulder, my finger moving, stroking and for me it was just like watching from the window, watching them watch us but oh what they saw, didn't see, didn't know, as if we were in some other place, bell jar, TV screen that anyone can watch but no one can touch and I felt like laughing, the voyeur inside out and Sophie's head tilting, just a little, *en pointe* chin and I saw her bite her lip, *oh* and kiss of moisture through her dress, warm fingertip and she sighed, reaching now to take from me the beer and drink the last of it, foam and pointing with the bottle at the people going by: "They don't know," she said, "nobody knows."

"Knows what?"

"What we know," and we rose then, got up and got home and slept naked by the breezeless window, slept till a storm woke us to stand, still naked, in the thunder and chilly drench, Sophie's hair stuck slick to her face and a puddle on the floor, water on the walls and "Listen to that!" her eyes sparkling, big smile in the strobe, body white with lightning flash and some voice, some guy yelling up from the street "Hey baby!": hey baby and when the lightning flashed again it was me he saw, just as naked and Sophie crouched laughing where he couldn't see, didn't know, couldn't tell and that was part of the game, too.

From then on it was something we knew we were doing, no more than what had gone before yet understood now, felt as conscious play; like a cipher decoded, vision once changed is changed forever, you could see nothing else, make magic of anything and in a way we did: our crummy jobs—both temps at that time, pre-AmBiAnce—and the hideous flat and the neighbors too loud, fighting or fucking above and through the jumble of their TVs and music, strange blend of sounds to us in our bed as we made stories around them, about them, made fun of the stories we made because everything was fair game, everything there to be mocked or scrambled, turned around on itself and inside out: nothing sacred but the jest because the joke was a joke on itself, on us too even as we made it: we knew about irony, we knew about the magic that's no magic at all but effort, grunt and strain and push out the laugh like a dead baby grinning at the farce and Sophie's own magic, I thought, was always stronger than mine, wilder—as mine was, what? Sharper? more focused, harder at its heart? Meaner, Sophie would say, she used to say I had a mean streak and maybe I did but never for her; I never hurt Sophie, I loved Sophie, she was the best friend I ever had.

We met at school, both on the verge of dropping out, first she and then me and while our friends were in class we used to sit and tell each other stories, chain-drinking coffee at Maestro's or the Luna Cafe, sharing a sandwich, broke then too and "I wanted to be a photographer," she told me, "for a long time I wanted it. Even as a kid," and me imagining teenage Sophie, her mother driving her to school: arms-crossed sunk in the seat, rebellious and sullen, too much lipstick, lips thick with it and "I wanted to make pictures of weird things, dead things—freaks, you know? Beautiful dead freaks . . . but when I told my advisor she came up with all this art history shit and Darkroom 101, *The Mechanics of Vision*," and the soft raspberry, slow-rolling eyes, "so I told her I could get more out of looking at one Arbus photograph than twenty hours in any class. But *then*," crust and crumbs, thoughtful head to one side, "then I decided I'd rather look at pictures of freaks than take them. So I didn't. So here I am," little two-fingered dance on the tabletop, pirouette to stop before me and fall to its knuckle-knees and then it was my turn to talk: about my willful departure from language history, English and Advanced Honors and creative writing one two and three, whatever creation imagined died a-borning because there was a party line to toe and I didn't, I wouldn't, I left: "Richard Rysman," I said, "Cady Sopowicz, the Georges," icons to us but who would teach me, show me how to write that way, *see* that way? and I left too, gave in, gave up, shrugged myself all the way across campus to the Luna Cafe, cheap coffee and Sophie's cigarettes—she still smoked then but gave it up not long after, partly for me and partly for her and partly because she got tired of bumming and stealing although there was no one alive who could slide a pack of cigarettes across a table and into a pocket with less notice or more technique—and still shrugging, dumb jobs, office temp and messenger and office temp again, Sophie and I for a brief time in the same office and then her job at AmBiAnce, a make-over salon and working there still, six days a week in high heels and sexy gray smock: hair cuts and styling, fabric samples and palette charts and "Blue is your *up* color," she'd say, card of little color chips like house painters use, very serious to the client in the fake Edwardian chair who would nod, nod, Sophie Sincere and her recommendation almost always a full course of action, exercise and diet, cosmetics and new clothes and she got a kickback from the gym, from the spas and shops she sent them to, bonus for pushing the most moisturizer and sunblock lipstick but "I like it," she said and meant it, too, she really did like helping people look better and once she was done with them they always did, some almost spectacular and Sophie would smile; she had a gift for transformation, another kind of game.

Every once in awhile she'd let me look through the client book, the Before and After pictures: "You're kidding," I'd say, "this turned into *this?*" and Sophie's smile again, it was amazing what ten pounds off and new hair could do but they almost always gained the weight back, almost always went lumpy again, frumpy again, as if what was inside would surface no matter what but "There's all kinds of reasons," Sophie's frown, "like they did it to get a new job, or to go to a reunion or something. Or they did it for a lover and now he's gone, or they got him and they just don't give a shit anymore. Guys do it too," one finger at me as if I might imagine otherwise, "guys do it all the time but they're so *lazy*," rolling her eyes, "they want us to do all the work, wave the magic wand. . . . You know what Po says? Po says sometimes she tells them to forget it, she tells them there's no hope. 'No hope for you, baby,' " in Po's cool gravel, chin tucked in, eyes wide in Po's charcoal stare. " 'I'm a technician, not a magician,' " Sophie's rolling laughter and it was true, Po was blunt as a bully sometimes, to the clients, the other workers, blunt to me too: wall-slanted and waiting for Sophie, paper cup of free mint tea and "You here again?" Po would say, poking at me with one split cherry nail, smock stained a rich and subtle shade, she never washed it, *I want them to know I been working.* "Why aren't you where you should be?"

11

"Where should I be?" eyebrows up, half-friendly, half-not. "At work, what?"

"That might help. Why don't you start putting in some more hours, make some more money so she can get out of here, quit playing with the blow driers?" and Sophie waving from behind the counter, blowing me a kiss and Po's voice dropping, flat octave: "You think 'cause you're so pretty she can't see anyone else." Her glance back to Sophie shrugging off her smock, tight white T-shirt, fresh lipstick for me, for me and "Maybe you're right," Po said, "maybe she can't. Lucky you," and "Ready?" me to Sophie and then outside, into the street, the heat and "Po thinks I'm lazy," squeezing her hand in comfortable complaint. "She thinks I'm not good enough for you."

"Well," and that dark smile, burgundy today, she got all her makeup free. "Are you?"

"No," my smile too, we both knew it was true, and false: what each would, could have done, been, become without the other was no issue, worthy or unworthy, yes or no or yes and no we were *for* each other, Sophie and me, and if the stance of the game gave us some other, temporary role—dutiful squeeze or lazy boyfriend, cocktease or predator or all of the above—then we would play that too, confident in the landscape of desire, all desires our own and in the end what we did or didn't do mattered so little, only what people thought could matter less: Po or other friends, at her work or at mine, all the way back to school: *you two*, they said, used to say, nods and mocking half-smiles and what did we care, what difference did it make to us what they thought? *Too close is not healthy*, that was Grace, one of Sophie's roommates before she moved in with me, Grace telling Sophie she ought to be careful, ought not to let me "subsume" her personality; as if I could have, as if I would have wanted to, why would I want that? I wanted her the way she was, the way she wanted me; the way we wanted each other, anytime, all the time.

Even now: see Sophie sidling in at my work, rare afternoon surprise: big smile, no panties and we called them fuck lunches, banging away in the storage room, the ladies' room, once we did it in a parking garage: cold concrete, hollow elevator sound and Sophie's breath in my face, quick slippery fingers, deep shuddering lock in my legs and Sophie's laughter later, in our own warm bed at night: *Did you see that guy? By the men's room, right, did you see him look, try to see?* But how could they know, how see when what they saw was less than surface, what they knew was nothing at all but *we* saw, we knew: contained and bounded by the game we made of every day, night and morning, made of what we had and what we didn't but most of all of what we were: us. We were us.

Not that we never had problems. Two strong wills but our strengths so different, our tempers different too and witness, say, Sophie screaming at me in a Vietnamese restaurant, long wait for a table and she was restive, silly-bored and nudging at the fake flower display, cheap plastic and she almost knocked it over, dust-gray ferns and fronds and "Sophie, cut it out," my own boredom soured to irritation, my voice louder than I meant. "Stop acting like a kid."

"Fuck off," sweetly and she did it again, poking and tugging and this time it went over, the PLEASE WAIT FOR YOUR HOSTESS sign toppling domino with a crash that silenced the room and Sophie standing hands to her mouth and giggling, *oh I'm such a bad adorable child* and I wanted to smack her, shake her, make her pick it up: "Stop being an asshole," I said, exasperation but it came out in a hiss, really mean and Sophie wide-eyed, shocked still for a moment but then back like a freight train, right in my face and "*You're* the asshole!" voice as loud as the room was quiet, "you're the one who can't ever make reservations, we have to wait wherever we go because *you* don't want to make plans, you just want to *go* with the *flow* and you know why? Because you're a big piece of shit, that's why! So pick it up yourself," and *bang* out the door, everybody staring and "Fuck you too," my sour mumble as I bent to yank the sign straight, left the greens where they were and outside to find her jittery by the car's locked door and we drove back in silence, silent upstairs and silent to separate, Sophie to the bathroom, me in front of the TV and it ended like all our arguments: crawling separate into bed, backs to one another to wake in the morning tangled arms and legs, our bodies warm and urgent with secrets hidden from our minds, conscious minds at which the body can only smile: *here is truth:* my cock hard against her leg, Sophie open for me, ready for me, rolling over for me to climb aboard and kissing her afterward, cheeks and chin and her eyes still closed, back to sleep to wake again in an hour, lovers again, friends again; everyone says you can't fuck your problems away but we did a pretty good job of it, Sophie and I.

And what fights we had infrequent, more than mostly over nothing, silly things because on the big things we dovetailed: money was for spending, nights were for going out, the game was to be played. My temping jobs changed but at heart were the same, same job, dull numbers, staring at a screen all day and Sophie at AmBiAnce learning how to sell whatever was new, learning how to handle clients who were bitches or creeps or lechers or only wanted someone to talk to, shampoo-sink confessional and "You wouldn't believe it," she told me, "you wouldn't believe the stuff I hear. I mean I don't know these people from Adam, right, and they start in about their boyfriends, how they hate their jobs and everything, they hate the way they look. . . . I wouldn't tell *my* secrets like that, not to someone I don't even know."

Filling her glass, cheap white wine but it wasn't too bad if you cut it with a little tonic, home chemistry made simple and "Secrets," I said, "what secrets? What don't I know?"

"You know everything," Sophie said; no smile, she meant it. "Everything there is to know."

Everything: since school, and what before? Almost no talk about her childhood, parents; I had never met them, ever, she never wanted me to. No hi-we're-in-town, no holiday visits; *holidays are for us* she said, tree-trimming parties and little candles shaped like stars, we ate Thanksgiving with friends or in restaurants then went out afterward to clubs, dancing till Sophie was tired. No cards to her parents (although to mine or to my brother: "Here," half-impatient, pen in hand, "sign this"), no gifts (otherwise a lavish gift-giver, Sophie, hours spent shopping, all the way uptown to find some bibelot for Po, or the perfect french-cut underwear for me) and only one small picture kept of the three of them, the family Sprause: fat dad in dark shorts blinking in front-yard sunlight, blonde mother with dark glasses, one hand on little Sophie's shoulder, how old there? and her shrug, "Nine . . . ten, I was ten." Blank-faced, elbows clasped in skinny hands, all her hair yanked back in ugly braids but still pure Sophie, you could see it, cheek curve and mouth the same, pouting mouth, soft underlip that I liked to take between my own, nibble and suck and "Cute kid," I said, picture in hand, "just take a look at—" but "I don't want to look," without turning her head. "I hate that picture."

On her lap the oversize greeting-card envelope, sick-pink and worn, fat with snapshots but no more family, only Sophie alone, Sophie with friends, blurry Sophie bridesmaid in a wedding: "My cousin Debbie," pointing to the bride, chipmunk cheeks and a headdress like bad architecture, arm in arm with Sophie in a sleazy yellow halter dress: "Crushed velvet," Sophie's nose wrinkling, good humor restored. "Can you believe it? I paid good money for it too. And that's Nat," to the next picture, teenage Sophie in black T-shirt and cutoffs, beautiful bare legs and the boy beside her in buzz cut and matching T-shirt, hand wide on her hip. "Nat was my boyfriend in ninth grade, remember I told you?"

Oh yes: Nat her first love, first fuck, scissoring legs and drunk on keg beer, back seat, back stairs and "I wish I'd known you then," I said, nuzzling at her neck, pale skin rubbed pink, "you and your cherry," and guess that past imagined, Sophie and I so young: what would it have been like? This life, our life so encompassing that it swallowed history too, hers and mine, we were what we were now more than we had ever been anything before, and though I had when asked given Sophie all my stories, parents and brother, growing up and getting out, they seemed exactly that, only stories: like a film recounted, a TV show, a mildly boring book: *this happened, and then this happened,* all of it vague and juiceless, without feeling or force: it took Sophie to make of me what I needed to be, me it seemed to do the same for her.

Family pictures . . . mine too but not too many, all of them jammed careless in the box of school records, old broken-elbow X ray, certificates from sleep-away camp and in those pictures the four of us always in the same configuration, as if there was one right way and this was it: me posed next to my older brother, our parents behind us but not too close and that was our family, desultory, distant, it had always been that way. Nowadays we might see one another once in two years, three, and no antipathy for me, from me, just our mutual disinterest, our understanding that nothing was understood, not their lives, not mine. "Temping," my brother would say, "right, that's what you're doing now," brain surgery or nude modeling it was all the same to him, to them, the same indifferent friendliness, same disappearing feeling once you set down the phone. *Alienated,* a girlfriend had once diagnosed, sixteen-year-old pre-psych naked on my sleeping bag, *you're alienated from your family, Jess:* so? and why should I care, what difference did it make to me? although from her I did learn to stop talking about them, or rather not talking: *Fine.* I would say when asked, *they're fine* but let's talk about you now, whatever your name is, your beautiful tits and your beautiful hair and the way you whimper when you come, let's talk about how it feels to lie this way, wet and warm, let's talk about the moon through the window, the sirens and the barking dogs, the way you're going west for the summer and maybe won't be back so let's make the most of what we have now, let's be together while we can.

And we were, whoever we were and then she was gone, whoever she was, momentary passion and the passion past, fucking since fourteen without real effort: *you're so pretty*, Po's scorn but true then too, pretty enough to make it all easy yet for me it was nothing but desire, no love lost or wanted, plenty of time for that: why worry? But meeting Sophie at school, oh that was different, that was something else right from the start.

See her: slow pout and big black hat, urban gypsy in tight skirts and opera cape, too much makeup, too much smoke and "Who's she?" to one of my friends, hangout buddy who told me her name: watching her walk, watching her go, saying that name to myself: *Sophie Sprause* and spotting her again at Maestro's, alone in a booth, her sleeves trailing spilled coffee, cigarette in hand and "Hey Sophie," my smile but not too wide, ready to slide in, slide next to her. "How's it going?"

That long slow gaze, raised eyes to mine: oh, beautiful and "Out the door," she said, "that's how it's going," and that was that and there I was, staring, stupid, half-pissed and half-tickled: thrall, it's called and it was. I followed her, I had to, she wouldn't wait for me: all the way from Maestro's to the flat she shared, cracked and rainy sidewalks, rathole porch with the requisite wicker chairs, me on the bottom step and "What do you *want?*" pure annoyance with her hand on the door: and my shrug, tilted smile, what to say? with a rapid scan through all my knee-jerk bullshit, none of that useful here and then it was too late, she was inside, door closing on me and the rain and I walked all the way back, hands in pockets, wet and wondering *what now?* because nothing I knew was like this, past experience no guide and all my thinking blurred circumference around that scornful figure in the center, elusive at the circle's distant heart.

So: pondering, turning the problem over and over like a monkey with a ball, *see me think* and when I finally saw her again—two weeks; do you know how long two weeks can be?—on some thrash-club dance floor, she and two girlfriends shrieking and tumbling I knew just what to do: nothing. Nothing at all but stand there, looking, looking at her and almost a smile when she saw me: "*You*," half-accusation, "you again," but when I followed her back to their table she let me sit: not beside her, Little Miss Just-Out-of-Reach but I bought her a drink, dark beer and she drank it, watched me talk to her friends, saw them laugh at my jokes and all the while my gaze on her: *look at me*, I was saying, trying to say, *just look at me because I've never seen anyone like you* and I never had, never would, never could.

Midnight, two then three and the club closing around us, lights too bright and "Come on back to our place," her friends' invitation, "walk back with us," and Sophie saying nothing, not yes or no and inside the flat more wicker furniture, cheap fake-surrealist posters, clearance-store wine rack filled with rolled-up magazines and her friends and two others all more than half-drunk, all their jokes and questions—did I ever go to Bingo's, did I know Russell Hawse?—just background noise because all I could see was Sophie, hiding in the kitchen, talking on the phone as if I weren't there, didn't exist: *so now what?* back home alone with my hard-on although one of Sophie's friends had more than hinted it might be nice if we were to, you know, *get together:* short brown hair and her breath in my face, handing me a beer but all I could see was Sophie, small figure past her still talking on the fucking phone: to whom? lover, boyfriend, girlfriend, what?

But the next afternoon she found me, library bench in the watery sun, short checkerboard skirt and Walkman and she let me listen, headphone stretch and "Vivaldi," she said, her face so close to mine. "You know Vivaldi? *The Four Seasons?*"

"*Aida,*" I said.

"That's Verdi, asshole," and back to Maestro's where she bought us coffee, let me share her sandwich, sit beside her in the booth and kiss her afterward, chaste child's kiss on her closed lips and then her murmur, cool as a dream: "Grace wants to fuck you."

Confused, aroused: be careful. "Who's Grace?"

"My roommate." Half a smile, leg barely, barely touching mine. "She says you're pretty." My silence and Sophie reaching, two fingers to press my cheekbone, the edge unshaven of my jaw and "You *are* pretty," she said, voice dry as if conceding an argued point.

"So're you," I said. "So what?"

"So nothing," the smile wider. "What are you going to do?"

"Talk to you," my own hands reaching now to touch her face, so soft and pale the skin beneath her eyes, fragile skin and after that it was like this, like now and she knew it, she told me later, that first night in the club, knew but did not, would not make a move, say a word to make it so because "What if," that small head tilted, bird's-nest tangle, "what if you didn't know? What if I was wrong?"

And when we made love, first time together and oh, to watch Sophie undressing, breathless to see her, dark nipples and violin waist, so *beautiful*—and then in my arms, under my hands, legs locked around me but as soon as she came she pulled away, face in the lumpy green pillow and me in iron dismay, oh God and still panting, "What's wrong, what's wrong?" and it took her awhile to tell me, cautious Sophie, how happy she was, on her side and shy to touch me, soft palms and those big knuckles framing cool around my face: "Hold me," whispering, "hold me tight," and I did, that night and the next and we spent all possible time together, walking to classes, to Maestro's, walking her home to sit on the porch in the dark and talk, whisper, giggle, kiss, those long legs butting, nudging at mine, big feet in slim wet-soled flats and hand in hand inside and to her bed, closing off the bedroom, chair against the door and her scent all over me, flesh smell, sweat on her forehead and temples and "Grace says," that wicked whisper afterward, hummingbird tongue in my ear, "Grace says there's such a thing as *too much togetherness*."

Who? and Sophie's voice in memory, *Grace wants to fuck you:* oh her and: "Well maybe *here*," I said, turning on my side, her face drawn close to mine. "So maybe we should be somewhere else. Maybe you should move in with me."

No answer but the smile, long and luminous and the books were the hardest to carry, books and tapes and two lamps, the collapsible bed Dumpster-donated and only Grandma's armoire the real problem but we solved that too, Sophie in T-shirt and opera cape arguing up the stairs, fat jug of cheap white wine and we drank it on the floor, heaped clothes and silly shoes and Sophie's head on my shoulder, legs stretched warm and bare beside mine and since then no day spent apart: in school then out, dancing at the thrash clubs, coffee and cigarettes and Sophie's ill-fated waitress gigs, Jim Java's and the Coastline, never working anyplace longer than a month and when we had money, any money at all we spent it, blew it: work a week to put gas in a borrowed car, blankets in the backseat and windows down, Sophie in weird blue plastic sunglasses, kids' sunglasses like the wings of a bird and one time we drove into the mountains, the Adirondacks, fucking in the dark on the cold sharp grass, headlights on patrol to send us stumbling naked for the car where we finished in blankets, wrapped cocoon and Sophie's murmur, *mmm mmm* those buzzing lips against my cheek; and waking to find my shirt missing, lost in the nighttime grass and so Sophie bought me a new one, garish green T-shirt with a picture of a butterfly target-center on the chest, which I wore till it stank and she made me take it off.

All the things we did, all tapestry, memory and in hindsight see what was the game unnamed growing, what? Wilder? No: more subtle, but the edge was sharpening, the joke a knife to cut from one day a reason for the next, everything shared and part of shared story, our story, our life and gone from school at last to live more or less as we did now, scraping money enough to move to the city, one-room closet that the ad called a loft; me with my aimless jobs and Sophie settling at last at AmBiAnce, glad to be out and away from temping, which was not her style at all: novelty, sure, but she had that with her clients, different people all the time but the same place, same work station, coffee cup and smock and joking with Po . . . and at first I was jealous of that camaraderie, jealous of the pleasure she found there, *how can she have fun with anyone but me?* Stupid, I know, knew it then too but how not to be when, back home, she would tell me all about her day, private jokes with people I didn't know or didn't like: like Andy, scut-work hair-sweeper Andy with his own hair down past his shoulders, California asshole in black jeans and white smock and he was so *helpless*, Sophie's half-laugh, he can't find a good dry cleaner, he doesn't know where to shop for *food*.

"Try the Dumpster."

"Oh Jess, don't be mean," but why not? I felt mean, not to Sophie but to Andy, Andy who would make a performance out of anything, Andy who told Sophie (who told me) that his first love was acting, he thought Albee was God, he wanted to work in the theater ("They have brooms there too, right?"—"Oh Jess, don't be mean")— and although I knew he was no serious challenge, no real contender still I hated him, soulful smile and clear-eyed, mano-a-mano handshake whenever I came in, hated it all enough to force Sophie into a defender's role not only of dumb Andy but of her right to make friends, any friends not also mine and oh, the yelling and the tears, Sophie furious—"You can't tell me what to do!"—and me in spite taking up with—what was her name?—Gira, right, Gira with her french-cut suits and her irritating laugh, fellow temp whom I used—I admit it—to be able to linger after work for coffee, for a beer, all the time with one eye on my watch, was Sophie home yet to see that I wasn't?

But she was smarter than me, smart enough to stay sweet, ask no questions, display no jealousy at all until finally I had to admit I was an asshole, humble nestle between her long forgiving legs and sometime after that Andy was gone, quit or got fired and she never seemed to miss him, never once mentioned his name. Later I heard that he'd gone back to San Diego and "Not a minute too soon," I said, to Po's nod in rare agreement: "Lazy-ass son of a bitch. All he ever wanted to do was sweep hair and look in the mirror."

But Sophie's friendship, comradeship with Po I never questioned, Po was good to her and by default to me too: it was Po who helped us find the flat, her sister's boyfriend's sister moving out with notice enough for us to borrow the security deposit, first and last month's rent, and moving in was a party, a parade of our minimalist junk except for Sophie's sarcophagus, Grandma's armoire again and "Who owns this casket?" Po's glower at me as if I must be at fault. Night turning to morning, more than half-drunk on beer and no food and we slept in our clothes beneath the open window, slept in the breeze and breath of the street below and I woke to Sophie's entrance, arm-tucked newspaper and bag of brioche as if she did it every morning, as if we had lived there together all our lives.

So: now: Sophie asleep in my arms, the sound of summer rain; same flat, different summer, still mostly broke but things a little better, more temping hours and Sophie in much demand, clients who told other clients who came in wanting the same miracles, Po assistant manager sending tidbits Sophie's way and that extra money spent on modest pleasures, music and lingerie and longer dinners at better places, Sophie eating tiger prawns, Sophie drunk on champagne, Sophie in my arms and fucking in the deep slow dawns and sometimes I would lie looking at her, just looking: time passed and nothing changed, the crease of her eyelids, pale shine of her hair clipped short, pixie, gamine and closing my eyes to think of where we might be, a year, two years, five years from now: here? and beneath the skin of comfort the barest ripple of, what? Disappointment? discontent? No, and no, because I knew it was Sophie I wanted, Sophie who wanted me so say instead a kind of restlessness, a deepening itch in the blood to take me where? because there was nowhere to go, nowhere else to be but here, sleeping to wake again to her warm breath, hands on my body, echo of the upstairs neighbors, their habits our landscape: clock radio in the morning, news before bedtime, we could always track them by their need to know, it's amazing what you can learn about people you never see. Not friends by any stretch, barely hello and goodbye but still a kind of disappointment, droll dismay when we realized—furniture screech, rental truck blocking most of the street—that the upstairs people were moving out.

"There they go," and Sophie at the window to watch the procession: building-block boxes, kitchen table, rolled-up rugs on parade. Furniture cheap as ours; the beloved TV. "You know I still don't really know their names?"

"Squeaky," I said. "Squeaky and Grumpus."

Head to one side, still watching and "Boy, she's really tiny," as if surprised, as if she had just noticed. "And he's so *big*. I always wonder about couples like that."

"You wonder about everybody."

"So do you."

Boxes trucked, truck filled and slammed and off: a week, two weeks of thunderstorms, dead humidity, nothing from upstairs and the strange silence of ghosts gone from between the walls: mornings without talk radio, nights without news or noise and then back from work on Friday to find another crop of movers sullen on the stairs and right behind the brisk new neighbor with his parchment lamps, framed MoMA posters and offer of a drink: "Soon as I find some glasses," pushing at his own, architect tortoiseshell, Goby's Desert T-shirt complete with grinning armadillo. "*And* the corkscrew, right?"

"Sure," I said, hands full of mail, magazines, and junk. "Or we could just drink right out of the can."

And once in new neighbor Jim was everywhere, at the mailboxes, on the stairs and always ready to talk: "Come on up for a drink," and so finally we did, Sophie beside me at the window to see our own view enlarged, one floor up made more difference than I would have thought; perspective is everything, what you see depends on where you are and there across the room see Jim, legs crossed in the leather butterfly chair, his shrug more to Sophie than me: "Sorry it's only beer."

"Sometimes beer is what you want," Sophie said, squeezing my leg and that was it for real conversation, all the rest was Jim Jim Jim. "You know when I moved here my friends thought I was crazy," long smile, too much teeth for the mouth. "I mean I had other options," but no, he had to pick our building, "branch out" and he would have talked all night but Sophie's smile calved us free, smiling all the way to the door then home again her wrinkled nose, perfect offhand slummery: " '*Only* beer.' Like it's poison or something."

"You know he didn't *have* to live here," I said, bending to take off my shoes. "He had *other options.*"

"That explains the furniture." Only half attending, picking through the day's mail, lingerie catalogs, gallery postcards. "Those horrible Bauhaus chairs. . . . Anyway we don't have to see him anymore, do we?"

And off again to a two-for-one party at some club Po knew, close to four when we got back, sour black brandy taste and Sophie jiggling the door key, stepping inside to stop at once and "What?" I said, too loud, too drunk and she shushed me with a palm across my mouth, sweet palm I kissed, nipping at her fingers and "Listen," softly, right into my ear. "Listen to Jim."

Ears still ringing, standing very still and when I focused I heard, what? Bumping, thumping; fucking? Yes: what else in that rhythm? and we stood in the darkness, Sophie's head tilted slightly, *thump*, *thump* and "Maybe he stops talking when he screws," bringing at once to me the image irresistible, some woman desperately shoving a tit in that moving mouth: *shut up shut up shut up*, I had to laugh and trailing Sophie to the bathroom, you could hear it better there: *thump thump, thumpthumpthump* and then Sophie's eyes wide, "What was *that?*" past Jim's *cri de coeur*, orgasm's bagpipes like a duck being strangled and "If I ever sound like that," my own murmur sick with laughter, "kill me, okay?"

"Oh no *prob*lem," and next day on the stairs, our up to his down and Jim pausing, one hand on the warped banister edge: "I hope we, I hope it wasn't too loud last night." Looking at Sophie. "I had a friend staying over."

"Oh, no," my own sunny smile, "no problem" and "The duck," Sophie's mutter through still lips, ventriloquist poise, "ask him about the *duck*," and oh the theories we concocted, gazing up at the ceiling as if at a screen, midnight movie starring Jim and his dates who came, or did not, in two categories, the yellers and the mute: "Diagnosis, please?" my question to naked Sophie who stood pulling clothes from the armoire—voyeurism begins at home—and her flip oracle shrug: "Strangers in the night," choosing at last a thin dress like black tissue paper, transparent as tears. "Express lane, five items or less, cash only."

"How he gets them in the first place is beyond me," and another shrug in response: "Who knows? Sometimes beer is what you want. Anyway nobody's like you, Prince Charming," batting lashes, wink of flattery's truth. "Listen, be my hero, I have seen *so much* bad hair today, take me someplace without bad hair."

"Can't be done," so we settled for Club Damage, What-a-Drag Night: amateur catwalk parade, glare and stutter of the misfiring strobe and at the bar three deep, elbows in, elbows out, Sophie grabbing slippery for her drink and all at once pinching my arm: "Look *look*" to see our neighbor Jim, red vest and no smile beside a woman whose presence, whose sheer proximity—to *him?*—was so incongruous that even we had nothing to say; until Sophie incorrigible, singing in my ear: "Oh, the cobra and the mongoose should be friends . . ."

Cobra, sure, and so, so beautiful: black hair chopped clean and sleek at the jawline, tall as me in black-and-white pinstripes, bright sickle-shaped earrings and Jim leaning close, saying something, wide smile but she didn't seem to hear him, seemed not to care that he was there; instead scanning the dance floor, the dancers' faux drag, with a kind of calm regard I thought I recognized and something else as well, something I knew without naming, without judgment, something strong as a smell—and all at once that moving gaze on us

on me

sharp and brief as a sting, wasp's kiss and gone and I felt, what? More than merely viewed, seen, instead *tallied*, totaled up, weighed in the balance and "Talk about an odd couple," Sophie's little smile, little sips of her drink. "Lady Beware meets the Urban Bore."

" 'What's Wrong with This Picture?' " but nothing wrong with *her*; no, she was something; and I found myself wanting that stare again, her regard: *so what's the verdict?* but "Why," my own gaze warm, "why would somebody like that be out with Jim?"

And Sophie's shrug, social scholar severe: "I don't know what's happening there, but nobody like her *dates* someone like him, I don't care how much money he makes."

"So what's going on then?"

"I said, I don't know. Come on," her hand in mine, class dismissed, "let's dance," to a slow song, hot song, Sophie warm in my arms and humming, humming, rag-doll dreamy and as we left the floor we saw them again, slipping through the crush, the woman in the lead and "There they go," Sophie said, "but I bet not to his place. Although nobody here knows that so it works either way."

"*You* know it."

"I'm not nobody."

So we danced some more, slow songs and fast, Sophie much the better dancer just like the old thrash-club days and in two hours, three we were back home, ringing ears and from upstairs no noise, no nothing, Sophie quick to sleep as I lay drowsing, thinking of the woman in the club, that stare so much like ours, measuring, considering as a judge: what had she seen? What did anyone see, seeing us?

Sleeping late, too late: rush and stumble, already a punishing heat and the day begun badly went nowhere but worse. Temping is a special kind of exercise, water-spider dance but normally it suits me, enough change to keep me interested, and without ultimate, fixed-track ambitions every job means only a bridge to the next: pay me, thank you, see you later. Or never. Some guys, guys at the places I temped, looked down on me, thought of what I did as mainly a woman's job—most office temps are women, even now—or assumed that I got into it as a way to meet women, or because I couldn't do anything else. I didn't care what they thought, I knew why I was there; and Po's one-time crack: "Well, it makes sense, you're just a temporary kind of guy," to send Sophie at once to my defense: "He is *not*," but "Hey," I told Po, unruffled, "what I am is flexible."

"Double-jointed," her correction, "like a possum's cock," but that day I felt no flexibility, no inner ease, only the pressure of sheer routine and lately my days seemed more tedious, my assignments requiring less brain power than ever, a monkey could have done them just as well; a cockroach, a rat, trained pet scuttling late and exhausted and was it only me or was everyone uglier, smellier, ruder than they had to be? and everywhere too hot, hot too in our building's vestibule, on the stairs rising into a smell like sweat and mildew, my keys jamming in the door and one cheap room air conditioner to cool the whole apartment which was nothing near cool, only a lesser state of heat.

And no food, no ice in the refrigerator, one cold beer and I drank it standing in the kitchen, my bag on the floor and past it the heaped clutter of magazines, unread mail, cracks in the plaster, crap in the drain: was this the best we could do, both of us so smart, so dumb? *What do you want?* I don't know. Something else.

And from the bathroom Sophie calling, pretty blind face blinking water and "You're late today," she said, towel in hand, faded yellow terry and see the rust on the showerhead, crud on the tiles, blind millipede dash past the toilet and I crushed it to a smear, take that you little

31

bastard and "Hey," Sophie said, "hey what's the matter?" Her arms warm and damp around my neck, hair still dripping, rivulet down breast and nipple. "Baby, what's wrong?"

"Nothing." Conscious of being dirty and stinky, underarm reek and no soap left except Sophie's weird pink goo. "Nothing's wrong."

Following her into the bedroom, where else was there to go? and "This ought to cheer you up," she said, handing the note to me: expensive notepaper, slanted handwriting to say *Come up for drinks:* "From Jim. Want to go?"

Scratching slow and hard at my ribs, sweat and dead skin, salt prickle of a cut and thinking then of Jim's piano smile, those off-white custom blinds to mask the sun, bet he had more than one crummy room air conditioner, more than he needed: *what do you need?* Something to happen, something to change, something to give us what we have to have and "No," I said, slow and certain. "No, I don't want to go."

"Why not?" honestly puzzled and from me no honest answer: why not go and drink his beer, wine, thick tutti-frutti liqueur I could never keep down or afford and "I just don't feel like it, all right?" which came out way too sharp and made her shrug too brief, all right *fine* and dressing fast, in and out of the room and "Well, I'm going," purse in hand. "Chinese, or what? *Dinner,*" to my blank face, as if I were not only an imbecile but a rude one. "Do you want Chinese food or *what?*"

"Whatever." Last trickle of the beer, piss-warm already and Sophie gone, me by the window and look at them look, guys to stare and whistle, *hey baby:* hey buddy fuck you, she's mine, mine with her silly sandals, mine with her beautiful ass—and above now the sounds of Jim's little party, half-imagined and half-voiced, a woman's laughter, *oh, do have another,* have a cocktail wienie and what the fuck would I have done up there anyway? Drink his drinks, abuse the guests, what? and now muted music, an almost bassless hum which I rose to drown with Sophie's old Crashbox tapes, clang and stutter, clatter and whoop past that blankest inner stare back to the days when this music was new, then and now and where was I, what had I come to, where had I been? Where was I going? Why, to the bathroom, take a nice long meaningless leak and don't worry about aim, what's a little dribble between friends, between the chips and the cracks and the rest of the shit and "*Hey!*" so loud I jumped: Sophie there in the doorway, hands on hips and "Are you deaf? I was *knocking,*" slamming the bathroom door for emphasis, big full-bodied bang half an inch from my approaching face and in the kitchen her frown extravagant, wisps of hair stuck damp to her skin: "It's hot as hell in here, why's the air conditioner off?"

"Because it's full of shit," I said. "Just like me."

"Oh *great.*" Unloading white cartons on the cramped island countertop, thick sticky rice and half-cracked chopsticks, hot brown goo and "I don't want this," I said, poking at a cartonful of vegetables steamed into shapelessness, "I wanted that other stuff, that stuff that's like stew—"

"If you don't like what I brought," level and cold, her own plate full and a bottle of something in the other hand,

33

"don't eat it." Crashbox snapped off, TV on to mingle with the echo above, party sound and she sat in the path of the windless window, watching the news and eating and "If you want to *party*," right in front of her now, too loud and blocking her view, "why don't you just go? Why don't you just head on up there by yourself?"

"Maybe I will," mouth full and furious, staring at me until I moved out of her way, TV whicker and drone through the news and more news, twenty people dead in a bus crash in Mexico, continued hot and humid through the weekend and Sophie rising, plate to the kitchen, shoes back on and "You coming?" she said but from me no answer, no look, stubborn straight-ahead glare and then she was gone, out the door and up the stairs and in the kitchen I scraped what was left in the cartons, lumps white and brown and sat on the floor to eat it, sat staring at the TV until the food was gone and the light was gone and "Fuck it," to nothing, to myself, and jammed behind the sauce pans and the popcorn popper (Christmas gift from my family, never used) was a bottle of Drambuie, three-quarters of a bottle of Drambuie which Sophie hated, which took me some time to drink empty, thick and warm its trickle, like medicine, like blood and "Fuck it," again, party sounds and people laughing, alto and soprano and sweat on my ribs, sweat on my neck and my back and "Jess," softly, "hey Jess," as I turned in the chair, slow and dull as a troglodyte to the sound of Sophie's voice, turning to see

the swimming image, dark eyes, dark stare

and Sophie's head smiling past that taller shoulder, standing behind a woman, someone I knew? no.

Yes. That woman from the club.

Her gaze: those eyes, the skin beneath as if bruised, angel's bruise barely there and bending to me now, bending to, what? touch me, shake my hand: long strong fingers and at this particular angle, this tunnel of light I could see right down her shirt, sleeveless white shirt, tiny black bra and breasts bigger than Sophie's, really beautiful breasts and "Lena Parrish," with her hand on mine as I realized with that same detached neanderthal calm that both of them were watching me, watching me stare at Lena Parrish's tits and "Stanley Kowalski," I said, not moving, my lips thick somehow and slow. Drunk: I sounded drunk. And stupid. "Nice to meet you. Want some Drambuie?"

"No thanks," in alto voice, glance now for Sophie who seemed far away, receding or removed and "We're going out," said Sophie, more or less at me. "You want to come?"

Slow headshake, back and forth like a wrong-speed metronome: "No," I said, "no, I don't think I do," and just like that they were gone, over and out and when I tried to stand instead a slippery vertigo, skewed numbness of thighs and ass and I must have been sitting there a long time, what time was it anyway? Late. Empty bottle, empty rooms, pink soap slop and into bed, wet hair and damp crotch and I knew I had been sleeping when I woke to find Sophie beside me, sweat-moist and naked in the silent trench of dream: hearing nothing, seeing nothing of my own motion as I reached to stroke that curving knob of hip, flesh and bone and a sound from above like crying, crying out, crying in orgasm and my hand now less stealthy, meant to wake and she almost did, troubled murmur but deep, deep in her dream as I pressed against her, half rolled her to one side, her body wakening to me as with one hand I lifted and held her thigh, parted her legs to the sounds above, slipped inside and held her close and strongly then, held her tight to another's cry, my own groan deep and Sophie waking at last as I came, woke to whisper and shift my hands to her breasts, woke to pleasure then sleep again, nestling tender at my body, silent face warm against the rhythm of my heart.

And morning, ah God and the grinding headache, sick aftertaste and Sophie in the shower, what time had she come home anyway? The Drambuie bottle still on the kitchen table, one spotted glass and Sophie sailing past me, naked and toweling, still mad? but no, see her smile, feel her kiss and "Hey hey," I said, reaching for her, hands on that slim wet waist. "Wait a minute. What happened yesterday?"

"What do you mean?" Not quite a smile. "What—"

"I mean with that woman, what's her name, Jim's girlfriend. What did you—"

"Lena," she said. "Her name's Lena, she was at the party—we came down to get you, remember? We—"

"I remember." Black bra; those bruised exotic eyes. "And you guys went out, or what?"

"Sure we went out. We're going out again tonight, all of us. And guess who she knows?" supplying then the answer: "Po! They're good friends, they met when she did her hair or something. Anyway we're going out with her for dinner tonight, so you come meet us after work, okay?"

Work; shit. "Sure," pulling myself upright, no time to make coffee now. "I'll be there."

And I was: later than I'd meant but still on time, hurrying up the street to see her, see them waiting, Sophie bright in red and somehow small beside Lena, who was just as tall as me, who could—and did—look straight into my eyes. Hand out again to shake mine, strong squeeze and "It's nice to meet you," I said. "Again. Sober."

Closer than another might stand, warm mix of seduction and aggression: *this space is mine*. "Well, third time's the charm," she said. "What-a-Drag, remember? At Club Damage." That gaze to Sophie. "Both of you."

"I remember." *Oh the cobra and the mongoose should be friends:* Jim's attempt at conversation, and she—what? ignoring him? No: as if he hadn't been there, as if no one had been there at all. "You were with Jim," I said, the name a subtle punchline, we both know what *that* means. "Just showing him the sights, huh? How the other half lives?"

A little pause, then: "Remedial humility," those narrow lips in half a smile as if I had done something smarter than expected, shown more wit than she'd thought I had and of course why suspect me of any, ill-met Mister Chug-a-lug and "Men seem," she said, "to need it more than women, don't you think? The odd reminder, the little dig."

My own smile, just the edge of the edge and "Well," I said, "well I don't know about *that*—"

and "Come *on*," Sophie impatient, already curbside with a cab. "Let's go," and bundling in, Sophie first and Lena to the driver, name of a place I didn't know. "Just a pit stop," she said, brief brush of her breast as she leaned across me, Sophie on the other side. "I want you to see my friend's show."

"What kind of show?" but Sophie was talking, saying something about Po (whom Lena called *Portia*) and what a small world it was and then we were there: a kind of bookshop-gallery, storefront full of overpriced art books, walnut-framed posters, and in the back room the opening itself: concrete floor and skinny sculpture made of what looked like coat hangers, black-coated wire and "This is Edie," Lena said, introducing us to the artist, skeleton chic with a shock of yellow hair, pointy collar and cowboy boots and her hand was cold, really cold, as if it were winter outside or she were dead.

"My pleasure," in a faint southern accent, her troubled gaze only for Lena and "Why didn't you say you were coming? If I knew, if—did Saul know? Because—"

"Oh, we can't really stay," said Lena, still smiling but soothingly, as if to someone ill or delusional. "I just wanted Jess and Sophie to see your work."

"Will you call me?" more troubled still, "will you at least—" and then Edie trapped on her blind side, a guy with a sheet of paper and a smile and "Listen, you're busy," and Lena disentangling, drawing away, still the smile and her hand then on my arm to lead me through what was already a crowd, Sophie behind us to breathe out "Boy is she *weird*."

Plastic glass, little sips of blush wine and "Not really," Lena said, "that's just how she comes across. Actually, Edie's very smart. She can get more money in grants than anybody I ever saw."

"It shows," I said. Wire-monkey sculpture, needy face across the room: looking at us, at Lena. "But I thought artists were required to starve. Or suffer or something."

That quirking smile, half mockery, half not: "Oh, she's suffering all right," and Sophie saying something too low for me to catch, Lena's laugh and then some guy in a black suit wanting to talk to her, wanting to talk alone and behind him some woman who knew her, another woman who pretended to know me too just to get next to her and they all seemed to want to touch her, squeeze her shoulder, peck her cheek, always that fast glance for us: *who are you?* and "Seen enough?" Lena said to Sophie, to me, as if no one else was there. "Then let's go."

And effortless through the crowd, Edie stricken across the room but too late, out the door, off to dinner at this crummy-looking Thai restaurant, which once past the scuffed exterior turned out to be pretty good: fat, red chaise lounges like in an old-fashioned whorehouse, heavy lacquer trays of appetizers and me between the two of them in the curve of the too-small red leather booth, Sophie spearing shrimp and Lena pouring wine, telling stories, she knew a lot of stories, she knew a lot about a lot of things: models and artists and writers, which galleries were good and which were shitty, who would be famous in ten years and who would be dead: long lists of both, cruel and hilarious and "So," I said, aware of my own ebbing laughter, "you think your friend Edie's headed for the boneyard, and you don't care? Isn't that kind of harsh?"

One finger tapping slow against her glass, circling its

rim to make a noise, minute wet cry of wine and "No,"she said, "not really. Why should I care, when she doesn't?"

"Would you say the same thing to her face?"

"I have."

"Oh." Which was no real answer but nothing else to say and in that pause Sophie up and off to the ladies' room, leaving the two of us in silence expectant, water and wine until finally: "She's really something, Sophie," those dark eyes at half-mast, picking daintily at her plate. "You two have been together pretty long, haven't you?"

"Always," I said. "Forever."

"I can see why."

"Can you?" meant to be playful but her gaze was not, was something else instead: the stirring of a smile, *what do you see* and I wanted to know, wanted to ask but didn't know how and then Sophie was back and we were paying the check, we were shrugging off cabs because Caliban's was not so far away. Walking in tandem, in trio, Sophie in the middle with her hand in mine to the usual line, dank purple walls, lights in epileptic rhythm and the guy at the door knew Lena by name, let us in to ear-ringing wrong-speed Patsy Cline and Lena and Sophie crammed on one side of the booth, black vinyl this time and " 'I fall to pieeeeeces,' " in chorus as the drinks came, Lena had ordered for us all: black beer in green bottles, citrus froth and "You ever had this before?" Nodding encouragement to our doubtful faces. "Go on, try it. It's good."

Strange and sour going down but a dark sweet after-taste like bitter chocolate, on the second round before I knew it, drinking toasts, toasting Po, and Caliban's, and

"Jim," Sophie said, "let's drink to Jim. Without whom, et cetera et cetera. You know, we were *wondering*," that bad child's smile, "about you two."

"So?" Looking from Sophie to me. "What's the verdict?"

"Well," Sophie said, "we didn't know what to think. I mean it's obvious you two don't belong together, anybody can see that."

And Lena's raised eyebrows—amused? offended, what? something there but too dark to tell and then some Lesley Gore crap and both of them in ecstasy scrambling out of the booth to dance as I watched, and drank, another round and this time plain Scotch and water, cheap little glasses like urine-test cups as the DJ played Dean Martin, One Red Bullet, Darrel & Dave and they danced together very well, Lena and Sophie, Sophie and Lena arm in arm and laughing, one reaching for the other to grab her close, yell something in her ear and in the men's room I had some trouble focusing, slewed piss in a small stray stream but it wasn't that I was drunk, not drunk but warm, very warm, warm inside and out. Thinking of Lena, of Lena and Jim, what was going on there anyway? and trying to imagine him fucking her, the two of them in bed but that picture wouldn't work, no, square peg in a round hole and back at the table to hear Sophie winding up our famous parking-garage story, elevator clang, cold floor and a smell like oil: and there before me more Scotch, Lena's shirt half open now, two buttons, three, wide mouth in a wider smile and laughing now at Sophie's story: "And we were like *uh*, *uh* and trying not to make any noise, you know, no more than we could help . . . not like, oh say Jim. . . . We heard you guys last night, you know." Head to one side, making of her hand a moving beak: "*Quack quack*" with a grin for me. "Fuck a duck."

And for a moment just a hint, just the barest sting of that stare as "You listen," Lena said, very cool, "to your neighbors? Having sex?"

"We listen," said Sophie, "to *everything*."

Silence: club silence, which means music and people yelling but at our table it was vacuum, the two of them face-to-face, nothing moving until Lena did, half-smile, meeting my eye with a gaze past deciphering and "Let's dance," she said, to both of us: sweat scent and the swirl of their damp hair, Lena's hand on my shoulder, long fingers, no rings and after that it was last call, let's go, into the dark drenched past humidity but too soft to be called rain, mist like steam cooled by that darkness and Lena shrugging off the cab: "I'll walk" she said and did, gone in half a block, dissolved; and Sophie's head on my shoulder, Sophie's fingers in my lap and she had me half-hard, half-unzipped and stroking me, eyes closed and stroking me and home too soon, fumbling for money while Sophie disappeared upstairs to stand for one back-lit minute naked at the window: "Have fun, man," sour from the driver as I slammed the door, went upstairs to Sophie's arms, Sophie's kiss, Scotch aftertaste and we fell asleep still joined, waking in an hour from no dreams at all to sleep again in thunder and silence, all the city quiet in the drizzle grown to storm.

"So what'd you think?"

Late afternoon, my bare feet in Sophie's lap; her Chinese robe. Headache again. "Of what?"

Impatiently: "Of *Lena*. What'd you think of her?"

Lena, yeah. Dark eyes, pale shirt unbuttoned, the cleft between her breasts. That alto voice. "I thought . . . " I don't know what I thought. That she was beautiful. That people liked to touch her, in restaurants and clubs and galleries, she seemed to have a lot of friends. "I liked her," I said. "I had fun. But I don't think you should've said that stuff about Jim, you know, about her and Jim fucking. I don't think she liked that too much."

"Mmm," past a mouthful of coffee, the sound she made when she didn't agree but didn't want to talk about it. "Well. Why don't you call her?"

"Call her? For what?"

"To go *out*," as if I were a moron and maybe I was; call her to go out, sure, why not? Just like I would call any other friend, *let's meet* but "We don't have her number," I said.

"Here," produced from her purse: three rings, four, no answer and Sophie emergent from the bedroom, pale scarf wrapped around her head, filmy as moths' wings, drooping and soft: "So what'd she say?"

"She wasn't home. I left a message," just noncommittal, *call us* and "I'm hungry," from Sophie so off to the deli, big sloppy sandwiches, brown stains on the black-and-white floor and "Do you think," Sophie said, "that she's attractive?"

"Who, Lena?" Something small and plastic floating red in my coffee; I fished it out. "Sure."

"Are you, you know, attracted to her?"

"What?"

"Would you fuck her?"

"*Sophie—*"

Insistent: "Would you?" and my own stern sigh, uncertain what she really meant, what she was really asking so "No," I said, "no, I—"

And that big bright shit-detector smile: "Oh Jess come *on*," and back to eating, greasy green-pepper sandwich, napkin-patting her mouth like a princess and back home again to the blinking machine: Lena, the background sounds of a party, club and "I got your message," her voice sharp through the clamor. "Come on by."

The address she gave turned out to be a kind of performance space, old theater with an arrowed sign directing us to a third-floor screening room, stairs even steeper than the ones in our building, truly Olympic stairs, even Sophie was breathing hard by the time we hit the landing. Some kind of premiere in progress, the film apparently over but the party just begun: dub music cranking on, what looked to be an art crowd spilling out past lurid posters, *EdVentures* in carnival script tacked at eye level above silver washtubs chunked full of ice, red wine in little bottles, beer and "'Scuse *me*," rudely, some stork-skinny guy in my face as I reached for the tub. "Your invitation?"

"What?"

"I said, let's see your invitation. This is a private screening," and my elaborate surprise and inner scramble, half turning for inspiration to Sophie who had apparently disappeared but: "Hey Jess," our tandem swivel to see Lena,

44

black cap and tight black T-shirt, long silver earrings like Chinese glyphs and "It's all right," she said, "he's with me," to the blond who shrugged, took a beer for himself before wandering away.

"If that guy's the bouncer," I said, "this place is in trouble."

"It's in trouble all right. He's the director," whose name was of course Ed, as the movie was about his, well, edventures: life, liberty, the pursuit of funding, trying to make a living by making a film about making a living by making a film and "Hey," I said, "why not hook him up with Edie? She can teach him how to get grants, and they could make a sequel called—"

"*EdieVentures*, right." Beneath the cap brim that brief smile, teeth hidden by the wide, thin mobile lips. "As it happens, Ed's not my problem. And anytime he wants advice from me he knows what to do."

"Whistle?"

"No, ask for it in writing. Where's Sophie?"

"I don't know," I said. "She ditched me," but "Liar," in my ear, Sophie's arm around my neck and the other hooking Lena, big hug and "Wow, what a bunch," Sophie said, "give me some of that wine . . . you know somebody in the ladies' room just offered me a part in a movie, she said all I had to do was get naked. Then *this* guy," pointing with her wine to a lean cadaver, old-style greaser looks but too clean to be wholly pure, "wants me to be in his band's video, he says all I have to do is go three-quarters topless."

"Which is about all he pays," Lena's shrug, "three quarters. Come on, I want you guys to meet someone," and gently towing us, arm in arm in arm to meet more of her friends, Annemarie and Jules, older, early fifties maybe, and very glad to see her—"We were hoping you would be here," said Annemarie, all in black, so tiny she barely reached Sophie's shoulder and of course she and her husband were filmmakers too, medical documentaries and after twenty minutes' talk I never wanted to go to the doctor again, instead went for more beer and came back to find Sophie and Lena cloistered with a new pair, two women, twin sisters from somewhere way out west in identically overpriced leather who were in the city "vacationing," but the way they laughed when they said it made it something else again. And we even got to talk once more to Ed himself, great drunken details of his plans for Hollywood release, long red schemes of outsider's cunning during which Lena made as if to yawn, prompting Ed's sneer: "Yeah, that's right, you've heard it all before. In fact she's been *all* the way around, right, Lee?"

"Right, Ed," suddenly sharp, pure grinning edge and "In *fact*," she said, ostensibly to us but that smile all for him, pointed at him like a gun, "I've been around so long I can remember Ed's days as a bike messenger, he used to hustle his homemade porn videos, he used to call himself the Hot Dog Vendor. Remember, Ed? And the time your little brother came to town—Michael—and he was, what, fifteen, sixteen? and you told him to—"

Hastily and too loud, much too loud: "Oh, fuck you, shut up," but he had obviously sustained a direct hit and they both knew it and without seeing the wound we on the periphery knew it too, watched him go, Sophie ticking tongue to teeth and "You'd never know it to look at him," Lena said, "but he does have some talent. Although not for films," and no need to stay after that so we didn't, went off to a club she knew: "It used to be some kind of school," leading us down broken concrete stairs, steep and narrow and "What school?" Sophie asked, "the Jane Eyre Academy?" Gloomy little dance floor, painful metal chairs but we made our own fun there at the table, just like the night before: as if with Lena the play expanded, the speed increased, we were more of what we were together when we were together with her.

And the blending duet, Lena and Sophie trading stories and me in the middle content to listen, to look, Sophie effervescent with wine and hilarity, Lena chin on fist and smiling, those dark and shining eyes: as if we could tell her anything, everything, the trivial to the vast: from Sophie's passion for sourball candies to my own failed stab at writing there was nothing off-limits, nothing that, once words were found, might not be said—and not only said, but without words understood: how rare is it, a friend like that?

The closing club, but the night not over yet so back then to our place, to sit in the light of one fat lamp like kids on the living room floor: and more talk, more stories, Sophie's story of how we met: "My roommate Grace was *crazy* about him," looking at Lena, squeezing my hand. "She kept giving me all this bullshit, you know, trying to break us up."

"And then what?" Long legs drawn up, bent head on crossed arms like a child hearing a fairy tale. "What happened?"

"Nothing," I said. "This."

"Nothing?" Sophie's pout pretend but "You're lucky,"

said Lena, "that's not the way it is for most people." Her pause. "That's not the way it's been for me."

Silence; and Sophie sidling over, moth's murmur and their heads bent close together and how could it be, my own honest wonder, how in the world could someone like Lena have any trouble with men at all? but the answer as obvious as asking, of course men would be all over her but would they be any men she could want? and like punctuation, illustration to make the point came from above the sudden sound, *thump* and *thwack* and "Jim's home," I said, reporting the obvious as Lena gazed without pleasure at the ceiling, made a face—then all at once a smile, wicked smile and "Show me," her whisper. "I want to see how you listen. To him."

Sophie scrambling to her feet, one hand out and leading Lena as I followed into the bathroom, silent-movie tiptoe to point at the ceiling, to stage whisper: "This is the best spot. Once he gets going you can hear really good."

Dark head tilting, bent so far back it rested on my shoulder; blurry from the wine, the beer and "You can hear," I said, "from our bed too."

"What else do you hear?" Lena's whisper, breath against my face; my hands on her hips, giving her balance. "Do you ever hear me?"

Silence from Sophie; my own silence and then "I don't know," I said, my hands warm where they touched her, a clear and particular heat and she stirred a little, just a little, rolled her head against my shoulder, back and forth and we waited, the three of us, for Jim to do something, screw someone, put on a show, waiting in the silence until Sophie's noisy yawns, open-mouthed like a little kid and "Oh, it's so late," in a drowsy murmur, "it's almost morning, why don't you stay? I mean why don't you just sleep here?" and it seemed the most natural thing in the world, pure common sense for the three of us to lie down just as we were, shoes off, clothes on, the rumpled landscape of our queen-sized bed and Lena on the far side, Sophie in the middle, the peaceful sound of their breathing and I slept almost at once, drunker than I felt, maybe drunker than I knew, to tumble past all dreams and wake in half-gray light, dry-mouthed and with a hard-on pressed against a long warm thigh, warm body in my arms

not Sophie

but Lena, tangled hair, black T-shirt twisted up above her rib cage to show the pale underswell of breasts; and past her Sophie, spoon-curled like a child, bare legs canted high, Lena's arm flung back across her hip and I thought nothing, nothing at all as I reached to gather them both to me, pull us all very close: legs and arms, breasts and shoulders, the scent of their bodies like the ether of dream—and waking next I was alone, sound of the shower and Jim's overheard TV, half rising to see Sophie, slick wet hair and drinking coffee in the long bright drench of morning light.

So the question, posed by memory to self: *what happened?* through the tumbled image—Lena's half-bare breasts, Sophie's bare legs (and hadn't she been wearing tights before?)—and my own sleepy grasp between all so exactly like a dream, bound by perfect sense till the dreamer wakes to see in sober daylight what sleep can never show:

the meaning of the rebus, explicating sense at the heart of the dream: *that* means *this;* oh, yes.

And wonder as I did—and I did—still for Sophie and me there was no discussion, no critique or even barest mention in the morning of the night; why? Normally our talk was everywhere, nothing left unsaid but past that morning—Lena's quick, almost stealthy departure, flick of damp fingertips, coffee in a borrowed mug—it stayed unspoken, pure paradox of something that in its feeling of sheer *rightness* was in the end too strange to talk about at all.

But beneath our silence complicit still my own half-furtive reveries, recalling the feel of her, her body in my arms, my cock pressed hard against her thigh; *do you think she's attractive?*

Oh yes.

Would you fuck her?

Now: see Sophie smile, wide and special-bright for Lena at the AmBiAnce door, Lena in white with a little black hat bending to kiss Sophie on the cheek, turning to me in my boyfriend's sprawl on the couch: "Hi, Jess," and a kiss for me too, sweet and briefer, crushed-flower smell; dark lipstick, darker than Sophie used. "Are you ready?"

"Sure," I said but the question was for Sophie who was already gathering her things, her purse, the dinner her arrangement—*We haven't seen Lena in so long,* what, a week? six days? but I was willing, I had been thinking of her too: dark stare, that alto voice and half-bare breasts (and how did *she* remember that night? would she say? should I ask?)—so out into the street then, the heat a great but diminishing blow and once in the cab Lena settled back with a sigh too deep to be pure fatigue, so deep that Sophie raised her eyebrows: "Bad day?"

Her shrug: bad day? Sure. Bad day, bad month, bad life, lots of things were going to shit, chief among them her rising rent: "It's just a fucking nightmare, in fact it's criminal but I don't want to talk about it," so we didn't, talked instead of Po and AmBiAnce, of Sophie's maybe raise, of my own growing hatred for Jim's car alarm, Sophie's imitation a flügelhorn moan and "Jim, right," Lena's narrowed frown, "don't get me started. Do you know he called me first thing Sunday morning—while I was still asleep, *trying* to sleep—to say *hello?*"

"Did you?"

"Did I what?"

"Say hello."

"I think he's sweet on you," Sophie's prim little moue, "I think it's all very serious."

"*I* think it's all very spurious."

The restaurant was called Bella Luna, which I presumed to mean beautiful moon and it was everywhere, windows and walls, woven into the napkins, etched thin on the glasses' stems and "We need another bottle here," Lena said to the waiter, Lena who had ducked out early from work, playing hooky to go see a friend's bookstore reading, some kind of self-help guy: *Find Your Wings* in primary colors, a bird heading toward the sun and "You never saw anything like it," flipping the book over to show us the earnest, smiling face, Over 500,000 Copies in Print and "I'd smile too," I said, "why not? He must be getting rich."

Crossly, "He is rich," pushing the book aside and the crowd, she said, had been pathetic, so sincere, so convinced that he could help them find their wings: " 'You can fly,' " in deadly mimic, " 'if you really want to, you can *fly*.' Why not try it from the penthouse, Tinkerbell ?"

"Now, now," I said. "Be nice."

"Why should I?" Heavy plates of coiled pasta, napkins the color of bone and "It's stupid," that cool and narrowed frown, "what the whole thing is trying to be is kink. But *dumb* kink, you know?"

"Kinky?" through a mouthful of noodles, Sophie's puzzled gaze but Lena shook her head: "No, kink is, it's like art, it's—well, it's a theory, really, my theory of life," her smile mocking drama, more wine in our glasses, tiny moons to rim the lip. "It's a way to see the world, to—like this guy's kink would be his self-help thing, right? It isn't only the money, he *wants* to help people, wants to be the one who makes them feel good—"

" 'You can fly,' " I said, "and whether they do or not they're happy and he still gets to cash the check. Enlightened self-interest."

"Right, sure. But everything . . . engages through that kink, that . . . angle . . ." Eyes closed, lips pursed as if annoyed by her own failure to make clear, to explain and "Like you two," she said, "you're each other's kink, right? You see the world through each other, you use each other to change the world, *make* the world. *Your* world: do you see what I mean? Like you're not just living, just like everyone else, you're making your life, *shaping* it like, like art, by the way you see things, the way you are. See?"

And Sophie's frown, mystified but not me: instead inside the inner flash that says *I know*, eureka smile and "It's what we call the game," I said. "Only it's not really a game, you know? And we were playing it before we knew what we—"

"Since you met," and not a question, she knew she was right and of course she was: we had been playing *as* we met, knew each other by, as well as through, the ability to play at all—and my smile said that, gave her my pleasure in her knowledge and her fingers then across the table to squeeze my own, other hand for Sophie and "You know, it's hard to talk this way to people," intensity now softened to a smile. "Nobody ever understands what the hell I'm talking about."

"We do," Sophie said. "We understand just fine."

And my nonchalance, well, what about Jim? "You ever try to explain it to—" and "Jim, right," her shrug, a look to Sophie who rolled her eyes. "You know he wants me to move in with him."

"Oh sure," my own grimace, too ridiculous for disdain but Lena's second shrug was rueful: "Hey, I might have to. For a stopgap thing, anyway. He keeps asking, and—you know they raised my rent again, I'm living month by month and I just can't afford it anymore," and Sophie saying something, nodded sympathy but for me the jealousy instant, narrow, black burn so harsh it shocked me, the way an impulse to theft or cruelty shocks: *am I that way?*

but still the idea unthinkable, past imagining to imagine her there, upstairs in his apartment, waking and sleeping, just out of reach

and "Don't," I said, my voice very flat. "Don't do that."

Her stare opaque: and Sophie's in odd mimic, twin gaze as if I had done something not only stupid but stupidly impolite and "What do you expect me to do?" said sharply, "live in the street? It'd be just a temporary thing, I don't intend to make a—"

"Don't do it," I said. "Move in with us instead."

Silence: and Sophie's grin ignited, eyes wide and "*Yeah!*" so her wine almost spilled, clapping her hands like a kid and Lena tugged between annoyance and a laugh, *yeah right* but Sophie insisting, on fire with the idea, no no *listen*, "Jess's right. Boy genius," with one of her swooping kisses, lipstick and garlic sauce and "Just think a minute," to Lena, one hand on her arm. "You'd save money—*we'd* save money too, and we could all have a great time together. It would be so *fun*."

Lena's gaze back and forth; a widening smile. "You're serious," she said. "You really mean it."

My own silence, questions tumbling but her answer was the only one that mattered: *will you?* and "Of course we mean it," Sophie's nod but Lena still thoughtful, the last of the wine and "What if," she said, "what if we don't get along?"

"Of course we'll get along."

"But what if we don't?"

"Then you can move out again."

"Or kill us," I said, making a smile, "and eat us."

"Or," Sophie said, "we can eat you."

Silence again, but a different kind, weights and measures and it made me think of that first look, first glance in the club: *what's the verdict?* and "Okay then," Lena said, "all right, I will," and Sophie squealed and hugged her, arms around her neck and Lena's smile for me then past Sophie's pale hair, her reach across the table to take my hand in her own, squeeze it tight

and reflexive as breathing, as the offer had been I raised that hand, slim strong hand to my mouth: and kissed it, warm and swift and secret on the soft skin of her palm.

2

THE PRINCE OF CHAOS

*P*o said we were crazy.

Trio dinner and she our guest, Medianoche with its flagstone floors and month-long waiting lists but Lena knew someone who knew someone, the manager's sister's sister-in-law; way too expensive still the splurge was worth it, the meal a celebration: but Po, our guest—their choice, not mine, for the first person to tell—still Cassandra-dour, sunk deep in the black-and-white booth, flicking crumbs with the tip of her damask napkin.

"You know it won't work," gazing at Lena, at Sophie; most sourly at me. "Lee, you're so smart, you can't think of anything else? Like the YWCA?"

And Lena unruffled, wine glass in hand; silver stem, calm fingers, hair back in that silver clip. "Or move in with you, right?" to Po's silence, my inner grin: then more kindly, "No, really, Portia. Why shouldn't it work?"

"Lots of reasons," looking at me again. "Like for one, money. These two," meaning Sophie and me, "have no idea how money works, you ever noticed that? And three's an unstable number anyway. Unbalanced."

"We balance," I said, "just fine."

"Oh yeah? For how long? You're not even officially in yet, right?" to Lena who shrugged: "Not till the end of the month, we've got some stuff to do."

"Like what?"

"Juggling furniture," I said, trying to stay friendly, trying not to get mad, we knew enough about money to pick up the check, right? and "Oh, don't be so pessimistic," sunny Sophie taking my hand, Lena's hand, linked chain. "Three's the perfect number, God's number," but Po was merely first in line as no one seemed to agree with us; Jim of course gone furious, Lena had told him our plans through one tense interminable dinner, all the objections she, and we, had heard before and heard too a lot of noise from upstairs, banging and door slamming and "Sore loser," I said to the ceiling though not loud enough for him to hear; why make trouble? and caught too by a moment's alien sympathy, *poor Jim*—but really, who was I kidding? Recall that restaurant surge, dark spark of primal jealousy and *poor Jim* nothing, Jim who did not understand as the others did not understand, the ones who laughed or looked blank, the ones who sniggered: *ménage à trois*, *three's a crowd* but "It's not *like* that," Sophie's great and flaring anger, "it's not that way at all! They don't see, they don't understand—"

and "Sophie," I said, each time it happened and it seemed to happen a lot—the friends met in clubs, at the movies, in a deli or restaurant, curious to our table, to our trio place in line—"Sophie, forget it," from my own largesse, leniency because how could they know? like watching an artist at work, painter or sculptor, color and stone and *what is it?* they want to know, there on the outside, at the studio door but what answer is possible? *It is what it is*, life shaped and consciously created and until Lena's articulation I had never called it more than a game, never realized that in the conscious act of playing it had become a deeper thing, the flowering of our long-ago dreams, Sophie the photographer, me the writer and if we had not done those things still we had not failed: we had done this thing instead, each day adding to that construction, that picture of the picture of us.

And ruffled Sophie calmed by Lena's cool amusement, who cared what people thought or didn't think? "Most of them don't think at all," one hand on Sophie's shoulder, pale nails unpolished, rising to brush at her hair. "Anyway, what do you care? They don't know us, they don't know anything about us."

Her shrug in answer, flickering of a smile: "I guess you're right," and she was, we all were, as right as our conjoinment: the next step, next move in the dance, the heart of the game because as we were the way we saw the world how the world saw us could not affect us, what other people thought could not matter at all; and wondering, how was it I had never seen this on my own, never moved past that nameless pure acceptance to a kind of conscious kink? but I knew the answer to that one too and its name was Lena, Lena who had come to show us, lens and mirror, just exactly what we could be, exactly what we were, Lena who in some untaught way would teach us what we could not learn alone.

Impatient then for Moving Day, the sleek new fold-out sofa—Lena's purchase—now delivered, see Sophie's daily pester for me to get rid of some of my junk, where're we going to *fit* everything and "Me," I said, "what about your stuff? Like your famous armoire, if we got rid of the armoire we'd have lots of extra—"

"Oh forget it," one hand to stop me, shut me up and then both arms tight around me, big squeeze and "It *is* going to work, Jess," her murmur to my ear. "No matter what anybody says. Right?"

"Of course it is," and I meant it; but *what will it be like?* to have that third presence, someone else in the house? Sophie and I alone together for so long; and not only here, in this place or any of the others but in that smaller, sweeter, more exclusive bubble, that place constructed by us for us: house of games, the house of kink now named and in the naming claimed by Lena as well. In seeing the magic castle, you may enter: *what is essential is invisible to the eye*, who said that? St. Paul? Saint-Exupéry? and now see the magic castle, the bubble built for two accommodating three. How will things change for us, for Sophie, for me? how will we change, playing this new game?

"We'll just make it work," Sophie said, her nod convincing and convinced, "we're going to be just fine," and then it was Friday, our last night alone together, fucking slow and desultory on the living room floor—spread arms, her gasps and little whispers, sweat glow on cheeks and thighs and "No more of this," I said, gentle tug at both her nipples, "no more going around naked," to her own smile, loose fist around my cock: "Well, not for *you*, anyway."

Saturday overcast, Sophie driving the rented truck but she had so little, Lena, in that drab flat: two square rooms and a tiny closet-bathroom, two windows facing north and all of it seen through my own strange drift of—what? disappointment? but then what had I expected? The cave of wonders, the Old Curiosity Shop? No wonder she'd never asked us over; impossible almost to imagine Lena actually living in a place like this, a dump really, unbelievable that the landlord could charge so much for so little but everybody always paid more for their place than any place could ever be worth, that was just the way things were and "Jess," Sophie peremptory, "we need a hand here," with piles of books still to pack—lots of my own favorites, Cady Sopowicz and Richard Rysman, Plath and Nabokov and some stuff I'd never heard of: John Doublas, *Black Middens*, *The Encyclopedia of Desire*—plenty of music too, expensive deck and speakers but beyond that just kitchen things and a couple of lamps, a small TV, elderly loveseat covered in red corduroy and "Leave that," Lena said, one-fingered flick of distaste. "It came with the place, in fact I think they built the place around it," so I left it where it was, skewed in the middle of the empty floor as she gathered the last gleanings—a paper sack of toiletries, wine from the dank refrigerator—while in the street impatient Sophie honked the horn: *come on!* and "Any last rites?" I said, bag in hand, sweeping wave one-armed like a game show presenter. "Last words?"

That narrow smile: "What took you so long?" and then we were gone, door slammed and the key on the floor, out to the borrowed truck and off for home.

Late, by the time things were carted upstairs, the fold-out unfolded and equipped: green paisley blanket and sumptuous red pillow, her silver alarm clock small as a windup toy, what time did she have to get up anyway? and realizing with dumb surprise that I couldn't remember where her job was or even what she did, she must have told us, how had I forgotten? Sophie slipping past to the bathroom, muffled gush and sputter of the tap and I crouched beside Lena—really here, here to stay—who lay now propped on one elbow, white T-shirt, man's T-shirt with a deep V neck and "Somehow," I said, "somehow I would have thought you were more the nightgown type."

"Peignoir," her drawl, "a scarlet negligee . . . what type would that be, Jess?" and I laughed a little, ambushed by my own stupidity, of course she was no type at all: she was Lena, purely Lena and for a moment—her gaze, barely half a smile—my strange déjà vu to those first meetings at Maestro's, Sophie in the club: *what do I do now?* but of course this was completely different, this was nothing like that at all so: my smiling shrug for answer and off to the bedroom, to bed where Sophie joined me, quietly, quietly, my mouth in her neck, her fingers pinching at my sides, and in the next room Lena as quiet, curled by the silence of her silver clock: just like I'd pictured, just like I'd thought it would be.

Then waking, near dawn's slow bathroom shamble and pausing in that lessened dark: to look at her, one look, sleeping beauty with the T-shirt a pale puddle beside the rumpled bag, bare shoulders and one long slim arm like the stem of a flower, fingers half-curled as if beckoning, twitching lightly as I watched as if in summons of a dream.

And in another hour, two, the alien buzz of her alarm, *what's that?* and then memory: oh, yeah, three of us now. Sophie crawling up and out, heading for the bathroom and past our open door Lena waking, long violin back bare to the hips as she stretched to resume the T-shirt, did she know I could see? Disordered hair brushed back two-handed, into the bathroom where as she entered I saw naked Sophie climbing out of the shower, mirror steam and scent of strawberry soap, the closing door like drawn curtains and nowhere for me to go but the kitchen, to make coffee for us, for us all.

And dinner plans: "How about if I stop," Lena fixing the clip into her hair, "and get Mexican, all right? and we'll get this place together." Smile for Sophie, for me: "See you later, roomies," and gone, Sophie back to the bathroom, dead center in the mirror and "Listen," I said, "what does she do anyway?" Ducking behind her, trying to brush my hair.

"Who?"

"Lena. What's her job, what does she—"

"She's a *corporate writer*," as if I must be dense. "*You* know that, she told us that a long—"

"No she didn't," and what the hell was a corporate writer? but Sophie's impatient nonexplanation—*you know, reports or something, presentations*—made nothing clear. Her bright, distracted kiss—"See you"—and gone, and before I left too (late already, what the hell) one last look around at all the new detritus, Lena's things moved in and come to stay: piles of books and her silver lamp, silver clock and red pillow, her white T-shirt lying careless to one side

(pick it up)

and feeling silly, giddy with a kind of adolescent glee I raised it to my face to find the scent of her skin, nocturnal curve of neck and shoulder, so beautiful; then let it fall to lie as it had been, calm as a question mark, white as a shadow's ghost upon the floor.

Our routine evolved without question, as if it had always been this way: mornings were Lena and Sophie in the bathroom, me making coffee, the three of us deciding what to do after work: and Lena always full of plans, ideas, there was always something to do. Gallery openings, theater benefits, open-mike readings; we went to the movies, foreign films and blockbuster one-guy movies (christened so by Sophie because "When it ends, everybody's dead except one guy"): passing the popcorn back and forth, Sophie's legs hooked high over seat backs and Lena slouched low and lower, one knee canted to touch mine as I sat content between them. We went to clubs, lots of clubs, much of it chiming for Sophie and me—thrash bars, piss on the floor—but some pure uncharted territory, places odd enough to dazzle: like Lady Bountiful, where most of the women were incredibly overweight (and most of the men were not); or the Spa, where the clientele was off-duty hookers, whores' night out and No Soliciting; and—for a brief while our favorite—Hysterium, where Tuesday night was always Spanking Night: get spanked on the dance floor and your cover is free, free drinks for your table if you're bare-assed when they do it and "Well?" me to Lena, "who's next?" to Sophie's giggle, bright eyes back and forth as "Oh no," Lena's head to one side, one hand light on my leg. "Only my *intimates* can see my ass."

And the next night downtown, ringside table at Punch 'n' Julie's where we watched two bulked-up teenage girls in bicycle shorts whack each other stupid with foam-rubber baseball bats: "You," my nudge to Lena, "you have a real nose for this, don't you?"

One of the girls now staggered to her knees, Sophie's shriek and Lena leaning closer, lips to my ear in all the noise: "The stink of kink," as the other girl, sweat-grim and panting, stood gladiator with the day-glo bat a sword to the other's throat: Lena squeezing my leg now, her curving smile: "We who are about to bunt, salute you."

Walking back from the club still talking too loud, rising moon and the tail of a rainy breeze, Sophie hands in pockets saying, "I don't usually like, you know, sports. But when that one girl sat on the other one's chest? Shit. You were right," to Lena. "That was *intense*."

And *she* was right, Sophie, that was exactly the word and not only for this night but for all the nights before and yet to be, the places Lena showed us, the people we met, all of them informed by that same intensity, her intensity: as if she were eager to give us her version of life, in bites and nibbles, drops and cropped pieces that we might then fit together as mosaic to our own lives, the things we knew and the things we didn't, hand in hand with the notion of growth and how right I had been about her necessity, how right we all were to live together, to be together and in the being become what we truly were, gifted by Lena as if everything she gave was a gift of self, something of her in everything she showed us, everywhere we went, a way to know her, a way to see inside: *look at this* like a work in progress and we did, and we did, and we did.

Not that we spent no time at all apart. Sometimes Sophie and I did things, met for quick dinners, ran errands; or sometimes it was Lena and Sophie shopping, or dropping in at AmBiAnce to gossip with Po, ugh; and sometimes Lena and I would meet, lunch or coffee, arm in arm in the way she liked to walk—she was a very tactile person, Lena, hand on my shoulder, arm around Sophie's waist, all those little touches, little squeezes and pats; *like a come-on* I would have said if things were different, if it were any other woman but not here because this was Lena, this was us—although of the pairings we did that least, Lena and I; why? Because then we made a couple, but not a "real" one? Because sometimes when she took my arm, kissed my cheek I thought *what would it be like?* Pandora's question, but here the question was safely moot for even if in honesty's bright room I could admit, yes, to wanting those touches, enjoying her closeness, the scent of her, the feel of her, well so what? because that was just not the game, never the issue; if anyone in our trio was the fifth wheel, the odd man out, it was me.

Although never, I knew, intentionally, no clear or purposeful exclusion, still from the beginning there was between them what I never shared or could: a kind of agreement without discussion, sometimes it seemed without talk at all and *how did you know?* I wanted to ask—how did you know she meant for you to call that guy at the bookstore, pick up ice cream at the grocery, send a birthday card to Po's sister? *I just knew.* Something in the air, in the hormones and never mind all the dumb-ass locker-room fantasies, the questions and the jokes: *so what's it like?* from guys I knew, guys met at work or clubs and when I told them it was just a roommate thing—no ménage à trois, no pussy sandwich—inevitable too their disappointment, disbelief: *oh come on* as if I lied simply to thwart their fantasies but "That's how it is," I would say, shrugging, "that's all there is to it," still aware as I spoke that I *was* telling less than the truth, concealed corkscrew layers of kink and not their definition either but how could they have understood that?

And further still past understanding was that what they thought they wanted, that life imagined past all denials as mine—two on one, the miniseraglio—was not about the man at all but instead at its center, its warm core a peculiarly feminine place so that where we truly lived, the heart's architecture of our life, belonged to Lena and to Sophie far more than it ever could to me. Drenched and bounded, immersed in the female, their ways and wants, their moods, their subtle sadnesses; a stranger in Girl-World but still the purest paradox: how be closer to anyone than I was to them, and they to me? and why wish for more when nothing could be better, when I could dream of dreaming nothing else?

And so no need to tally time in twos because by far the best times, the most fun of all was the three of us together, Sophie and I content to follow Lena's lead and why shouldn't we, when it was taking us where we wanted, where we needed to be? Forget all the carping, neighbor Jim's acid mailbox smile, Po's dry frown and "You know you're even starting to look like her," to Sophie off-duty, me impatient by the AmBiAnce door. "Like those slingbacks, which you used to hate, remember? and red lipstick now . . . and you too, Stonehenge," curt nod at me. "She's getting to you too."

" 'Getting' to me, what's that supposed to mean?" Fucking Po. "You know people who live together pick up stuff from each other, that's just the—"

"Oh sure," that slow roll of her eyes, "just natural give and take, right? So tell me, when's the last time you went to, what's that damn greasepit called—Diesel's, right— when's the last time you went to Diesel's?"

Diesel's: gummy cheese fries and cheap tap beer that always smelled like disinfectant, always gave us headaches, Sophie and I used to dance to the jukebox and Sophie now looking to me as my shrug echoed her own: "I don't know," I said, "what's that got to do with—"

"I bet you don't go at all anymore," said Po, "or to that other pit either—Miss Kitty's, right? Sophie, you used to love Miss Kitty's. Why'd you stop going?" and for her question no answer, we just didn't, what difference did it make?

"I'll tell you what the difference is, it's that Lee doesn't like them, am I right?" and my rise to lean deliberate on the counter where she stood counting out a drawer, *ten twenty thirty* and "I see what I see," she said, "I know what I know and I've known Lee a long time. A *long* time," and echo of that tone, where? yeah, *EdVentures, Lee's been ALL the way around.* "But it's none of my business," a final shrug. "You want to act like she does and talk like she does, you want to be her, go ahead. You weren't all that shit-hot to begin with, and *you*," to Sophie hanging up her smock, "I'd rather see you copy her than *him*."

And pushing harder than I should have at the door, green-glass door to swing and bang and I could do my own diagnosis, thank you very fucking much, I knew perfectly well what Po's trouble was: she was jealous. Jealous as Jim of the three of us together, the way everything she'd said would happen hadn't and even more so—of course and absolutely—of Sophie's bond to Lena: for hadn't Po always considered herself Sophie's mentor, big sister, best friend besides me? Glad to tell her how to dress, how to juice suppliers for free samples, how to handle asshole clients, answer questions, give advice—and now someone else to take her place, someone closer now than she ever was; natural her jealousy, anyone would be.

Back home to find that Lena had stopped for pizza, black olives and sticky white cheese, Sophie struggling with the wine and Lena there behind her, hands on her hands, helping her work free the cork and even if, I thought, even if Po was in some way correct, even if it was the kind of thing Sophie's college roomies used to bitch about—subsumation, was that it? two turning to one?—how could that be *wrong?* Sifting through memories of clubs and movies, Bowl-a-Row Night and lectures on classical music and if we had changed under Lena's tutelage, if we had let go of places like Diesel's or Miss Kitty's it was only a function of balance, of replacing this with that, going here instead of there because the locus, the function of the game, our game, our kink had not changed at all but in fact—as I knew, as it should—had deepened, still irrevocably the game yet different, made for three to play instead of two.

So forget it, I told myself, forget Po: and joined them then on the living room floor, sharing sections of the paper and "Listen to this," Lena shifting to schoolteacher voice to read aloud: " 'Regardless of its ultimate share of the marketplace, the female condom must remain a potent symbol of caution in an age of plague.' Also makes a great food-storage bag," and then she told us a story, about a sex club she and a friend had once visited, more than a little curious and "It was," she said, "the most depressing thing you ever saw. Sweaty guys with tits as big as mine, and their wives all *smiling*, handing out these flavored condoms, and we just sat there in our little towels with flowers on them—with *stains* on them—pretending to take notes because we told everybody we were researchers, we weren't there for the sex at all—"

"Then what were you there for?" leaning warm against her to feel her shrug, that long half-smile and "I don't know," she said. "Kink, I guess, what else? Anyway, when the club closed we went to this all-night coffee bar and my friend said impotence could also be a *choice*, and *I* said—"

Overtaken then by Sophie's giggles, crescendo crow to invite Lena's own but I was thoughtful, and later I asked if she had ever gone back there, ever seen those people again.

"What, the swingers' club? No, never," collecting her pizza plate, the discarded papers and "Why?" teasing, stopping short to lean against me in the doorway, her back against my chest. "You want to go?"

"No," I said. "I want to show you something."

So was Po right? Admitting nothing still I had to see, answer the question, put it to rest so "Let's go out," my next-morning's invite, Lena sipping coffee, Sophie in the bathroom putting on her face. "We can meet after work."

"Sophie works till nine tonight."

"No," I said, "I mean, you know, just us. Me and you," and "Oh, my," nudging me with her shoulder, soft dig against my own, "a date? This is all so sudden, Rhett."

But she was there on the dot in front of this week's building, DATATRAC in streamlined caps like a caption above her head: "So what's up?" as she took my arm, all in black today, black suit, hair in her favorite silver clip. "Where to?" but I didn't tell her, I wouldn't say, big secret until there we were, on the sidewalk before the peeling pink awning of a two-story sex boutique: Curlie's Downtown Stud Shop.

And Lena's stare, head swiveling in disbelief: "I left work early for this?" but "I know, I know," as I pushed at the door, 18 and Over Only in eye-level stick-on letters. "But bear with me here, this is better than it looks."

"It would almost have to be," and inside the smell strangely like old clothes, dead air uncirculated and in barely half a minute's browse at the wall-to-wall magazine rack "Oh look," she said, holding it aloft, "*Jug Juice*." Which turned out to be a lactation stroke-zine, the most amazing pictures on the cheapest possible stock and she had sussed the trick instinctively, How Low Can You Go? and better at it than Sophie, better even than me, a nose for sleaze unparalleled: black-and-whites hideous and grainy, weird Danish horse porn and "Hey, here's one for us," waving something big and day-glo bright beneath my nose: a two-way dildo, leather waistband back and front and pretending to quote from the label: "For the three-some who has everything."

"Is that what we are?" leaning over her shoulder, her smooth hands on the weird green plastic. "A threesome?"

"Well, we're not a couple," tossing the dildo back to the counter, "are we? There's you two, and then there's me. . . . Oh, look, it's a blow-up doll. No, wait—it's a blow-up *torso*," examining the package, "just tits and crotch. No head, so you never have to make conversation: 'A Boon to the Lonely Bore,'" and so on down the counter, thumbcuffs and leather blindfolds and Make-It-Last Oil, her pretty scorn to scatter a clutch of teenagers hunched under the video monitors, all of them rattled to see a woman in there, a beautiful woman unembarrassed by the skanky magazines, the tacky sex toys and see me grinning in her wake, enjoying the joke on both levels: oh this was the game all right, prime kink and strangely sexy too, to be with her this way, in this place, nudging and joking and handling all the merchandise, laughing so we roused even the somnambuiistic clerk sitting glued to his radio, reggae and static and "You got to buy somethin'," peremptorily to me, "or go. You too, lady."

"It all looks so wonderful, how can I choose?" and emergent into the street, fresh air and "That," two fingers fanning her face, "is what they call *atmosphere*. You sure know how to show a girl a good time."

"Wait, there's more," and the rest of the afternoon, pale light gone to sunset I showed her my version of the cheap: all the places we used to go when we were fresh out of school, terminally broke, and lots of it gone now—the used bookstore, Paperbucks, become a peep-video outlet, the Salvation Army thrift store now some kind of titty bar—but much was still the same, Dollar Drugs and Proud Paul's still 24-Hour Food, sign as old as the grease in the fryers as if no time at all had passed yet there I was with not Sophie but Lena, and time *had* passed and things had changed, different now inside and out and "So tell me one thing," Lena said. "Why are we here?"

"Chance," I said, elbowing out of my coat. "Blind, random Darwinism."

"No, stupid, *here*." One finger pointing at the cruel fluorescents, sticky booths and broken jukebox and what could I say to her? That I was just a lovable cheap date at heart? That I was proving Po wrong? and so for a minute silence, half a shrug and "I don't know," not entirely untrue but she deserved more and so "I guess I just wanted to show you stuff," another shrug, *you* know, "show what we were like, what I was like when—"

"Coffee?" in two ugly cups, cup and coffee the same dogshit brown and "This way they never have to wash them," Lena sniffing at the boiled-steam smell, and as the waitress walked away I said, "Hey, don't complain, at first I was going to take you out to Chicks."

"Chicks? What's that?"

"It's a topless bar," and why, after Curlie's, this adolescent blush? as Lena pulled a sour face: "Oh, be still my heart. I bet you say that to all the girls."

"Actually I don't," head down, stirring my coffee. Round and round, silver spoon, why the hell had I brought it up anyway? "I never took anyone there, I never even took Sophie there."

"Really," but it wasn't a question which was good because I had no answer, I didn't know why I'd never shown Sophie or even told her about Chicks: dumb red-velvet sweatbox where the music was lame Top 40 and every dance was a table dance. I hadn't even been inside for years but I still knew where it was, even had—why?—the discount card creased pink and furtive in my wallet: ten visits and you get a free drink. Stupid, but I never threw it away, kept it like a memory and why in the world would I want to take Lena there now? To demonstrate what an asshole I could be? *You liked Curlie's, now try Chicks!* and "I don't know why," I said, looking up to look away, back again to see her smile bloom, a softer smile than I had ever seen from her and "I do," she said, taking my hand, fingers laced warm with my own. "It's a kind of gift, isn't it? To show something that means something to you, something you've never shown anybody before. Even if it's silly. *Especially* if it's silly. Right?" and of course she was, so right that there could be no more embarrassment, she had rescued me from myself and so we talked instead about our afternoon-turned-evening, the Meet the Past tour she called it and "I can just imagine you," sipping the bad black coffee, the former Jess-and-Sophie special—grilled cheese and soggy fries, the cheapest thing on the menu—lying dingy before us on a faintly stained white plate.

"Sophie showed me some pictures once, of you two in her old apartment—she was wearing some kind of Renaissance hat, and you had such long hair—"

"Sophie and her hats. And her famous opera cape," and led by her questions, always the right questions, I told stories, silly things we'd done: dress-up parties with clothes from Goodwill or Council Thrift, our Sherpa walks in the snow, the ill-fated plant-watering service: "Get rich slow," sipping my coffee, sugar gritty as sand at the bottom of the cup. "Watch plants die. We ended up spending at least twice as much as we made, just replacing all the stuff we killed," but it was funny now, remembering our dismay, Sophie and her borrowed sprayers, how were we to know they'd been used for chemicals?

"Well, you could have asked," but she was smiling, reaching for a napkin and "You're so lucky, to've had Sophie all that time, to be together. I never had a friend, you know, that way. I knew a lot of people, I never had problems meeting people, but never like that, a *good* friend, a best friend." No smile at all now; gazing at me. "I haven't had a best friend since I was six years old."

Which hurt me, somehow, as if I should have been there, somehow should have known and never mind the way people talked to her, touched her, hung on her because you could be more lonely, more infinitely apart in a crowd where, knowing, you stay at last unknown, but instead I put my arm around her, pulled her close and "You do now," I said, "you have two," and then a question of my own, change the subject to her own school days, *hard time in collegetown* she'd said once, where was that?

"Oh, school," dryly, "school was such a waste. . . . I

spent most of my time hanging out with these people, these guys who—they had this business they were trying to start, right, and so they started selling coke to make money. It's not like they were dealers, really, they were chem majors and it just seemed like an easy way to—"

"Dealers? What were you doing going around with dealers?"

And Lena's answering shrug: "I didn't 'go around' with them, I just knew them," so offhanded that for me all at once, Damascus jolt came full and concrete the idea, the *fact* of her past: like a giant picture with a million details, all the hours, days, nights spent with others, people I didn't know, would never meet: lovers and friends, school and work, clubs and parties and excursions to unnamed destinations, each day a place, each year a dwelling, houseful of rooms I had never seen, doors and mirrors and passageways to go deeper and deeper, narrowing whorl to the heart of her heart and inside myself then the need to see them, see all of them, know her from the inside out, the way I knew Sophie, knew myself. To *have* her, whole and entire: and I would have said more, asked more but all at once she seemed sad again, seemed to want only silence so I stopped talking and kept her close, her leg pressed against mine, my arm around her shoulders; thinking of how it must have been for her, so beautiful and so rare, so terribly rare which means *alone*, alone in all those rooms of memory with no one to give her what she really needed, share what she really was.

And to be here like this, so close to me, so dear made it seem as if she had been with me always, her past somehow my own: warm in the booth as those countless, drowsing

78

hours spent here with Sophie, rag-doll head on my shoulder, hand in my lap, dexterous, teasing, touching hand, my own in mimic and sometimes we could hardly wait, racing one another to get home, get to bed and once or twice we had not waited, slipped concealed beside a Dumpster, hidden by the back of a van, open coat and lifted skirt, and aroused now by those memories, yesterday's passions unchanged, I turned my head—without thinking, I swear—and I kissed her.

That warm parting mouth, nothing like Sophie

nothing

and I could have drawn back, pulled away

but I didn't, still there and Lena reaching, soft fingers to touch my cheek, just the tips of her fingers and "Jess," her whisper, "you're my friend now too, aren't you? Aren't you?"

"Of course I am." Feel my heart hammer and no thoughts past the hunger, the heat of vast surprise which was really no surprise at all, was it? Was it? "You know I am."

"Then don't be afraid," she said. "Don't be afraid of me."

"I'm not," as she tilted her head, crushed flowers faint and warm

don't

don't be afraid

and I kissed her again, the way she wanted; warm narrow lips, her fingers loose and fisted light and I was hard, so hard, one hand beneath the suit coat, my fingers on her hip through the black slide of her skirt—and then her head turning, slow turn to rest gently on my shoulder, one hand slipping like a child's into my own and we sat that way in silence, food forgotten, sat until my heart slowed and Lena said at last, "We'd better go."

Outside much colder now, dark edge to the wind and I felt so strange, as if something big had happened, as if action was now to be taken but what was there to do? and Lena linking arms with me, the way we always walked and "Sophie should be home by now," checking her watch, the name from her mouth so easy and natural and in such contrast to my own, what? guilt? Was I guilty? No. Yes. Of what?

Jess, you're my friend now too, aren't you?
Would you fuck her?

"She might be, you know, wondering . . ." Trying to sound normal, like she did. "Because it's kind of late."

Flash smile, as if at a joke unwitting and "Oh, Jess, don't worry," her kiss on my cheek chaste and brief as a sister's. "I'm sure she isn't wondering at all."

Back home in silence then to the stink of scorched pizza, Sophie pinball from mutter to shout to a pout of self-pity because the customers were all creeps, she was dying of a toxic migraine, she was going straight to bed so goodnight, everybody, don't wait up, get lost. And Lena studious with her briefcase, armful of work and off to the kitchen, teapot shriek of boiling water: "Jess? You want tea?"

"No," the newspaper unread before me, "no thanks." There on the floor like I always sat, just as if nothing had happened but nothing *had* happened, had it? One kiss— all right, two kisses—in a mood of confidence and nostalgia, what was that, armageddon? The end of the world?

Don't be afraid of me.

And rising then past the sounds of her motion I crossed silently into the bedroom to climb fully dressed into bed, to reach for Sophie and hold her close: familiar the feel of her, her breasts in my hands and I slept still holding her, slept to dream like an open door: of Lena, long, lurid dreams in which we kissed endlessly there in the coffee shop booth, her tongue in my mouth, my hands rapid and fierce on her body, tugging at her jacket, mauling at her skirt, one dream daisy-chain to the next—and waking then abrupt as nightmare, wide awake to slip from Sophie's grasp, my cock stiff and hot and tight

and silent step from the room to stand as silent, breathing loud and look: at that sleeping face, face of my dreams sleeping naked there beneath the paisley quilt and what if I bent, just now, and

touched her

kissed her, just a little kiss on her cheek and she would stir and say *What are you doing up?* and I would say—no, she would say nothing, she would just know, know what I wanted and she would lift the quilt, warm quilt and underneath her body as warm, open for me, ready for me and

her flickering eyelids, my blundering hurry, into the bathroom to sit breathless, wait in shame to calculate the stretching moments: three minutes, five, is she back to sleep now? so out again, to glance—just one glance—to where she lay in shadows

and I saw that she had moved, rolled in her sleep to tug free the coverlet, make bare the mound of one breast: rounder than Sophie's, palest skin and dark sweet nipple and the face above still wrapped in silence, in the fathom-less confines of dream

and no sound made as I passed her, away and gone into my room, our room where swift past Sophie's breathing I closed the door, slipped back into bed to lie like wood, arms martial at my sides and *what's the matter with you, what's the MATTER with you:* as I tried to calm my breathing, calm my heart beating fast as a burglar's, a trespasser in the oldest room of all.

Alarm's cry, morning and pulled from a thick dead-feeling sleep by the feel of shame itself like a dream: *peeping tom,* dumb fantasizing jerk but Lena didn't know, neither of them knew or ever would and so breakfast like always, Sophie grumbling over work, Lena making plans for dinner, how about this place Sultana's, Middle-Eastern food with dancing, how about that?

"You mean like belly dancing?" Sophie's damp head to one side, towel around her neck like an athlete's, a prize-fighter's. "I love belly dancing."

"What about you, Jess, you want to try Sultana's?" White blouse buttoned high at the neck; the smallest smile. "Or would you rather go out for cheese sandwiches?"

Looking only at the table top, coffee cups, fat sugar bowl and "Sure," I said, my voice distant even to me. "Sultana's sounds fine."

First to arrive at the restaurant, hunched in the wrap-around booth, dragging still like Marley's ghost my all-day anger, dull disgust like a headache in the heart and all at once Lena, brief shoulder-squeeze as she slid into the booth beside me, reached to take the glass from my hand, Scotch and water ordered but undrunk: "So, where's Sophie?" as if everything was normal. "How was your day?"

Just lovely, thanks; I spent it thinking of you. Incidentally you have a terrific left breast, really incredible, I'd like to see them both if you don't mind. "My day," looking anywhere but at her, "my day was just tip-fucking-top." Faint lipstick mark on the rim of the glass, cosmetic taste as I drank. "And Sophie's late. As usual."

"Jess, what's the matter?" Her smile half gone, not sure, leaning close enough for me to touch; *hands off.* "Are you upset about something?"

"Why should I be upset?"

"Beats me." The waiter came; she ordered her own Scotch, no water, no ice. "Maybe because we had such a nice time yesterday? Maybe you feel guilty or something?"

A nice time, sure. "Or maybe," I said, "maybe you shouldn't talk about 'cheese sandwiches,' wink wink, in front of Sophie. Maybe that's the kind of thing that really—"

That stare purely level, the depth of those eyes and "I'll talk," as level, "about whatever I want, whenever I want, to whomever I want. Which includes Sophie. And if you want to feel guilty, if you want to make a big secret out of nothing then I feel sorry for you."

Nothing? Her mouth on mine: *don't be afraid of me.* "I wouldn't call that nothing," and back, fast: "What would you call it then?" and what could I say to that? What *would* I call it? Hunger: I want you: and "Hey," Sophie breezing in, bending to kiss and envelop me in some weird chemical smell: "Oh, sorry," when she saw my face, apparently they were using some new treatment at work, some triple-strength hair coloring "but it works," serene, "so what the hell. The clients don't care how they smell anyway, and—"

"Have you ever heard," I said, "of rubber gloves? Maybe Po could break down and buy you a pair. Maybe two pairs, in case one has a blowout. Or there's this stuff called soap and water . . ."

Her pause, head to one side in what Lena called Sophie's bird look, you don't know if she wants a bread crumb or to peck out your eyes. "Nice to see you too, ass-hole," and to Lena, "What's *his* problem?"

And Lena, Lena not a bird but a cat, slow chiseled feline stare and then away as if nothing concerning me could ever begin to have relevance to her and what if, I thought, what if I said what I was thinking, a little table talk to start the evening off right: *hey Sophie, guess what we did yesterday?*—and the waiter then to tell us that the dancing would start in just a moment, we should just sit back and relax.

"Gee, thanks," I said, "these pins and needles were killing me," to Lena's raised eyebrows, Sophie's sigh like a neon sign: *Jess is a jerk* and I was and I knew it, exiting then to go stand in the men's room until I felt I could maybe go back and sit between them with my mouth decently closed until later, when I was calmer, later at home where I would take Lena aside and say to her, say—what? *I don't want anything bad to happen, I don't want anything to change* and I would be very calm and reasoned, I would clear the air, make everything the way it should be . . . and crossing then to the table under cover of spotlit darkness, the dancing had started, waiters moving like ships in a channel, silent to serve from trays as big around as hula hoops and "Look at that," Sophie's whisper to Lena, both of them ignoring me in favor of the dancers, "look, isn't she gorgeous?" and they kept on ignoring me too, all through dinner and the way home and *okay*, I thought, *okay that's fine with me* although it wasn't but what else for me to do?

And at home my plan's evaporation, unable to talk, to speak, to say more than goodnight as they sat talking on the fold-out, their murmurs road and river, landscape and background like the quiet talk of those who speak another language, whose discussion holds a meaning one cannot guess or know: and that night like last night, tomorrow night and all its brothers, red genie burst hot from the bottle—why? and why now? yet beneath all my questions, my logic and deprecating scorn still came that endless, mindless yammer, wet dreams like a teenager who's never been laid: Lena on the fold-out, in my cubicle at work, stretched in the back of a midnight cab all closed eyes and dark nipples, both hands out to beckon me in: and waking from that storm to sit across from her at breakfast, to eat dinner with her, to watch her walk around the house and no matter how I tried to pretend that nothing was happening, pretend that I had control—presto change-o, simple as that there was no control, no way to stop what had now begun in earnest—but *are you really trying?* to stop thinking about her, stop asking like a finger finds a sore that darkest, simplest question, inquired at last by flesh of the hungry mind: *what would it be like?*—how would she look, feel under my hands, my mouth, tongue and fingers, nipples and cunt

stop it

and was this after all the real reason for that altruistic invitation, *move in with us* and my harsh red jealousy a flag, unspoken warning from self to self: *this is not what you think it is*, only the body believes as I chased the prior absolution of propinquity for what I had been secretly wanting all along, wanting since I met her and now enacting only the long-expected—ménage à trois, *just you wait* and never mind my smugness, Jess who never cheats, who would never dream of cheating and especially not here, oh no, oh my, is just another guy, another kinkless, game-poor asshole who can't imagine any farther than the end of his cock: sure, go on and kiss her, dream of her, dream of fucking her and here comes the snake into Eden, *your* snake, big joke and everyone knew it would happen, everyone *wanted* it to happen and now you want it too, don't you? Don't you?

But am I the only one who wants it?

Don't be afraid of me.

And what about Sophie, trusting Sophie my best friend for so long, partner in kink, co-creator of this art of every day—and I tried, then, reached back through memory to find guides, to ask *had it been this way with her too*, in the beginning, this slavish, wordless hunger? but no true comparison because it had all been so different, so little impediment, her own brief reluctance and then all day every day, no walls, no doors, no reason to stop—and was *that* the real attraction here, the idiot lure of the forbidden? Could I, with vast infant cunning, hiding motive from self and self from motive go on now to jeopardize what we three had made just to force from *no* the slick relief of *yes*? Could anyone be that selfish, that heedless, that dumb?

More than anything I hated the thought of being dumb.

Then *stop it*, I told myself, *don't be alone with her, stop thinking* but good intentions were nothing: for every minute safe on the tablelands, the place where I might stand apart and—*you poor fuck*—grant to myself if not pity then a kind of cold compassion, there were hours, nights spent in the trenches, no way to shut it off, no way to keep from looking and wanting what I saw: there for me, there every day and the net effect a deeper helplessness, comfort nowhere, between them all abraded with desire and desire.

How can this happen?

You want it to happen.

Don't be afraid of me.

Sometimes, times alone I would sit—eating lunch, on a break—and think of what to do: *maybe you should go away, just leave, maybe Lena should leave* but take one look at Sophie, Sophie in the middle so *talk to them, just tell them just sit down and say we have to talk* but imagine then their faces, the same look shared—dismay, disgust—and I knew I couldn't do it, would strangle in the trying, simply could not bring myself to say the words: what words: *I want you, I want to have you both.*

And so my usual solution, which was no solution, *let it go* and on my feet again, another walk around the block—

"Again?" Sophie on the fold-out wrapped in an old

chenille blanket, long bare toes tucked into that pink co-coon. "What're you, training for a marathon or some-thing?"

"I'll be back," while passing Lena in the kitchen, Lena by the door to gaze and say nothing, black jeans and blouse so thin I could see her nipples through the cotton, dark nipples slightly hardened by the draft beneath the door: *oh God* and gone, down the stairs and did she know, did they both know what I was thinking, guess my dreams and at their tandem talk and laughter I would think: so has Lena told her, are they laughing at me, angry at me, sorry for me, *what?*

Stop it for the millionth time, *just stop thinking* as I went again around the block, wind undercut with moisture, not quite rain but then it started, big drops and cold, rain in my eyes like tears of self-pity so back home again, trudg-ing past them in their pink chenille cocoon as they shared a magazine, my smile to theirs purely false and exhausted as I crawled into bed, face in the pillow like a mournful child's and Sophie in silhouette to climb upon me, rub my back with those stern girlish hands, fingers reaching to tickle, tickle between my legs and "Hold still," her solemn smile in the darkness, "I gotta get that bug that's up your ass."

Pulling her down, pulling her to me and what would she think, my sweet Sophie, what would she do if she knew that when we made love I sometimes made of her Lena, those breasts imagined, swept and bucking to trai-tor's orgasm, who's fucking who? but—*oh so smart, don't kid yourself*—maybe she already knew, already forgave, understood . . . and wasn't that another little-boy fantasy,

88

the love unconditional, the all-forgiving goddess? Right, sure. Try it sometime, tell me what happens.

And even at work "You're not concentrating," from that week's supervisor, some prick with last year's haircut and a discount suit and *Hey, buddy*, I wanted to say, chin like a fist in his face, *hey buddy I'm concentrating plenty, I'm concentrating so hard my head's about to split* but of course he was right, I was fucking up, I had to get myself together and stop thinking, stop worrying, stop analyzing Lena's every move, Sophie's every frown, every tiny twitch of my ever-hungry cock: sifting through gesture and motive, it was not my forte, I was not the analytical type which of course made it all that much harder, made me all that much wilder, driven to ground and *enough*, that inner cry, *enough is enough and I really can't take this, I can't take too much more of this shit*

but I was still there, wasn't I? Like Lena, like Sophie; every morning, every night.

Pleasant dreams.

"So let's go out," mumbling to Sophie, head nuzzled between her breasts, the covers pulled like a tent above our heads, a barrier to keep out the rest of the world. My sleepless eyes itching like an allergy, ache like a hinge in the small of my back and "C'mon, Sophie, just me and you. Like a date. Like we used to. Okay?"

"Jess," drawing back to raise my face, fingertips to my chin and she was smiling but not her real smile, something else there in her eyes and "Baby, what's the matter? You're acting so weird lately, you're—"

"Weird," I said, "me and you on a date, what's so weird about that?" and inside past the grin I tried to make normal *oh, Sophie, please,* my face again between her breasts, *please, Sophie, just say yes.* Because I want things the way they should be, the way they used to be but you have to cooperate, I can't do this alone and "All right," her own smile dubious, "sure, we can go out."

"Tonight," I said. "Let's do it tonight."

And from Lena no questions, no comment past a friendly "Have fun" as Sophie in sweet black and me behind trundled briskly out the door, out into the night, out for dinner and dancing and my grim verve insured that everything went wrong; no cabs and no reservation, second-choice club and dancing set after set, wanting her to want this as much as I did, to show somehow some sign that she realized my great inner struggle, to win me over, win me back, make things the way they used to be and "Jess, what's the *matter* with you?" Sophie pettish at last to pull her fingers from my grasp. "I don't want to dance anymore, I'm tired."

"Don't you love me?" Splash and spill of champagne in our glasses, last of the second bottle and already my head hurt, an ache like lead between my eyes. "Don't you want to be with me, am I boring you or something? Can't you be happy for one night without Lena?"

And her face then very still as if I had insulted her, hurt her in some clever new way unknown even to me and "I can be ex*treme*ly happy," articulating with great precision every syllable of every word, "without Lena. I can be happy without you too if it comes to that, I can be *ecstatic* just all by my*self*—" and slumped in my own failure I closed my eyes, slow champagne swallow, brick by brick, somebody ought to drink it and it might as well be me because none of this was really about Sophie after all, was it, none of it meant for her pleasure but instead just guilty reparation in escrow for the times to come: and her voice winding down finally, not finished but done and "I want to go home," sullen as if I would deny her that too as I had denied her, what, her ability as a human being to entertain herself or whatever the rant had been, I had just stopped listening, I had had enough for one night too.

And so back home, easy enough to get a cab this time, everything's easy when you don't care anymore—and Lena sleeping when we came in, paisley coverlet to the chin, beautiful face like a bas-relief in the flicker of bathroom light; and off to our own cold bed where we lay with heads averted, twin trenches back to back, her long feet tucked under as if she could not take the chance of even that unconscious touch.

No talk with either in the morning, no word until after lunch, a message from the receptionist as I passed with felon's trudge: "Some woman called for you": Lena? but no, only Sophie's brusque reminder that I was to hurry home, we were expected at an opening for one of Lena's friends and "Gee thanks," to the receptionist, the note creased tight in my hand. "Thanks a lot."

"Hey hey," her narrowed eyes, "don't blame me, I just write them down," to which I said nothing, absolutely nothing at all and maybe, I thought, maybe I can't relate to women, any kind of woman at all, maybe I should just go off into the desert or become a Buddhist monk but instead went home as requested, into Verdi turned up much too loud, Sophie nowhere to be seen and Lena from the bathroom urging me to hurry but why should I? why rush off to where I had no desire to be, another ridiculous opening, performance art this time with, said Lena, spoken-word interludes *and* jelly-filled balloons, the curator was an old friend of hers who had just been hired by some museum as a graffiti preservationist and "Do you know," emerging beautiful from the bathroom, fixing the clip in her hair, "he knows eighteen different ways to spell *fuck*? In English alone?"

Shirt half-open, reaching for a beer, the dark citrus beer learned from Lena and "He must be very proud," I said. "Very *fucking* proud."

And Sophie then austere in black, heels so high she was shoulder to shoulder with Lena and "Well?" when I didn't move except to drink. "Is this like a new look for you or something, the Unkempt Look? Or are you planning to button your shirt so we can go?"

"No," staring at her, not loud, not mad. "I'm not."

Lena's gaze between us, careful and kind and "If you change your mind," she said, "the postcard's on the table. Galerie Cerise."

"No thanks," and the beer was empty but that at least was something I could control: more in the refrigerator and stores all over town, uptown and downtown and "I'm my own performance art," I said, "shows every hour on the hour," and "Come on," Sophie's head averted, hand on Lena's arm, "forget it, let's just *go*," with sudden odd emphasis, the word swallowed as if in tears and Lena bending then to kiss me, soft kiss hot on my cheek and gone, closing door and who, I thought, could blame them, either of them? Why would anyone choose to stay home with me when the alternative was a veritable festival of art, *jelly* balloons, my God, and a man who could say fuck in eighteen languages, it was more than worth changing clothes for something like that and I was just a killjoy, that's what I was, an oversexed self-obsessed stick in the fucking mud. Why shouldn't Sophie be angry, weep tears of disgust, why not? All I had tried to do was restore our relationship, all I had tried to do was show her a nice time but of course that could barely begin to compare with flying jelly, right, and Lena at her side, maybe we were both secretly in love with Lena, sure, why not?

And for tonight's solution to this ongoing problem, this endless triangular noose why not try beer, beer after beer and a bottle of wine, wine we'd been saving for some nice dinner at home but fuck that, fuck the niceties, be a sodden slob who doesn't have to think or wonder, flay himself, crawl up his own asshole looking for a way out and I sat there until the news was over, the late-night shows were done, they still weren't home but so what? Big girls in the big city and they could stay out all night long if the mood overtook them, toss jelly balloons at the stars if such was their pleasure because I was certainly nobody's pleasure tonight, not even my own.

And rising then for bed, brief but fierce the urge to vomit but in the end I wasn't that drunk after all, just drunk enough to scrape my shin bloody on the bed frame, to entertain myself with a ramble of self-pitying scenarios, the game gone wrong and all of it my fault: art turned to kink turned to heat turned to dust, only dust without it, nothing left . . . and visited again by dreams, Lena but

Sophie too this time, both of them in this very bed, our bed but where was I? Watching, crouched in a corner watching as if through some little hole, oh my, how Freud and they were touching each other, still in their party clothes, Sophie's hands rooting under Lena's skirts, Lena's dark head bending low, lower and I reached to join them, reached through the mists and waters but found only my own flesh, my solitary cock and then the picture changed, dwindled down to Sophie's face, Sophie's eyes owlish in some other dark and *go back to sleep*, she was saying, *Jess go back to sleep* and that part, I saw, was real, really Sophie on the edge of the bed, pulling off her pantyhose and "It's late," her whisper warm and slightly slurred, "very very late," and then she was under the blankets, hands locked loose around my chest, breathing in my ear and as my eyes closed all dreams left me, left me then in darkness and an hour's worth of peace.

Their morning voices, I had slept through the alarm; tired and sick, sick and tired and "You coming by today?" Sophie bright to Lena as I tugged twice at the chair to move it, find a way to use it to sit down. "To meet Kelsey?" *What time did you get home? Who's Kelsey?*

"And the best part," still Sophie, "is that he's really nice. Guys who're that cute are almost never nice," was that half-gaze for me? a dig, a nudge? "But *he* is. And he really is gorgeous, all that long blond hair and now he's growing this little goatee, it's so—"

Long blond hair, right. Shades of—what was his name, the erstwhile hair-sweeper? Andy, right, another long-haired blond and "How about lunch?" said Lena. "We can meet then."

"Meet who?" I said, silence made by the question. "That guy? What for?"

"Because he's a *cute guy*," Sophie singsong in the way she knew I hated, her defective robot voice. "Because women like to meet cute guys."

Automatic my stifled dismay, lurching brain in protest: *you can't do that* but of course she could and why not, why shouldn't Lena be introduced to a cute guy, why shouldn't she meet anyone she chose and "What's the matter with you?" Sophie staring at me as if I were even more of a moron than usual, "what's your trouble?" and "Nothing," pushing back from the table, from them. "Nothing at all. Enjoy your day," which was of course unseasonably cold, grim promise of the winter to come and why shouldn't Lena meet whomever she wanted, do whatever she damned well pleased?

Because I don't want her to: could not picture her with some stupid blond with a goatee, past fathoming her desire for anyone, anyone but us, *but me:* and furious at her, at Sophie too and at myself: why no relief, when surely this was the best thing that could happen, this would solve all my problems, take the matter right out of my hands so *why aren't you happy, stupid?* and home that night to Sophie only, scooping greenish pilaf onto a plate: "Hi," brief but not technically angry. "You want some of this?"

"No thanks." Ice water instead, I had been swilling water all day, still dehydrated and as casually as I could: "So where's Lena?"

"She went out."

Sprinkle of soy sauce, tiny *ting* of fork. "Out where?"

"With Kelsey. They went to dinner or something." Pouring herself a drink, red wine almost black in the silver glass and "You know," smiling at me, *smiling*, "at lunch they seemed to hit it off really well."

"Oh, really?" *Shut up.* "Did it ever occur to you," refilling my water glass, my back to her, "that she might be doing this just to humor you?"

"Oh, I don't think so," and just the barest edge, as if she knew, as if she was saying it on purpose to hurt me, sow the salt inside my sores. "She seemed pretty happy about the whole thing, and of course *he* was ecstatic. Who wouldn't be?"

"Of course." Dropping ice cubes like bombs, sloppy the splash and "What a good friend you are," I said, "just a regular Little Miss Matchmaker. Maybe you can fix Po up too, maybe you can set up your own little dating service, exclusive clientele, no reasonable offer refused—"

"And what," her slow swallow, clearing the decks, "just what the fuck's the matter with you, I mean what is your *prob*lem? What do you care if she goes out with him? Are you jealous or something?"

"You know, that's just like you," calm, well-reasoned, the beating of blood in my brain; *shut up.* "That's always the first thing you think, and I think it's because you're basically insecure, you know? I think it's because you have a basic problem with—"

"*I* think," still smiling, the smile of great rage, "I think you should stop acting like an asshole morning, noon, and night. Unless you can't. In which case you should just shut *up.*"

Which was excellent advice, but none I could apply: and flicking through channels trying not to think, staying up late but not too late, not late enough because Lena was still not home—and in the morning resisting the urge to say anything, to ask at all but Sophie determined to ask it for me: "So what time'd you get in?"

"Not so late," her yawn, so beautiful, was she even more beautiful today? "Maybe two. I'm feeling it now, though. Thank God for your coffee," and one hand out to ruffle my hair, stroking fingers and *stop it*, I wanted to say, *get your hands off me* but I wanted her hands, her touch, yearning like a child, like a fool and that moment more than ever told me flat as a blow to the body what I wanted, the red voice of need speaking straight from the back of the brain and yet see Sophie, there in her baggy blue blouse, bright eyes *but this*, I thought, *this has nothing to do with Sophie* which was a lie and I knew I was lying but—say it, go on—I didn't care because I wanted her, wanted her, wanted her now

and pushing away from the table, not another word and they might have called after me, my name or maybe not and then I was gone, out the door to a day's worth of pictures, cinema verité but spun on an axis changed and now it isn't you at all, is it? not you but some other face, other body in that picture, touching her, fucking her, long blond hair and *he really is gorgeous*, did she think he was gorgeous, had he fucked her yet? Why shouldn't he? Why shouldn't *she*, if that was what she wanted?

A colder wind, shadows falling early because the earth was turning, axis in motion and my dry hands fumbling with the mail, the keys, dragging half a day's work like a stone in my bag, the day gone in waste and anger and inside to find all empty, no one home and me restless from room to room, sit to rise to move again to the window, twitch the blind like fingers helpless to the itch beneath the skin: *where is she?*

and like a granted wish, a prayer answered the key in the lock, the opening door

and Lena alone, coming in to smile at me.

"Hi," and clicking closed the door, briefcase down and I said nothing, looked once to look away and something working inside me, grinding, rising, a barometric rage and "Well?" I said, "so how was it?" Hunched like a troll on the fold-out, my bag beside me like a broken sack. "Your date last night. How'd you like it?"

"Not so much," shrugging, "but he's okay." Shoes off, the hooks of the long jacket gleaming silver in the light. "He's taking me out to dinner tonight, some Jamaican place, he says he wants to teach me to eat with my fingers." Pale blouse, champagne color and her hair so very dark, freed from its clip to lie against her face, my Christ she was so beautiful and my voice like a stranger's, sick with envy like a mouthful of stones, bones and "You don't sound very happy," I said in that strange new voice. "Didn't you have a good time?"

"I told you, it was just okay. Nothing more, nothing less."

"Then why," rising, "why do you go out with him?" Stop it, this is none of your business: it is my business: voices in my head. They say crazy people hear voices that tell them what to do: I know what to do, *I know what I want* and Lena cool and almost offhand, finger and thumb to play with her necklace, small drops of silver like some rosary unknown and "What do you expect me to do, Jess? how do you think it is for me? You know I listen to you two screwing all the time, I can hear you through the wall," and abrupt and vast her mockery, voice a whispery, sugary moan: " 'Oh baby, make it happen, oh baby *yes*' "

looking at me, looking right into my eyes

and soft again that alto murmur: "So what do you expect? You have Sophie, and Sophie has you, but who's supposed to be for me, hmm? Who's going to do it for me?"

I am, did I say it out loud? There before her like a scene from the dreams, motion past thought, my hands on her shoulders and "I am," I said, and I kissed her: hard, very hard, kissed her so I couldn't breathe and then as if plunging past some trench, some depth unseen but charged with all desire, all I had ever wanted or dreamed as want I kissed her again and harder still, my hands up her back, on her ass, kissed her mouth and her face and her neck, crushed flowers and dragging her down: *enough* then and there, here and now on the floor by her shoes and my jacket, her work papers, reports crumpled and spread and Sophie could come home at any minute, walk in, walk in and see us

see me

grabbing at Lena's blouse, pulling off her bra, her arms locked around my neck and lifting her, raising her as she tugged at her panties, tugged them half-way down but "No," I said, no I want you naked, I want you to be *naked* and she was, she was, open for me like the dreams, wordless and smiling and "I can't," I told her, *I can't wait, I can't last* with my mouth against her cheek, her ear, sliding my tongue across her skin and I wanted to bite her, I wanted to taste her, I waited so long and "Why did you wait?" her voice breathless, hips canted high, "why did you make us wait so long?"

And holding her tight and tighter, crushing her to me so it had to hurt but I didn't think, I couldn't stop and her arms around me, strong fingers digging, digging at my back, my hips, pleasure's clamor gone to shriek, become scream in the body

and then we were still, my breath harsh and wet as if from a beating, her sweat on my skin, her face in my hands and feel the shudder go through me, paralytic, un-controlled; like the insect's drench-winged palsy as it creeps, all fright and hunger, at last from the torn cocoon.

"I love you," I said, to her silent face. "Lena, I love you."

Her closed eyes, breath on my cheek; her smile. Sticky thighs, damp flesh to peel back carefully from mine; the sway of her breasts as she rose, as she gathered her cloth-ing, pantyhose and bra and my eyes closing, deep breath in and out and now the sound of running water past the bathroom's open door, trickling water and I should wash, too, *destroy the evidence* but I did not move, lay where I was, arms crucifixion-wide against the floor as if motion was no true choice and perhaps I even slept a little, ex-haustion's doze because all at once Lena there beside me, hair tied back and wearing clothes, different clothes, some pale dress and "Jess," her whisper, the moth's touch of her kiss, "Jess, it's time to get up."

Looking up at her, looking into her eyes and I said

nothing, what was there to say? and so our kiss swift and chaste and off to the shower still sweet with her scent, shampoo smell and tumbling water as hot as I could get it, cataract spray and in its heat I felt I could stand forever, muscles lead-warm on my bones, all thoughts dissolved past words to a single humming sigh, the body in satiety, that little inner voice shut down at last: until another voice, Sophie's voice, Sophie's laughter and I closed my eyes, closed them in the water as if seeking some immersion, some greater depth at which I need never open them again.

And—as always, now incredible—our trio dinner, plump garlic shrimp and Sophie's tales of her workday, chopstick prod and I smiled and I ate and Lena smiled too as if we had not just screwed ourselves empty on the floor beyond this table, as if nothing had changed or ever would—and waiting, as I ate, as I smiled my dry felon's smile, for the truth to announce itself, shriek free like some fierce black bird to circle the room, to land at my feet but then what? then what will you do? Cry? Beg forgiveness, say you're sorry? but I wasn't sorry, was I? Because true contrition demands remorse, demands the wish to have the sin undone and *would you not have done it*, that voice inside my head, *do you wish you hadn't?*

And near as breath the tactile memory, the feel of her, the way her breasts moved, would you give that up? would you?

No.

Then why are you guilty? so calm the question and its answer there beside me, Sophie, my Sophie who drank most of the wine, who asked, arch, about Kelsey: "I thought you guys had a date tonight?" and Lena's graceful shrug: "I canceled," rising to take up the empty plates, bright ball of soiled napkins. "I decided I'd rather stay home."

Stay home: to write reports at the kitchen table, one knee bent beneath that white dress, angel's profile and I passed without stopping, without speaking, took up my own bag full of papers—dropped there, when? two hours ago, forever—to read through, make notes, catch up and "Herc," Sophie's nudge, coffee cup and not mad anymore, settling down beside me to read a magazine and it was as if somewhere inside myself I stood apart, watched from that darker promontory the way I sat, worked, turned to take Sophie's kiss and were they all false, those motions, did what I had done make a lie of what I did now? No: but why then this dislocation, here from there, time unstrung and spooling only from that moment, that writhing on the floor as if between her legs I knew another kind of birth, knew as surely as the infant, as the corpse that there would be no going back, that truth or lie, black bird or utter silence still nothing would ever be the same again.

Shoving papers back into my sack and "I'm tired," I said, "I'm going to bed." Door almost closed, undressing in that dark and Sophie now to join me, to lay atop the covers, fingers playing on my body and see, oh, that traitorous desire, half-guilt and half-excitement, see me strip her and kiss her with the knowing passion of longtime lovers and all the time comparing without conscious will the way their bodies differed, different textures, different scents: *she* is this way, *she* is that and I made her come again and again, my sweet Sophie, my wronged darling, made her sweat and groan and shake her head from side to side, tiny curls so pale, so unlike Lena's and when at last she was still, panting softly in my arms, I heard above our breathing another sound, a secret sound like

the opening door: to show me Lena there in back-lit pause, hair down, her face not visible but I saw that she was naked

and stepping calm as an executioner she crossed the room—two steps, four—to stand for a moment in darkness, then with that same exquisite calmness lie next to Sophie on the bed.

And all I did, could do was stare, clubbed still by the pounding of my heart as Sophie stirred, turned, open eyes and half a smile, smiling for Lena who reached one hand to stroke her cheek, tap two fingers to her lips—*shhh*—and draw up the covers about her, the two of them, the three of us

and then past all fear or wonder it *clicked* for me, the rightness of it, echo of that first night like a key in a lock, lock in the door behind which lives the one life that is yours, was meant always and from the start to be your own and when at last you see it there is no confusion, no disorder or surprise: *oh*, you say, *oh, so this is how it is, this is how it was meant to be:* this room, this bed, drowsy Sophie still damp from my touch and beside her Lena, Lena reaching now across that body curled between us to take and link my fingers puzzle-piece within her own.

"Of course I knew." We three at dinner, Sophie in the middle and wine poured for us, saffron shine beneath fake stained glass and one window right above us, two fair ladies at table reflecting red and gold and "How could I not know?" rolling her eyes in mock of a moony swain, Lena's laughter and "Oh come on," I said but I laughed too, easy with comfort, it could all be funny because it was over, because we had landed, heart's miracle, where we should have been all along, where we had been but oh, the difference with that last door opened, last step taken to make dance from stumble, art from meat and "Of course I knew," Sophie again and serious, "but what was I supposed to say? It's not like I was jealous, but really—go ahead, or what? is that what I should have said?"

"Come on," Lena's murmur, half to herself. "Come in," but "What if," I said, "what if I had just—"

"We had to wait," Sophie's glance swift to Lena, "because she said—because we knew it would happen. Not like *people*," with a swifter frown, "all the garbage people talk—it would be something *we* made, like—"

"Kink."

"Right. Right! and even if it took time for things to happen, for all of us to be together it would still be worth it, everything we had to go through to get there. . . . We knew it would happen, we were there already." Her glance for Lena: gratitude, relief? "We were just waiting for you."

"To do what? Go crazy?" but if in my own relief there was still that tang of anger—when I saw how easy it was, to reach and take, how absurdly easy it had always been and my own struggles shown to me now as the waste they were, pain's torque to twist me stupid and stupidly lost, a man awash in plenty eating his own heart in the dark—still being here made up for everything, made of that pain only a place I had been and need visit no more, a place worth no memory because here were no secrets, no desires unknown, only Sophie and Lena, Lena and Sophie to eat with me and talk with me and take me hand in hand back home, through early dark and rising wind, past our door like any other door to our bed where we could lie together, just that, lie together like children and "We need each other," said Lena, Sophie cuddled on her side, her face turned close to mine, "we belong together."

And I was nodding, closed eyes and mouth reaching, soft, soft, to kiss like a promise those narrow lips when from Sophie a sound, face bunched and knotted and "You were *hurt*," she said, one cold hand groping past Lena to find me, "we *hurt* you": wretched, her pain some mystery born of mine and "Sophie," my own alarm, half rising on one elbow, "Sophie, I'm okay, it's all right now," and Lena's wordless whispers, one-handed stroke of Sophie's hair, her face, wiping at the tears and "I love you," Sophie cried, wrenching then from both of us to roll away, alone, roll to the edge of the bed where she lay in fetus-curl to weep so her body shook, deep sobs and more alarmed I reached for her, gathered her to lie between us as slowly, slowly Lena's calming hand to stroke again her cheeks and forehead, her wet and closing eyes and soft the murmur, the voice of all comfort, *Sophie, Sophie* as I kissed her as softly, kissed her hair and folded hands, soothed her to quiet and a kind of sleep.

And our gaze to one another, Lena and I across her body as from that other dark wind struck the windows in faint and rattling whisper as if all the secrets of the world were loosed that night to fly, find home or haven, heart's nook to nestle and to grow and "She loves you," Lena's murmur, Sophie's hand in hers sweet and guarded as a child's. "She was very worried about you."

"What about you?" said softly, softly. "Were you worried too?"

The wind, rain's stutter like flung bones, the tiny bones of tiny creatures and "I don't worry," she said, the room's dark a caul before her eyes. "I just wait."

Change was what I expected: new ways, new rules unspoken—what now? and who sleeps where?—but although the surface might have shifted still the locus held unchanged, brought no subtraction: instead there was more of everything, and deeper, oh deeper than I ever could have dreamed.

Maybe we went out less, now that the game had truly come home, and there was like a closed door no more talk of Kelsey: "So what about him?" Sophie's nudge as if asking was the answer and "Oh, Kelsey," Lena's almost-smile and the whole exchange so subtle, so sly a feminine mockery that my own smile felt unsure: because I didn't see, not really, didn't get the total joke but in the end it could not matter because what could Kelsey, what could anyone from outside ever have to do with us?

Because that expansion, that deepening was, I saw now—now that I was able to see—a function of pure progression, the natural culmination of that whole gone wholly exponential and Lena—artless between us, in bed, at the table; feeding me apples and raisins, laughing at Sophie's jokes—somehow come to represent the process of kink itself: the riddle guessed without knowing because in some way she *was* the game, its passion and finesse, played by instinct, played for keeps; open hands and hungry core, the inner smile that asks of you all you have to give, a love demanding both generosity and greed, bordering on, what? danger? or call it risk, yes, risks always at such depths and hunger, oh new hungers born from each new day, more each day than the last imagines. I had thought we were as deep as we could be, but I had been wrong; only Lena, wiser, had fathomed the necessary, as if our sex was the last ingredient, the final drop to make of potion brew.

And in that potion's alchemy I came to see, to believe that Lena, catalyst and guide, was in some way for me—just me somehow, not Sophie—the next step. Sophie the first and sweetest, yes, Sophie to save me from my aimlessness, Sophie to make me real but Lena now in some new way the step beyond, the step necessary, essential evolution through means of purest kink, past control and glad to be and only she could take me there. And faithful, all this time, not from fear, some lockstep sense of duty but because there was no one like Sophie, never anyone to compare but through Lena that nucleus of first connection, Sophie to me shown now in retrospect, magic mirror of what is to make what was come clear—the same wit, the same skewed vision, same sense of chaos at the heart where control lies not lost but abdicated, given over to the service of the fire—but now, become what my love for Sophie had made me, I was prepared to become something else, something wilder, something whose nature, whose art I could not yet understand.

And looking at others—at work, on the streets, on the stairs of our building, the whole mass of the excluded—I felt not smug but overwhelmed, lost in a kind of helpless wonder: *how can you live without this?* as if granted heat in a world of ice, world within worlds, this paradise of kink and it was everything to us, to me; it *was* me, it was where I belonged, the only place I could ever hope to be.

And although it seems assumed that ménage à trois means, is, nonstop fucking, still for us that definition lost all boundaries, failed to contain us because for us it was contained, subsumed in that greater bond; call it instead a kind of marriage, and if sex is the heart of any marriage still it is not the whole: *we* were the whole, here in this room, this bed, this hour and the notion of boundaries— where you end, where I begin—was not considered, did not hinder or truly apply because our true beginning was Lena's entrance into our bedroom, that silent courage as she lay beside Sophie to the music of my leaping heart.

And so the first time we made love as a trio—long legs drawn up, closed eyes and stroking hands—was not less momentous but less *remarkable*, it was what should happen, there were no surprises left. Although that was not completely true, was it? because the night that they made love, each point of the triangle merging at last, that vision was for me so absorbing that my solo orgasm occurred almost as afterthought: it was all so *different*, the current and the arc, the way they paused to nuzzle, whisper, sigh, Lena's quiet laugh, Sophie's fingers soft to that narrow smile and a moment's return, the déjà vu of my drunken dream: Lena and Sophie in party clothes, my own rapt frustrated gaze but this, oh this was nothing like that, heat to that light, light to that darkness and when they had done they turned to me, opened their arms to take me into their heat, share with me everything they had shared with one another because now no act could be complete until it was completed by all.

And still in that intensity—of giving, of guiding—Lena showed us new ways of giving to one another, new ways to play: not so much new positions (although I was—admit it—slightly jealous to see Sophie try things so readily for Lena that she would not, had not tried for me alone: "I thought that made your back hurt?" and her sleepy smile: "Not *this* way") but a new attitude, a languor, a time-out-of-time feeling as if we stretched the time around us to accommodate our play, our passion, our lust: that's an old-fashioned word, isn't it? Lena loved it. *Lust:* not the tame sweetness of making love or the animal grunt of fucking, but somehow both and somewhere in between, the limitless hunger that can never be fully fed, only appeased for now, for today with this body, this touch, this heat, this cry: and slumber then in that vast fulfillment, satisfaction replete, to wake again as eager and as hungry as before.

It was a hunger I knew best served in trio, as now those times we spent apart seemed to wear a kind of resonance they had not had before, waked into being a worming thread of jealousy: like last night, after-work trudge into a dark apartment, no food, no them and "Where were you?" when at last they entered, snow-damp and glistening, peeling off gloves and boots and "I *told* you," Sophie's kiss, "shopping. We left you a note," pointing at some scrap, pink curl of paper unseen, and see now Lena's slowest smile, sliding hands, cold hands down my pants, tweaking at belly and balls and "You could have come with us," her cold nose against my cheek. "We asked you, remember?"

"I don't remember anything," as Sophie's hands climbed me now, Sophie's warm and open mouth and we lay there on the floor, under-door draft and their peaking nipples, cold, wriggling toes and afterward my own damp pleased inertia, lying where I was to watch their quick efficiency, sorting from the scattered clothing bra from bra, blue panties from white, long tremble of a stocking traded one to the other and for me another note in the endless anthropology, litany of comparisons in which neither was more nor less than the other but both so different, so beautifully unalike. As just now, making love: see the differing ways pleasure took them, Sophie's starfish sprawl and gulped half-sentences, Lena's silent arrowed concentration and was it imagination, my imagination or were there subtle changes when each was in my arms alone? because although our lovemaking, our lust was almost invariably practiced as a trio—not because it was wrong for Sophie and me, for Lena and me, to make love as two, but because as in everything we preferred ourselves complete—still sometimes that solar flare, the strange half-guilty glee as Lena—spread against the counter, tumbled on the couch, Lena who seemed past all experience to grow ever more desirable, as if the act of possession opened doors unglimpsed before—was in that moment only mine: and did she feel it, too? a kind of deeper focus, a fiercer, less forgiving heat? Or was it only what Sophie styled, in mingled drollery and contempt, one of those *man things*, just the simple caveman pride at having both of them to please, separately and together, mine and mine and mine alone?

Did it matter? and to whom?

Elbows on the floor, damp and chill and surfeit: *not me*, from self to self and back again. Not me.

The next day more shopping, Christmas shopping and this time they made me go too, fetch and carry and "Jess," Lena peremptory past the crackle of paper, wrapping paper in festive greens and golds, "we need a hand here."

"Who just carried all the fucking bags upstairs?" but it was rote protest, I didn't really mind: sit on the floor in a pile of presents, help them wrap and sort and "Who's this for?" holding up a sexy calendar, half-bare breasts and winking smiles, Modelicious! and "Your brother," Sophie said. "We got him the same thing last year, remember?"

No. "Sure," I said, quick flip through the oversize pages, ooh la la, and "*Last* year," Sophie said, "Jess's brother got *him* a ski cap. With a tassel."

"What'd they get you?" Lena asked, bows stuck to her fingertips, strange blossoms stiff and bright, "a bun warmer?" to Sophie's shrieking laughter, more than the mild joke deserved but Lena was laughing too and maybe, I thought, maybe it was some kind of private joke but what jokes could be too private for me? or then again maybe it was—

"—about you?" to me, Lena's quick fingers prodding in my side. "What do you think?"

"About what?"

"Give me that," taking the calendar, "it's fogging up your thought processes. I said, we're giving this," some fancy vest, all black lace and shiny buttons, "to Po, and *this* to—"

"Po? Give her a lump of coal. No, a lump of—"

"Oh no," Sophie shaking her head, "not the vest. How about that little crystal thing, that chime-thing that you hang over the—" but "No," Lena more definite, the vest was for Po and "Why'd you even ask me?" I said, "why bother when you already—" but they were onto something else now, some glass bibelot for my mother: strange to think of Lena choosing a gift for *her*, a woman unknown and distant past meeting, a woman who would surely understand none of us, the way we lived at all and from its gift box I lifted the little crystal chime, gold cords and iridescent dangle, in a million years with a million dollars I would never have chosen this but Lena serene, as sure of her selection as she was of everything else and "Okay," Sophie's shrug as she folded the vest, "this for Po, then," and I pulled at the length of paper, I cut, I folded, I did as I was told and when all the boxes were wrapped, the parcels ready to mail Lena off into the kitchen, back with two bottles, cold bottles green as deepest water and "Look," she said, "a treat for us. Champagne."

Slick silver labels turned toward me, expensive stuff and "I got a bonus," Lena's shrug, "at work. For being the smartest ant in the ant farm. . . . Sophie, honey, why don't you get us some blankets?" and, lights off, we cuddled to watch the snow, snowflakes leaping tandem to the bubbles in the glass, the window in palimpsest ice, nights' cold written one upon the other and "It's so beautiful," Lena's whisper in that warmest dark, "it's just so *beautiful* . . ."

Silence, sweetness: then "Move over," Sophie to me as she wedged closer to Lena. "I need more blanket, I feel cold."

"There's enough blankets for all of us."

"Move *over*," and so I did, moved so my arm left Lena's shoulder, moved so Sophie was almost in her lap but I said nothing, pretended not to notice, sipped at my champagne past the tiny prickling surge because it seemed like Sophie was doing this more and more, engineering these kinds of competitions to have more of Lena, more than she needed, more than her share. Childish and selfish, and what difference should it make where Lena sat or didn't, who met her for lunch, who lay next to her when we slept together?—and what to think when she chose, as she sometimes did, to sleep alone on the fold-out? Was I supposed to know, to do something about it? but I never asked, never asked Sophie either, halted by some reticence unexplored (because what if she knew something I didn't? what would that make me?) and deciding, what else, to leave mystery to itself, Lena's mysteries like so much else of her, like her past: not something I could know, those endless suites imagined whorl on whorl but every turn, each chamber closed to me, only the bright room of the present marked boldly with my name and Sophie seeming baffled by my interest, my desire—expressed, lightly, lightly, by jokes and questions, little nudging brief asides—to know more, see our life through what hers had been but "What difference does it make?"

Sophie wanted to know, shrugged shoulders in the cold, leather cuffs rubbed bald against her wrists. "I mean what're you, a journalist or something? A detective?"

"No," mildly, rich cloud of breath above our heads like a thought balloon—and flash memory, my own childhood annoyance that unlike cartoon characters our thoughts could not so easily be read: "But why *not?*" to my brother, who himself annoyed by my persistence hit me hard on the head with a rolled-up magazine, which more or less characterized any serious encounter we ever had, which is why we never had many—but it was exactly that, *those* kinds of memories I was after, little tidbits, little clues to show me in the Lena I loved the Lena who had been, the Lena I would in the truest sense never know without those clues—and "No," I said again to Sophie, taking her arm, squeezing her hand, "I don't want to investigate anything, not like you mean. I'd just like to know, that's all. Just like I know you. Just like you know—"

"That's different," hauling us, hands linked, into the path of a delivery van, red curse and swerve and "Different how?" I asked to her shrug: "It's just, it just is. And anyway," she said, hunching lower in the jacket, turtle shell, "what she *was* isn't what she *is*," with which I so patently did not agree—because what are we then if not a collection, self stitched to self by threads of past lovers, past journeys, hopes and greeds and terrors still, like scars, like memory, present in the fabric of the current day, in the choices we make, the hungers we indulge—that the disagreement troubled me: how strange to find us so divided on such a fundamental point, as if the Sophie I knew was not the real Sophie but someone else, someone

114

different, as the picture of the forest holds drawings hidden of snakes, of wise beasts watching, and what you see from the outside is never all there is.

So I let it go, dropped the subject; but not with Lena who with a smile deflected my questions, that graceful sloping shrug like Venus in the water, Venus reborn and I thought of people we had met, people she knew—like artist Edie, filmmaker Ed, others in clubs or in line at the movies, people whose faces changed when they saw her and how not to want what piece of her they held, what Rosetta fragment kept like a souvenir that when produced and studied always brings a certain smile, a certain feeling twinned equally to pleasure and loss? because having her once meant wanting her always, and losing her—losing her was something I never considered because how could such a thing apply to me?

And back home, my bag banging hipward, upstairs to find—cold hands, bright eyes—Lena and Lena's kiss, Sophie jiggling at the key and "Listen," Lena said, "I have an idea for tonight": a dance contest sponsored by some oldies station, dances from the fifties and everyone in period costume, even the people who just came to watch: poodle skirts and DA hairdos, letter sweaters and bobby socks and Sophie stomping and cheering like a fan for the winners: a husband-and-wife act, varsity jacket and saddle shoes, both of them at least thirty pounds overweight and courting infarctions as they did the Stroll or the Lindy or whatever the hell it was; sweating like crazy in the lemon light, modest trophy held between them, loving cup.

On the cab ride home, cheerleading Sophie now thrown-switch gloomy, head against the window and

115

"You know I used to go to dance class," voice low and child-small. "Every week I used to go."

"You did?" Lena's interest immediate and warm, "when?" and for me a sudden little twitch: I hadn't known that, how could there be something about Sophie that I didn't know? and her shrug, looking out the window, away from us both and "I don't know," she said, "when I was ten, eleven. . . . My parents made me go, my mother. She said it would help me to, you know, get along with other kids, learn how to act. Be a lady. Shit," lower lip caught between her teeth, embarrassment's gesture recalling all at once a younger Sophie, Sophie swathed in cigarette smoke, frowning out from beneath her hat, a gesture oddly tender to me and "All I learned," she said, then a long pause as if choosing, classifying *learning* and *knowledge:* "I didn't *learn* anything, really, I couldn't even remember the steps, how to do the dances. My mom was so—like I was wasting the family fortune, or something." Shaking her head, that frown again. "There was this one girl, though, she only came to a couple classes but we used to sneak into the lavatory and smoke while they were changing the music, compare dresses, you know, see whose was stupider . . . her name was Deirdre," with the smile of lost pleasure retrieved. "Deirdre Bacon."

"I bet you were so cute," Lena angled sideways on the seat, half-turned from me, "right, Jess? Patent-leather dancing shoes, frilly dresses—"

"Frilly, right," Sophie's humor restored, "with *slips*, can you believe it? Half-slips, with lace," and "Don't ask me," I said, "I wasn't there," but neither answered, went off on a tangent of grade-school fashion and the subject was left to lie until that night in bed, Lena up working late, fold-out papered with spreadsheets and reports and we off to bed alone, drowsy Sophie and my cool murmur in her ear: "So how come you never told me? About dancing class?"

"I did," her mumble obscured against my chest. "I told you today."

"I mean before. Why didn't you ever tell me before?"

"Because," turning in my arms to face me, eyes half-open in the dark, "because I didn't think it was a big deal. And it isn't."

"Then why'd you bring it up today?"

"I didn't 'bring it up,' it just occurred to me."

"So what else don't I know?" I said, leaning up on one elbow but "Good night," her back to me, abrupt and dismissive as a child, a kid, ten-year-old Sophie in her frills and patent leather, sneaking smokes in the bathroom with fellow bad girl Deirdre Whosits and what else unknown when I thought I knew everything, what other fragments lay somewhere unseen? First Lena, now Sophie. Blue-beard's wife.

And in the morning my breakfast comments, I thought I was being subtle or at least funny about her secret past as a dancing girl but Sophie instantly unhappy, slamming out early, no plans made, no good-byes and from Lena a frown censorious: "What's the matter with *you?*"

"Nothing." Pouring more coffee. "Nothing's the matter with me."

Hands brisk with folders, loading her briefcase. "Then why'd you make fun of her that way?"

"I didn't make *fun* of her, I was just—"

" 'Show me some steps,' " her chilly mimicry. " 'Maybe

we can enter a dance contest.' Really, Jess," that chill of disapproval and in answer my own inner prickling, annoyance at them both and "So it's okay," I said, "for *her* not to tell *me* stuff, but I can't—"

"Tell you stuff? That happened, what, fifteen years ago? Get over it." Very close to me now, folders forgotten, face-to-face like adversaries and "Even if it mattered—which I can't see how it does—that's still not the way. If you wanted to know something why didn't you just ask?"

"I did! I did ask her. But she wouldn't tell me, she got mad—"

"Well then," decisively, *this case is closed*, "you should have shut up. You can't force someone to confide in you."

A vacuum pause, then: "You know," my tone flat and pleasant, "Sophie's been walking out of rooms at me since the day we met, it's not a new problem and I know how to deal with it. So if you really want to be helpful then why don't you just—"

"Fine," sharp, offended in an instant, briefcase snapped shut and out the door and "Fucking *shit*," my own voice to silence, not even sure why I had made such an issue of it, what difference did it make? but I knew what the difference was: the idea that there might in Sophie be places I had never been, facets untouched; secrets. Why secrets, between us? and that day gone in brooding, sitting in my little slavey's cubicle for lunch and I ate nothing, did little work and none of the usual hurry to get home, instead my hesitation doubled: would they both still be mad at me? and what would that be like? Sophie's furies I knew, quick to flare, quick to die but Lena the unknown quantity, all possible ground gone terra incognita because we had never been angry this way before, the trio divided—because, yes, I was mad at them too, hair-trigger Sophie so obviously in the wrong for being secretive and what was so bad about my asking besides the way I asked? And critical Lena with her guilt-dispensing frown, why couldn't it be Sophie's fault too, why should I shoulder the shitty end of the stick? Because I was the odd man out? Because I was *the guy?*

Wet shoes, the streets pure slurry but no hurry to get home, up the stairs and my threshold pause to hear their voices, quiet voices that ceased as I entered, the silence of business unfinished. Lena at the kitchen table, Sophie on the floor, sullen self-protective slump in the TV light and I went straight to her, knelt down enough to look in her eyes and "I don't care who you dance with," smiling a little to show it was a joke, not a joke, "as long as you dance with me."

"You're a lousy dancer," but her own smile as she said it, one arm around my neck to bring me close, to kiss me on the cheek: all over, all done with now and "Go get dinner," gentle fingertips' push. "You're already all wet and nasty."

"Nasty, right," but from the table "I'll go with you," rising without a smile, hat and coat and now what to do about her? Apologize, make a joke, what? and no words, just walking; hands in pockets and she waited outside, away from the crowded, wet-dog smell, Szechuan Express-to-Go and moving as I emerged, no words, no smile and was this, I wondered, the on-the-road version of the silent treatment, was she still mad at me or what? and so to break that silence I touched her, one elbow clandestine and "Our first fight," I said, "our first real—"

And turning, turning straight into me, shoulder to shoulder like a blocker and she pushed me back, off the sidewalk, back to the wall and window of some pizza place, Hot 'n' Good and she kissed me, not some small discretionary peck, *kiss and make up* but a real kiss, hungry mouth and hands in my hair, one thigh caught warm and tight between her own and when I opened my eyes there were people watching, sidewalk nudging, catcall laughter but I didn't care, I was glad, I wanted them to see: *see how she loves me* and then walking again, tandem stride and Sophie's perennial complaint—*you go too fast*—with Lena did not matter: no matter how fast I went she was always able to keep up.

And back home Sophie sharing out the food, plates and cups, little jokes to bring much laughter as if such cushioning was somehow necessary to find again our places, to start the dance anew: and that night we slept together, arms and breasts and pleasured breathing, pink-and-black comforter, comfort and joy: as if all of us, none of us had ever been angry, as if division was less threat than a dream of falling, of tumbling helpless through a colder sky, the dream from which we wake to smile, secure inside our stationary skins.

The next week was dismal, work and nothing but: *Meet us at Driscoll's* the notes would say, or *Loft party* and a phone number but I didn't go, home too late and too tired to do anything but shovel slop into the microwave, leftovers scooped out of cartons, paging aimless through the paper and sleeping where I sat until hands on my shoulders, Sophie's hands and "Wake up, Jess," into my ear, "it's time to go to bed."

And groaning, rising to Lena's murmur: "Poor boy," and into my own bed too tired for dreams, hearing nothing until the morning sent me back to work, slave to the grind and worse than the drudgery—finite, therefore bearable—I missed them, missed the three of us together: like being lost, cut adrift and their little invitations no solace, did they need me to have fun? Apparently not. Scatter of notes and creased club flyers, concert programs, postcards from galleries—this one for tonight, another of Lena's artist-friends, the name half-remembered, the postcard black and white: an optical illusion, two facing profiles, man and woman and if you looked at it a certain way you could see a woman's naked body as the space between, bare back, bare ass and "What's this?" gulping at my coffee, irritable and rushed and "What do you think?" Lena taking the card from me, the true amusement of her smile because she liked those kinds of things, now you see it, now you don't, funhouse trip-you-up and every hall a hall of mirrors in which you see yourself reflected in ways you never could have dreamed and "Fairly trivial," I said rudely, "that's what I think."

Her smile undimmed: "I'll tell him you said so," and maybe she was telling him now, she and Sophie both . . . and shoving at the table detritus, junk mail I had no time to open, more gallery postcards, an empty bag from some lingerie store, Sweet Illusions with a hot pink notecard advertising another Amateur's Night very soon, what the hell was Amateur's Night? and no time to ask them that or anything, no time to wonder if they missed me at all, if they ever bothered to consider that it might be nice for me to have someone to talk to when I got home instead of slumping like a discard, staring at the TV where some grinner in a brown suit was advising me that this evening's temperature would be hellishly cold: "Snuggle up!" and snuggle with whom, where the fuck were they, anyway?

Sleep's tumble right where I was, park-bench hunch and half-waking sometime later: to dark, hands touching to move and warm bodies there, just as they should be, legs twined in my own and from a deep, sodden sleep my wakefulness like coming to, middle of the night and cold somehow beneath the covers

to turn, half rise to see them, the one body their bodies made: Sophie's hungry nestle, Lena's claiming arms and where, I thought, where in all this comfort was room for me, where was my place? Out watching, where I was? out in the cold? and see them breathe, hear that sigh—from which? who knew?—as with slow cunning hands I parted them, loosened one from the other: Sophie's murmur, half a frown even in sleep and I lay down again, Lena now gathered against me, Lena whose eyelids flickered as if in the deepest waters of dream: *dream of me*, I thought, and kissed her, on the temple, only once.

After Hell Week my next few assignments seemed, were, easy: handling backed-up correspondence for some minor Cultural Council adjunct, sending faxes and sending out for lunch; then a stint as a receptionist at a major bank's branch of a branch, "Good morning," and send them to this office or that, drink lots of coffee and leave precisely at four but still it seemed I saw little of them, Lena and Sophie, as if the new patterns engendered by my absence bred like a twin a reluctance to change and "Where were you?" said again, home from work to empty rooms, the two of them coming in late and together and "We *told* you," Sophie's careless kiss, Lena shedding her bags, packages, how much shopping could two people do? although these two, ah, Santa's little helpers and both of them willing to cross town in a midnight blizzard for a wreath handmade of feathers, little ornaments that lit up from inside, endless strings of white lights like tiny stars and the tree itself twined with lights enough, I told them, to burn the whole building to the ground but "It's just the holidays," Lena consoling me now, shrugging from her coat, flipping expert through the mail. "You'll see, after New Year's things will slow down . . . oh, look," to Sophie only, holding out a card, dull-green envelope and see Sophie's face harden: "Oh *great*," to throw it back on the table unopened, "the annual communique. 'Mr. and Mrs. Scrooge request your presence at dinner, where we will be serving Tiny Tim on a bed of crutches. Be there or be dead,' " and turning away, turning past Lena who reached to take and open the envelope (addressed, I saw, only to Sophie): red wreath and printed text, "Happy Holidays" and scrawled beneath in bright green felt-tip "Love to Soso from Daddy and Mom."

"They still do it," Sophie's murmur, her back to us both

and then into the bathroom, closing the door and "Christmas and birthdays," my voice kept soft although Sophie could not possibly overhear, "it never fails. She doesn't like to talk about—"

"I know," thoughtfully, looking at the card and for me the mental picture, lone snapshot of the Family Sprause: blonde mom, fat dad, Sophie in braids and mutiny and in contrast my own family's desultory contact, their cheery and meaningless cards, ski caps and popcorn poppers seemed somehow innocent or at least innocent of the intention to wound or make trouble, to cause any kind of feeling at all. And Lena's family? who knew, another room closed to me, closed off like Sophie in the bathroom and *don't*, I wanted to tell her, Lena card in hand at the door, *just leave it, leave her alone* but saying nothing, silence to both in the tempest erupting, tears and slamming doors, slamming out of the apartment with Lena close behind but I knew better, knew not to chase where no pursuit was wanted; by tomorrow she would forget or make herself forget, until the next time, the next card, the next yank on the cord—and thinking again of Lena's family, who were they? Parents, divorced or still together, remarried, dead, what? and siblings, brothers or sisters (and caught breath at the idea: Lena's sisters, what might they be like?) but love them, miss them, deny them it was the same, she never talked about them or told us anything at all.

And see my loves returning, slipping back inside quiet and glum: Sophie off to bed at once and Lena to the bathroom, door closed and kept that way until I went to bed, heard the faint click of the fold-out as in bed Sophie wrapped in blankets, defensive as a pupa in her pink-and-black cocoon; and me stranded in the gulf between them, warmed with nothing but my own discomfort, unable to help either one.

But the next day all forgotten, Sophie all smiles and pinching my ass: "Hurry up, baby," to some work friend's Christmas party, a DJ and a ten-foot tree and "C'mon," hugging me, "it's so pretty outside, let's walk," in her silver cowboy boots for twenty deadly blocks but I gave in, glad the cloud had passed, glad to walk with her this way and listen to her chatter, tugging me this way and that, go here, go left and the building when located as dour as ours, scabbed brick and graffiti but inside all tinsel and glitter spray, the door opened on Lena's greeting— "Come on, come in"—as if the party was hers: and my pause past that entering moment to stop and look, just look at her in her slim black suit, rushed from work but she didn't look rushed, smile for bright Sophie in her wake, Sophie in spangles and big, glossy bow, gift wrapped—and following then, catching up as they poured from a huge ceramic punchbowl, golden rum in little silver cups, one for me too and "Merry Christmas," Sophie's toast and Lena's smile, cup to cup like a private kiss: "Merry Christmas, Soso."

And my own dismayed surprise—as if she had hurt Sophie secretly, or spat in her food, why that unhappy name? but Sophie's smile at my surprise, looking to Lena as translator, interpreter of some language she herself would not speak and "Oh it's just stupid," Lena said: the nickname dreamed up by Sophie's father, used when someone would ask *so how's your daughter?* and he would make with his hand a little rocking motion, *Only so-so. Get it?*

125

"I got it all right," Sophie's murmur, "I wasn't *that* dumb," but not angry either, last night's fury not only drained but seemingly removed, excised and the name itself sea changed by Lena, laved with love enough to draw the sting and "Why didn't you tell me?" I said, trying not to sound annoyed, not to be annoyed. "Why didn't you ever—"

"Well," Sophie's shrug, again that look to Lena. "You never asked."

I didn't think I was supposed to: but that was no answer either and it seemed unkind to complain, selfish if not churlish and I let it go, drank the toast, drank the rum and watched Sophie prance off to flirt a little with the DJ, bright eyes and wiggling ass and "What's the matter?" Lena's nudge subtle, hip to hip. "Don't you want to dance?"

"Not right now." Rum fumes, a summer smell: *you never asked.* As if I should have known. "But you can. You and Soso."

A twinge as I said it, not what I meant or at least not in that tone, so sour and clipped and "Sometimes she likes to tell me things," her Venus motion with one shoulder, not quite a shrug. "Things she doesn't tell other people."

"I'm not 'other people.' "

"I never said you were."

More rum and the music louder, some novelty tune about be-boppin' reindeer and "Tells you things," my voice slow, trying not to sound offended, only interested, "like what? What kind of—"

"You know," although apparently I didn't. "Work troubles, things with Po . . . personal stuff."

And what did that mean, whose idea the division: *personal*, and what else? Nonpersonal, unclassified, OK even for me to know and "Does she talk about," how could she, "about us? About me?"

And, incredibly, Lena's nod: well, not often, once or twice, just to talk over problems and "*What* problems?" I said, disbelieving, too loud, a circle of heads turning and what was worst of all, more so even than the knowledge that Sophie had problems with me was that she could, and had, shared those problems with someone else, other than me, *before* me and I turned away, turned for the door and "Jess," Lena calling after, "Jess wait a minute," but I didn't want to wait, to stay, to listen to whatever explanation Lena might give, let Sophie do her own explaining, let Sophie

and out into the cold, yanking on my coat: "*Jess*," her hand on my arm, my bicep, holding me back and "*Stop* it," as strongly, "all right? Just stop it."

"Stop what?" Snowing again, on her hair, in my face, snow myriad as secrets, all the things I didn't know and "Stop acting this way," her hands now on my shoulders, face level with mine. "She loves you, you know that, that has nothing to do with this. All that stuff with her family, her stupid father—"

"I don't care about that," although I did and as more than gateway too, whatever touched Sophie touched me but "What I care about is what she says about us, about— secrets, it's not right to have secrets—"

Hands tightening, "It's not secrets," as if she would shake me, force me to see and behind her I heard my name, Sophie's cry and "Jess," clumsy plow into both of us, footing lost in the piling snow and "What are you *do-ing?*" she said, amazed and indignant, as if I was the one in the wrong, "what are you—" and "What about you?" I said to Lena, ignoring Sophie because she had done it first, hadn't she? ignored me in favor of Lena, showed her secrets to someone else. "Why didn't you tell me, why couldn't you—"

"Tell you *what?*" Sophie's demand, "what are you guys—" and "Sophie," Lena not loud but sharp, "go back to the party, all right? Right now."

"I don't want . . . Jess, what's—"

"Sophie, *go back*," harsh as a blow and Sophie's eyes widening, mouth open as if in outrage—but turning, slip and stumble in the silly boots, shiny heels and back to the open door from which people were watching, people we knew, people surrounding her now and "You know," Lena said, rum scent and voice lower still, "you know maybe I can help sometimes, Jess, maybe you ought to think of that before you go storming off, maybe you ought to consider that she might just be blowing off a little steam when she—"

"When she what?" because I had to know. "What kind of steam?"

"Like the way," deliberate, "the way she feels when you make fun of her job, sometimes, or complain about Po—Po's a bitch, so what? But you make it *her* fault. And that hurts her feelings. And she complains to me."

"And so what do you say?" but like a pierced balloon my dwindling anger, unstable gas dissolved and if that was all it was, well. Not complaints about *me*, not really; just work talk, circular rants I had heard before and Lena's

128

frown in tandem to my smile, my silly shrug relieved and "All right," I said, "forget it," conscious now of the cold, she was wearing no coat, we were sprinkled with snow. "I didn't mean . . . I just want to be with you guys," arms around her now, holding her close. "I just want you to, you know, tell me stuff. Need me."

And in that embrace her rising hands, cold hands to cup my cheeks, fingers tapping slow against my temples as if that might help me focus, give me vision, make me see: and then her kiss forgiving, long and slow as if there were no cold, no snow, no watchers avid in the door and "I need you," she murmured, lips still touching mine. "I need you very much."

"A party," Sophie said, "a *big* party with plum pudding, and champagne," gag gifts and midnight carols but Lena's veto prevailed: "Our first Christmas," she said, "should be for us," and so Christmas Eve cross-legged on the floor before the tree as Sophie poured the wine, heady and gar-net-dark, myself as Santa to hand out the gifts: shimmer of a silver package, a gaudy golden bow, "From Sophie" to Lena, "From Lena" to Sophie, their pleasure in pleasing each other, in the gifts they gave to me: camel-colored cashmere, a black leather cap, a book by an author whose name I didn't know and "He's really twisted," Lena's sly sweet smile. "You'll like it, I know."

Some packages too from my parents, another dumb appliance (a five-speed blow dryer and why would anyone want one?) and from my brother and his family a red box, Morning's Light Farms and Sophie wrestling with the cardboard, staples impervious and "Watch your hands," from Lena with a kitchen knife to hack a way in, chunks of paper packing and "It's a cheese wheel," Sophie cried, busy with extraction. "Colby cheese."

"What's a cheese wheel?" although I was pretty sure I knew, and Lena's shrug: "At least it's not a whole cheese *car*."

And my gifts to them, well. Savoring the wait as I savored the smoky wine, the picture they made: Lena in a dark blue satin shift, Sophie in gleaming green, quilted queen's robe and "What about your presents?" Sophie said, flushed cheeks like a child's and "Presents?" to tease her, "what presents," but anxious now to see their faces I gave them the boxes, two for each and "The little ones are serious," I told them, "the big ones are for fun" so of course they went for the big ones first, twin pink boxes from Sweet Illusions: peach froth for Sophie, rosebuds and tiny ribbons, and for Lena white silk cut low, thinnest silk like a whisper to the skin and "Now," I said, wine glass in hand, watching them, "now open the little ones."

Tugged ribbons, heavy crease of golden foil and "Oh, Jess," Sophie's sigh, cupped palm to hold the earrings, twist filigree of gold and lapis green and Lena's pleasured smile, the ring thick braided silver, frost-bright and "Put it on," her murmur, hand extended: and I slid the ring down her middle finger, gentle tug to check the fit, gentle kiss on her warm palm and "Me too," Sophie leaning forward so I might adorn her, guide the stiff stems of the earrings through the minuscule pink holes: and taking up the peach bustier, queen's robe discarded on the floor: "Do this," she said. "Do this too."

Play and shimmer of the colored lights, the candle-light, earrings' gleam and she knelt naked before me, eyes half-closed as if enchanted: and I dressed her, edged lace tugged in place around her breasts, the wee old-fashioned hook and eye, little rosebuds tight and soft and Lena then slipping free of her shift, white gown and waiting for my hands, for the ancient whisper of pouring silk, loosed hair caught to one side to slide across her shoulders the narrow straps, false buttons like tiny nipples and "Beautiful," I said, to myself, to them both, rapt with desire and the knowledge absolute that there was nowhere else in all the world, in all of time that I would choose to be: this night, this room, this scent of wine and burning candles, this instant that with all my heart I wished would never end but only spiral onward like waves in the water, like snow falling changeless on its sister snow beneath: like moments each subsumed into the other, creating a constant, the shape of the world.

New Year, the annual new start: and my own resolutions kept quiet but firm: not to notice Sophie's possessiveness, or complain about our time together—less than before, surely so; was I the only one who noticed? Trudging to work and back, barrens and midwinter deeps and wondering as I went *what happened?* To my idea of the next step, kink's art to lead me deeper into my own heart, the larger change that Lena was presumed to bring: where was it? Not here, not now in this atmosphere of dry coughs and torpor, edging bridge of discontent through one day's landscape to the next and for me the feeling that we were stranded somehow where we should not have been, gone lost in a place where those discontents instead of dwindling grew to blossom: Sophie's little-kid clamor for Lena's attention and approval, always at my expense, and her apparent new conviction that nothing I did could by definition be right: the videos I rented, the dinners I proposed, the clothes brought home from the cleaner's and "They lost two buttons," agitated, "again. *Jess*, you're supposed to check this, you're not supposed to just *pay* for it like it's—"

"*Sophie*," in mimicked whine, "next time go pick it up yourself," as if two buttons were the end of the world, big fuss for nothing and looking to Lena who refused to meet my gaze, take my side—or, true, Sophie's either but I was so manifestly in the *right*—and Sophie's mutter graceless in passing, blouse in hand and the next day out for dinner, Lily's Garden for unspecified Oriental, soggy egg rolls and dull wine and Sophie saying something about hair dryers, their vacuum-cleaner sound and "I remember," head dreamy to one side, "I remember my aunt had one of those old bouffant ones, you know, with the cap you put over your curlers? Big pink cap like a mushroom, puffed full of air" and little Sophie half under the coffee table, eyes closed pretending she was in a cave, a snowstorm, her aunt bouffant at the kitchen table smoking Viceroys and reading *Woman's Day*, *Family Circle* and "So what's the point?" my question with what I thought was a pleasant smile. "What exactly are you—" but Sophie instantly sharp, on the defensive and "It doesn't *have* a *point*," she said, "why does it need a point? It's just a story about how I like the sound of—"

"Well," still patently pleasant, still my smile with wine glass in hand, "it's kind of trivial, isn't it?"

And Sophie's gauntlet glare, chopsticks thrown down almost on my plate and Lena our unwilling mediatrix, faintest frown of distress and "It can't be trivial, can it," looking at me, at Sophie who would not, "if it made Sophie happy?" and "I didn't say *she* was trivial," my rising voice, "I just meant . . ." but *Let it go*, that wiser inner voice but not without resentment at another failure presumed—*oh, there he goes again, insensitive Jess*—but let's face it, it *was* a pointless story, little Sophie tranced on the floor watching her auntie smoke, blow-dryer soundtrack and so what? So what? but be honest, now, while they're off in tandem to the ladies' room (to talk about me?), be honest and admit that what maybe makes you angriest is that Lena gets it and you don't: echo of connection effortless and strong, strong enough to do without me: the closed sorority, *table for two* but I didn't say that, said nothing, went home to pretend to read the paper, their background murmurs and then Sophie ostentatiously to bed, yanked covers, *don't bother* so I didn't, instead led Lena to the fold-out to strip and fuck her in total silence, head back, breath forced through clenched teeth and she took what I gave her, all I had to give and afterward her arms to hold me close, face-to-face and "I love you," I told her, heart pounding dizzy and hard, "I miss you. I *miss* you, you know?"

Half-sigh, the beat of her slowing pulse: "I know," and she kissed me, "I know, I know," but with a kind of melancholy unseen in her before: cryptic as a hint subtle past all reclamation, the change begun already, on the way—*what change?*—but all I could do, did, was hold her, bundle us together in the blanket, cramped intimacy of the fold-out and sleep with her there, sleep to wake to Sophie's silence, Sophie in the doorway staring dry-eyed at us both.

And then—O brave new year, what was *happening* to us?—see my evening's slog, another vast and miserable storm and this week's job all the way across town, wet-dog journey and all I wanted was to get home, be here where I was: but see Sophie's smile beneath a big black cap, pose struck in the kitchen, something wrong with that smile and the black cap raised, big flourish—"Ta-dah!"—to show a head so shorn I swore out loud: "Fucking *shit,*" bag dropped and approaching, the pale fuzz like scorched earth and Sophie bubbling on and on about her new look, big change, big surprise and "Did you do this," I said, "just to piss me off? I mean did you even think for one second that I would *like* the way . . ."

And her eyes wide, backing, turning sharp on her heel as if I'd slapped her and "Sophie," I said, angrier still, "oh Sophie come *on,*" because this wound (if she really was wounded, past that theatrical retreat) was unintentional, I had only meant, what, that she was too beautiful to have such ugly hair, too beautiful to look like a Marine Corps reject—and remembering those curls, tiny baby curls, grown long enough for me to tug, to play with, over and over I had said how I liked them while she moaned how ugly they were—and now see her off to Lena for comfort, Lena who stared at me above and past that head denuded, Lena who, it turned out, had done the cutting herself: "*I* think she looks terrific," coolly, "very clean, very—"

"*Clean?*" I said, "what's clean got to do with anything? She looks like she's been prepped for surgery, she—"

"You sound like Po," Sophie's shout almost tearful, fierce segue to mimicked Po-voice: " 'I been cutting hair for fifteen years and you let *her* cut your hair, what's the matter with you, why'd you let her cut your hair?' What's the matter with *me?* what's the matter with *you* is what I should have said, what's the matter with *you* and you too," accusingly to me, "how dare you be such a shit? How dare you—"

"How dare I disagree with you, that's what you mean," and it went on that way, dreary ouroboros for what felt like forever and me stranded there in my wet jacket, no dinner, no peace and finally I lost my temper, finally shouting back and "Shave your fucking head," I said, I yelled, "be bald for all I care, what do I care? And *you*," as angry somehow with Lena, Lena who had jointly perpetrated this idiocy, Lena who should have, what? stepped in, made it stop, made *us* stop but now purely inscrutable, that narrowed stare and "You can't expect Sophie to do what you want," arms folded in the doorway, like a gateway, like a guard. "You can't expect to tell her what to do."

"Oh yeah? and who can? You? We lived without you for a long time, Lena, we could probably—"

But that was too far, much too far and I hadn't meant it, not that way and "Lena, I'm sorry, I—" but firmly she put off my hands, my touch, folding me back on myself and "Let's just forget it," as firmly, turning to include snuffling Sophie as well. "Let's just forget about the whole thing."

Which we did: and didn't, who forgets fights like that?

especially with the constant presence of that tennis-ball head but even once it had begun to grow back—sprouty, patchy, *the chemo look* said snide Po and for once I agreed— still nothing said, nothing from me which was my constant mode these days, winter's heart like an endless illness, late March and still the snow, the ice underfoot like crumbled glass, cold hands and long nights in which all it seemed we did was bicker, carping and sniping, Sophie and me about whose turn it was to get the papers, who had left the cof- fee maker on, who had forgotten to pick up clothes at the cleaner's or groceries or tickets to a midnight showing of *La Contessa* and "I didn't even want to *go*," Sophie sullen, folded arms and showy glare, "so why should I have to waste my time getting the fucking—"

"Because," Lena's tone pure reason, "you said you would," and Sophie in tears, her only answer, but every time she wept I felt it less; circle and spiral, on and on and my own bleak wonder like fingers curious on the body, landscape of the thickened lump: *what is this?* and when did it begin to grow? And if I knew, if I could pinpoint, say it started *here* or *here* would that help, make a difference, make it stop? Or had we already gone (gone where?) too far?

And if I had no answers then maybe what was needed was a question, asked of self in those odd, clear moments, the tired mind ungeared and waiting: in line at a deli, in the elevator, getting coffee or the papers and what if, I thought in the cove of that moment, what if all these things were connected, all the troubling small details— Sophie's imp's gift for irritation, Lena's habit of silence grown, our bleak disharmony—all facets only, torn edges of a larger view and my own contribution this scrambling perimeter stumble, unsure what I was seeing, mapless and going farther from where we should have been, drawn step by step to

the next step

which was what? where? In closer or away, step back, step down into the feeling of balance lost, undertow greed *because it's all starting to come apart*

because it's over, don't you see? the three of you, that kink: it's over.

"No," out loud, right there in line, hot plastic cup and the tremble of coffee, steam in my face and *no* again to myself, no you're wrong: but too late, the idea a virus in idiot growth and *it would explain a lot*, explain the tears and the silence, the way I felt in the middle of the night, waking to see Sophie wormed to center yet again, arms around Lena like a child with a toy, selfish child, *mine it's mine*

and "Excuse me," from the cashier, dog-faced blonde in a red bandanna, "you gonna pay for that or what?" and I paid and I sat in the first seat I found, greasy table uncleared, lunch scraps and balled napkins and I burned my mouth on the coffee, no taste beyond the scald and *no*, again but quietly, the voice we use to smother what we fear, *that's not how it is* because it was never, ever supposed to happen to us, protected from the stumble and the fall because it was more than sex, even more than love: it was kink, our game, like art created—because if it wasn't, if it could fall apart like any other dull affair, if that edge, wedge between Sophie and me could in the sundering drive Lena away as well, could strand us alone and game-less, no life, what then? What were we, if we were not the trio we had been?

What was I?

Slow, slow through the rest of the day, a feeling like pressure, subtle aneurysm's squeeze: and upstairs, tracked slush to their rush and clatter, getting dressed, getting ready for something and "Kelsey's birthday party," Sophie in passing, crop top and ugly new harem pants, olive green harem pants like some misused parachute and "Oh come on," exasperated at my failure to, what? comment? smile? cheer? "Don't say you didn't know because I told you myself, I told you this morning, I made a *point* of—"

"I didn't say that," as Lena came in, black dress almost to her ankles, hair swept high, so beautiful—but sad, somehow? or only tired?—and eyes closed I leaned to kiss her, soft brief respite, brief reward of her mouth to mine but at once from Sophie: "When you're done playing kissy-face maybe you could get changed and we could all get out of here before the—"

"Changed?" Looking down at myself, black pants, black jacket, so what's wrong with this and "Oh, I don't know," head to one side, Sophie's bird look and watch out for your eyes, "maybe something a little more *festive?*"

"Sophie," Lena's frown, "why don't you just—"

Instant flare: "Just what?" and "Just go," I said, "I'll meet you there," which was nothing I would have said before, we would have gone as three or not at all: and Sophie turning at once away, back into the bathroom past Lena's murmur unheard and I could have told her, could have said it all right then, spilled out my worries and malformed fears but instead my shrug in answer, pouring a drink, snow on the windows as they pulled on their coats and "You have the address?" Lena's hand on my arm, little squeeze and Sophie beside her tense and still, refusing to look at me, refusing to meet my eyes and then they were gone and I was alone and *see?* the sorrow of that inner voice, as I drank neat vodka, thought of changing my shirt but fuck it, fuck her—and when had I ever thought that way about Sophie, such weary dry dislike? when had I . . .

and "Shut *up*," I said, aloud and beleaguered and I left the vodka, out the door for the snow and the street, salt pellets underfoot, grind and slide and thoughts in echo, back and forth and here it is, "Happy Birthday!!!!" in tropic green above the door, some shit-box sixth-floor walkup, screech and smoke and I spotted them at once, wedged in a corner with the guest of honor, blond birthday boy Kelsey and at my approach Sophie gone sullen, hanging on Lena who seemed tired, unlike herself and "Happy birthday," I said, my gaze at once to hers. "Many happy returns."

And Kelsey's loose nod of acknowledgment and largesse, already very drunk: "Champagne in the kitchen, man," but all I found were empty bottles, keg of beer dripping like a broken faucet and at the back of the refrigerator a bottle of gin, cheap gin, so what? Singing in the living room, happy birthday to you and who should nudge into me but Po, high-collared red blouse, little gold earrings like antique coins and "You," she said, nodding to my glass. "Where'd you get that?"

"In there," pointing to the refrigerator. "How come you're not singing?"

"Because I don't feel like it." Pouring herself a drink,

thick chunk of cloudy ice. "So how's it going with you? I don't see you so much anymore."

Like you care. "Fine," I said. "It's going fine."

Eyebrow arch, *oh really?* and "How'd you like Sophie's haircut?" but oh no, I thought, I'm just too smart for that one and "I think she looks great," smile but not too wide. "Why? Don't you like it?"

And her own smile—contempt for my lie?—and the shrug small and delicate, queen's motion, queen's distaste and "No," she said simply, "no, I don't," and left me there, alone in the kitchen to drink my gin, top off the glass until it was time to go home and the trip accomplished in silence, squashed close in a cab and Sophie, face turned to the window, begun very quietly to weep: *go ahead,* I thought, *go ahead and cry,* tears to bring neither help nor change, tears that fell on and off throughout the night but I did not turn to her, there beside me in the bed, did not reach for her, did not say *Sophie what's wrong* but instead lay quiet, false sleep until I felt her rise, leave the bed, leave the room and I knew where she was going—to Lena, to sniffle and pout and be soothed like a baby but I let her go, did not follow, slept at last in the silence she left, a thin dry sleep without dreams or comfort, waking to a headache and the sound of the shower, to Sophie at the table who did not smile when I entered to sit beside her and "Sophie," I said, to say something, to start, "Sophie I want to talk to you."

Coffee cup, dull shrug; she looked as tired as I did. "All right. Let's talk."

"Not now. I want," and my pause—*would she?* (and how

sad, oh God such *evidence* not to be sure) "I want you to have dinner with me. Just the two of us. Okay?"

"We're supposed to go out for dinner," gaze rising to fall at once: as if I were something she had seen so many times she need never really look at me again. "Lena made reservations, some Sicilian place that she—"

"All right then, lunch. Have lunch with me," and silent now as Lena entered because it was Sophie I had to talk to, only Sophie; *but why?* from the conscious mind, why her and not Lena too, why not sit down all three and talk things out, smooth things over? Because we two had the history, had been there from the beginning; because we *were* the beginning, Sophie and me? Or because Lena seemed somehow an innocent, affected by yet somehow apart from this trouble, this anger sprung from Sophie, this discord and dismay? and when I left I kissed them both, warm mouths, parted lips—and were there tears, again, in Sophie's eyes? or just the light, the angle of deflection, *oh shit I don't know I don't want to think about it now.*

And in the noontime coffee bar, five minutes, ten, fifteen and was she going to stand me up, was that her answer?—but here she came, flushed face as if from real hurry and maybe she had: still wearing her AmBiAnce smock, dropping hard into the booth and "I got here," she said, "as fast as I could. The fucking traffic . . . ."

"I know, it's ridiculous," and what's next? the weather? Nice day we're having? as I reached across to take her hand, cold fingers, ugly new nail polish the color of wet sand and "Sophie," I said, "I wanted, I wanted us to . . ." To do what? and what do I say now, how to say what I

141

mean? Stranded by my own silence and wanting her to help me, speak up, say something but she did not speak, barely held my hand or my gaze and then the server came, forty-two coffees and on special today the walnut scones, the boysenberry tart with heavy cream and from Sophie a faint smile: "Oh, I want everything."

I want everything

and she did, too, didn't she? Didn't she? Wanted Lena to sleep with her, talk to her, shop and party and dance with her and she wanted me too, wanted me to sit down and shut up and fuck her when she was ready (but not when she was not and be sure to know the difference); wanting to be always in the middle, in bed and in cabs and in restaurants and in every conversation we ever had or ever would and

"That's it," I said, voice flat and dry past the surge of my pulse, the black eureka leap: *I see.* "That's exactly what I mean."

"What?"

"You want her," I said, "all to yourself."

"*What?*" Loud, too loud, too blank: what else there, just behind those eyes? "What're you *talking* about?"

"Lena," and oh, the calm of my voice, grave but conversational, *that tumor's going to have to come out.* "You want Lena for yourself, you want to push me out, get rid of me, get—"

"Jess, that's . . . you're crazy, you know it? You're just *crazy*," and getting louder, people looking, nudging but I didn't care, I didn't care because *I see now*, I knew: knew it like a hard-on, like a broken bone, the X-ray shadow that shows like a map how your life will finally end: everything shown to me, *sure*, *of course* and almost relief because now it made sense, all the little incidents, her sullenness and spite, making me the odd man out, the bad guy because if you want to hurt someone it helps to hate them first, doesn't it? And all those tears, why not tears, why not cry when what you're doing is so wrong: so wrong because it all could have worked, could have stayed as it was if not for Sophie's neediness, Sophie's greed to tip us past balance, make us all fall

and "I don't know what you're *talking* about," crying now from anger, paper napkin in her fist, blame like a blow for me but *oh no not this time* not me Sophie because I don't buy that anymore: and out of the booth, sliding out easy and smooth and I didn't say anything, left her there, let her pay for her own fucking blueberry torte and I realized I was shaking, seismic tremble through my flesh, adrenaline grind and I started to walk, just walk because I could not go back to work, not this way, not now and who cared what they thought, they can't fire me, I don't even work for CompuTrac or DataSys or whoever it was this week, I can walk all day and all night if I feel like it and I did, walking past the burn in my chest, in my heart, walking to nowhere because there really was nowhere to go

and Sophie's next move imagined, coffee-shop scuttle and rushing off to call Lena, call and say what? *Jess was mean to me, he made me cry, he said I want you all to myself* but she couldn't say that, could she, not to Lena because what would Lena think then? what would *she* say, what solution might she then propose and maybe I should talk to her, maybe I ought to call her first, stop at a pay phone, the sound of her voice . . . but walking instead as if I had somewhere to go, to be, long stride Lena's kind of walk, effortless rhythm past the inner twist, skewed echo of that first turmoil, remember? Walking it off, the clamor of my cock, denying the hunger, the clamor of my need but this, oh this was even worse: because then breaking through had felt like being born, coming into a life already waiting, all I had to do was lift my hand—but now it was murk and confusion, no clear road and *what will we do?* to the cadence of my steps, if we can't go on together what will we do? What will *I* do? imagining, trying to guess a life beyond this life created, kink smashed and me left scrabbling, back to the beginning, no one and nothing and *no*, I said to myself, *no* like a mantra because it must not happen, *no* because I was more than that, I had to be more

and suddenly stilled and halted by the sense of a monstrous simplicity, a darker light in which the question could be, must be put: if it can't go on then it has to stop; if we can't be three then we must be two

but which two?

Which one?

Stranded now, chain-link park and trees still leafless, all of it clear as a drawing, black etching, tip of the knife into metal like flesh—and such a small question, *which one?* a question to swallow the world, swallow me whole and I would have liked to pretend, say later that I hesitated, agonized, had to think but I didn't, I didn't, I knew right away because no matter what happened *I want her, I have to have her, I cannot let her go:* no life guessed past her, nothing past her but nothing at all because that was the next step, the real step, the last step: the choice, the hand sunk harsh into the fire to grasp the tool that makes the scar: *I have to have her.*

Sophie or no Sophie.

No matter what.

3

THE CIRCLE IN
THE FIRE

*D*ark now, and still moving, hands in pockets; walking home.

In a kind of ether lightness, inside and out: streetlights, headlights, hurry around me as I moved through crowds but not of them, waiting at a corner for traffic to clear, dart and stride and a warmth at my chest, heat but not from walking, hands in pockets and the closer I got the more I felt it, rising tide of, what? Pleasure, peace? No: *relief*, a stronger word for a stronger feeling, the feeling of knowing that a step would be taken, something done to make it all stop; that no matter what else might happen, what sorrows or unguessed pains, this at least did not have to go on.

Dark rooms and empty, neither of them home—and remembering: *Lena made reservations*, some Sicilian restaurant and there the tabletop note but better not to go, not to join them, better to sit here alone and wait. Making coffee, not a drink, dark sweet coffee and thoughts in slow exhausted circles, thinking of what I would say when they came home; what would I say?

I want you.

Go away.

See Sophie's hat forgotten on the counter, magazines and mail, curled lists in Sophie's handwriting and past that crust of thin relief the pain unseen below, black water and what *would* I say? *I'm sorry, Sophie,* it just isn't working; sorry, sorry but—and the sheer alien taste of those words, how possible that I could even think this, surrounded by her artifacts, domestic detritus of this life, our life made and shared? How could I just not want her anymore?

Head down, small cough of steam from the coffee maker and like vertigo the sickening reverse, the feel of being *against* Sophie, of loving someone more than her, desire at her direct expense; and masked then by the Janus face of grief, how can that be, how can that ever be? Sophie my first darling, first friend and best and the key in the lock, opening door: *which one?* and half-rising, trying to be ready but it was Lena, Lena alone, Lena who without a word, gloveless hands outstretched came straight to me, arms around me there in the chair, my head pressed to her breast, cold wool coat and buttons like bones and "Jess," less breath than a whisper, "Jess, Jess," to hold me tight then pull gently away, hallway sounds and now Sophie, red eyes and stiff fingers to yank at her boots, nothing said to me or to Lena and off into the shower, a long shower, water like a voice in a language I did not speak and no one spoke, a pall of silence as if someone had died, as if something had happened past all power of speech to change: and like clockwork we three to bed, Lena and Sophie and me all bundled together, Sophie like a stone between, a wall, stiff and naked and I lay on my side staring at nothing, at the clothes on the floor, Sophie's blue slippers like small feet in that dark and at every motion, every sound, every sigh my own breath faltered, caught and held and waiting: for someone to turn and reach for the light, sit up and say *We have to talk about this, we have to talk about it now.*

But no one did and not me either, staring at the clock until exhaustion gave me sleep: and reel on reel of dreadful dreams, stumbling outside from a building on fire, crumbling in an earthquake, dissolving to dust and split boards like bones around me and it didn't take a shrink to figure that one out: why not dream of dissolution in a state where balance, parity, was intrinsically lost? and in a different mood I could have found it funny, not funny ha-ha but funny cut your throat, the way we laugh at irony as we dangle from its chains but when I woke it was still dark, an hour or more till light and despite my dreams, beneath them a feeling of arousal: *not now* from the conscious mind but my cock was hard, stiff against the mattress, against the slow pull of my hand and out of bed then, quiet to the door, quiet into the bathroom

but quieter feet behind, someone else awake and it was Lena, Lena pushing lightly at the bathroom door, sliding inside to put her arms around me, mouth to mine and her name from me in a wounded whisper, *Lena* as I kissed her, *Lena* as in swifter motion she enfolded me, legs braced to the sink, her eyes half-closed as if still in slumber, sweeter dreams than mine and I held her, squeezing, kneading, tighter and too tight as if she were my dream, dream flesh beneath my hands that no touch could injure, no passion bruise and when we had finished and stood, slumped, propped together her whisper again: "Jess, sweetheart . . . we have to try."

My silence, the headache throb of my heart and "Sophie told me what happened," fingers warm against my cheeks, my closing eyes. "We went to that restaurant, she kept hoping you might show up—"

"No," I said. "No, I couldn't, I just—"

"I know, I know," those loving fingers, that touch and all of it directed at me, unshared, all mine and "We have to *try*," again, the whisper urgent, "no matter what. Because I think—I really do, I think we can make it work again. Like it used to be," there on that plane of my silence, my eyes closed in the inner shadow of some great unscalable hill, climb certain but in sorrow, all my dark winter's work to get this far, see where next to go—but see her, now, my heart's desire, there at the bottom, calling to me: *Come back*, oh come back and "Lena," I said, "I don't know if it *can* be how it was, things have changed, we, *Sophie's* changed, I mean you have to see that, she's gotten so—"

"Sophie," a sigh, "doesn't know what she wants." Head to one side and for the moment uncanny it was Sophie's bird gaze, Sophie's motion until her head shake, brief and sure and all herself again, confident and calm and "*I* know," hands moving now to stroke my chest, slow circling palms as if to soothe the heart within. "I know what she needs. I know what I need," grave gaze as if I alone could fill that need, give her what she wanted, what she asked not only for herself but for us all and "I love you," my kiss defeat as she slid away from me, slid herself free of me, feet on the floor to stand face-to-face. "If this is what you want, fine, I'll try. Just—help me. Help me," and her kiss then a covenant, a promise between us, just she and I and the work of restoration, she and I together at the bottom of the hill.

Together: and we managed a start at least, giving Sophie lots of space, lots of time, what patience I could muster and Lena pure nurture, ignoring the bad moods, bad tempers, encouraging with tenderness the April grace of those rare Sophie smiles, moments gifted by small jokes or tiny kindnesses, moments when it almost seemed that Lena was right and we could be together again, the rift repaired, tightrope balance regained and in those moments Sophie glimpsed for me through that newer lens, washed poignant in the light of future loss and *what will she do without us?* as she laughed with Lena, smiled small and swift to me: hand in hand in hand, the trio again if only in this instant, this street, this warming afternoon where the gray rocks of snow at last had melted to show beneath that flecked cornucopia, old flyers and street garbage, mementos of the fall in which we had walked together, talking and giggling in our bubble, our snug envelope of kink and thought it, we, could never change: and oh, I thought, oh you selfish bastard, you used to love her, you used to *love* her; what happened? Little chin pointed up, pale hair half-curls again and that flash glance to me, to Lena where the glance rested and found root, Lena in whose ear she had to whisper, the observation shared while denied to me—and that denial to activate, again, the old brute grind, envy another souvenir of that dead winter, still alive, still turning on itself like a snake cut in two: and feel Lena's hand in mine now, sweet secret squeeze to say *I know*, Lena who understood what it was like for me, who knew I was trying so hard to give her what she wanted, what she asked past my own inclination, my own desire to make an end, to cry out *this isn't working, this is over* because for every good day five were bad, for every one of Sophie's smiles a tax of tears spilled seemingly without provocation, for every hour spent glad in trio twenty more where all I wanted was to grab Lena and run and never look back.

You can live a whole life that way, if you want to.

But think of it: scraping constant on that grindstone of frustration, Red Queen's race and now for me the new deprivation: no lovemaking, said Lena, nothing that might disturb the balance and "We have to be careful," that careful sigh, "we can't upset her right now." Kissing me clandestine in the kitchen, slow caress and "What about me?" my protest but rote only and she knew it, knew I would go along with her, do what she asked even though I wanted nothing but her now, my desire exponential, fed by our discretion and of course between Sophie and me there was almost nothing, not that way, not anymore as Sophie these days seemed somehow beyond desire, permanent resident of a country where fucking was too frivolous an act to be practiced by the natives and me stranded outside with my cock in my hand, warm between their bodies, still curled impossibly trio and on Sophie's insistence: as if she wanted to keep an eye on us, keep us apart; and unable to rest in that silence, breathing their twin scent like the ghost of our old passions I would rise, lightless search for the calm of the fold-out, where sleep at least might be.

Spring taking true hold now, season of new beginnings, fresh starts but not here, not for us: nothing here but Sophie's tremors, Lena's patience like dripping water wearing me, not Sophie, down, the atmosphere at home such a cauldron—Sophie's scowl perennial, what will set her off this time? so better to say nothing, sit and look at Lena there to smile in sympathy, sweet smile, sweet the shape of her breasts through her blouse . . . and me like a rock, stone block reading the paper, a magazine, flipping through the mail but instead thinking solely of her, incessant fantasies like the good old, bad old, hot old days but this time of sheer escape, Sophie dissolved somehow and Lena and I off somewhere, some new place, new apartment where we would lie together all night, every night, nothing between us but the gloss of our own sweat, sleeping to wake still holding her, Lena all mine as she was never now, so rarely even there alone with me.

And my own wonder sometimes, to undercut those fantasies, dry question posed without answer: such pleasure possible, such pure relief but Lena still unpersuaded: why? Was it some flaw or fault in me, my tenderness unable to compete against Sophie's tempers and storms? Was it something she saw that I didn't, something she knew? because I tried, oh did I try: but Lena was stubborn, Lena believed hope was possible and not wanting to push her, anger her, drive her away instead I had to woo her, draw her to my side, make her mine past all other, lesser wants: because as it was, had been, like marriage between us so now its dissolution, chosen or not, was still a true divorce, and me with Lena, why, that would be what people call an affair, wouldn't it? The maddening little touches, shared glances past Sophie's sullen gaze, kissing in a restaurant booth while Sophie was in the john; calling home from a pay phone, calling Lena to meet me—for coffee, for a drink, some scrap of time spent alone together, time to talk freely, without whispers, without having to stop because Sophie had just walked in—hunched there in the rumble and scream of traffic, desperate, enfumed but she had already left, bored tinny receptionist shriek, *she's gone for the day* so I chanced calling home, ringing phone and if it was Sophie or the machine I would hang up, give up, trudge back and sure enough Sophie answered, thin voice as if from miles away and *"Shit,"* my snarl as I banged the phone, turned too fast from the booth and into a trash can I hadn't seen, stumbled almost to fall and behind me a laugh in passing, it all must look pretty funny, pratfall despair but not to me, harried and driven, sweat on my forehead and home to find them watching some documentary, *Dance Today* and sharing Thai takeout, cozy as hell and for me in the doorway the urge gigantic to slap off the TV, kick over the table, splatter and drench and turn on them to say, to say . . .

And Lena's gaze on my face, rising to come to me, ostensibly to pour more wine, ask about my day (about which Sophie could no longer even pretend an interest, whether I had made an extra million or been mugged it was all the same to her) and in her motions a weariness, a kind of tired strength so resolute it made me want to weep: what was all this *doing* to her, the tension of riding the middle, the edge of the edge like a high-voltage wire and in the kitchen, spilled wine and I gathered her to me, anger-rough and held her tight, tight, held her and said in a voice I did not try to keep low: "We have to do something, we can't keep on like this. This is no *good*, Lena, this is—"

And her sigh, head back and "Maybe it's my fault," she said, "maybe I should never have moved in with you. I think about that a lot, you know, I think about how things were for you before I—"

"Don't say that," but she did from time to time, sighs and shrugs as if she felt culpable, responsible for the whole disintegration, Sophie and I together and presumably happy until she came—but that was foolishness, no fault ever hers and every time I told her so, did the best I could to make her see that her coming gave to me what I could have had from no one else, not even Sophie: trenched depth of passion and of need, dark light to give me skill beyond the game I thought I'd mastered, to show me game within game, heart within heart, desire nested, breathing, in the hungry arms of kink and "Don't say that," I said again. "Sophie's the one who's the problem here, it's her fault that it can't be the way it was, ever, we'll never—"

But "We can't just abandon her," head on my shoulder, rare and precious in my arms. "She's very unhappy, she's—we just have to keep on doing our best, and everything will be all right. Right?" and kissing me, narrow warmth of that seeking mouth, taste of wine and my cock springing hard to life, kissing her harder, hands sliding down to draw away as Sophie entered, slammed cupboard doors and sour face and I left the room to keep from talking, keep from saying what was curled there in my throat like some new tongue, black appendage made to speak words no one wanted to hear and sometimes it was as if I had never loved her, never at all, as if she were some cruel and alien twin who had subsumed the Sophie I, we, once had cherished and left instead this dour new stranger with her cloud of self-pity who demanded, and got, all of Lena's patience and the dwindling drops of mine.

And so as I once had thought to outrun desire by walking, up and down and around the block now I chose working, volunteering for extra hours, dumb, time-intensive jobs I could have done in my sleep but that ate up the minutes and kept me from thinking, or at least from thinking too much. Coming in early, leaving late and "Keeping busy, huh?" from the receptionist, leaning over me with another cup of coffee, bitter vending machine brew but she kept on buying it, trotting it over to me so what the hell. Blond hair a few shades past Sophie's, pale eyes and heavy tits and "Busy bee," I said, what the hell was her name? *Lisa*, right. "Busy me, that's me, Lisa."

"Don't you ever, you know, just sit back? Take some time for yourself?" Leaning low, no bra and if I leaned as well, just a little, I could see almost everything, dark nipples' crest and this her shtick since the day I got there: bringing me coffee, complimenting me on my ties, asking my opinion of a movie or a club: *you ever go there?* and my own distant wonder, how long had it been since I had just had fun with a woman, just a few laughs, a date, a night out instead of my daily Jacobean soap opera, tension junkie proud of pain as if the outside world was intrinsically *easier* than where I stood now, easier to navigate and survive; as if that enclosure in which I lived, built of flesh and sorrow, confliction and desire, seraglio of whispers and longing had somehow become me, or I it: spectator, participant, and act all in one but how in the world to explain that to this woman, bright smile and loose yellow blouse and as far from me as two people in the same room, the same world ostensible could be, speaking the same language but without communication, *you can't imagine* and "Sometimes," I said, "not much. I like to keep busy."

Silence, then: "You live with someone, right?"

"I—yeah."

"Two someones," her smile turned coy, turned on its edge, "right? That's what Rico told me, you know Rico? He says that you live with two women and you, you like *date* them both."

Date, right; fuck was what she meant. Coffee in hand, no gaze for her or her tits there on view and "Yeah," I said, "yeah, that's it, that's right," and "Oh," she said, "oh, wow, it sounds so *romantic.*"

And I laughed. I didn't mean to but out it came, a dry snide sound and that was the end of that, she thought it was meant for her, aimed at her but where the humor really was was in my bathroom at home, bent over, jacking off to my own stifled grunts, thinking of Lena, angry at Sophie: *it shouldn't have to be this way:* oh *romantic,* sure. Like Keats coughing tubercular blood, like the whisking guillotine: like dying for love.

But that night, freak spring storm of thunder and flung snow, Sophie cocooned and thick with sleep, her back to me, to Lena: who with caution almost painful turned then, eyes open, wide awake, to place my hands upon her breasts: exquisite gift, slow bedclothes rustle, my own thick breath and "Let's go," a murmur barely sound, "let's—" but Sophie stirring, moving as if she heard and we subsided, Lena's pulse felt in my hands, my palms, rhythm to rise and her hands then on me, silent and expert to the trebling pound of my heart and Sophie near enough to touch, to smell the heat on me, smell our lust and *stop it*, that voice inside, *not here, not like this:* but was it that too? the lust for betrayal, like discovering within oneself a taste for human flesh, savoring the wrong—and still I was mindlessly hard, I could have come in an instant, almost instantly did, slick and wet on her hands, warm strong fingers and my fingers thrust inside, swift and brutal, *in* and *in* past her bowstring thighs: semen smell and her own caught cry like a dream-shout dwindled in the waking instant, my breath imprisoned and held as if I might burst from the pressure within: subsiding, slow and slower, our hands linked like prisoners, like conspirators

and Sophie still sleeping, nestled head like a tired child's and for me in that moment, clear past all passion or relief a wretchedness intense as nausea, deep enough to turn me away even from Lena: but to what? where? Nowhere, nowhere to go but in, deep like a chambered heart, crawl and stumble in a tiny place, a place like my own life, cramped and disfigured like bound feet, limbs that cannot grow but still like some magic box that space to contain the world entire, all the world and all its vistas, all its pomps, *I do renounce them* for the chance of having her, having her all to myself.

All mine: please: and soon. All mine.

Sun's heat like summer and me sweating in my jacket, walking up to AmBiAnce to meet Lena and Sophie, one of our shared excursions just like the good old days: dinner, a Japanese place around the corner and then to the theater, something called *Dog Pound* with an actor Sophie liked, some snaggletoothed blond who used to come into AmBiAnce when she was first starting out. Tickets in my pocket and I was early, so: sofa perch and wait around just as I had done so many times yet strange now the distance, as if I were an actor too, playing the role of the Boyfriend, Lover, Betrayer, but who was I really? Double roles, double agent, familiar headache behind my eyes so I picked up a magazine, lifestyle stories about people who made more money than I would ever see, spent it in places I'd never go and past the radio and blow dryers, running water the sound of strident Po, ragged edge of real anger, she was really laying it on: and then in answer another voice, Sophie's voice sawing through the clamor, tight and too high like the keen of an animal trapped and "*Why,*" slamming out of the break room, "why don't you just get the fuck off my *ass?*"

All the stylists, clients in frieze to watch their entrance: Po fierce and fiercely silent, red-faced Sophie clenching a paper towel and ready, I saw, to cry: and seeing me, swung gaze as Po saw too and "Speak of the devil," loud enough for everyone to hear, "it's Mister Excitement himself. Maybe *he's* the trouble, huh, Sophie? Maybe it's all his fault you can't get in on time, you keep screwing up, maybe he's your big problem in life—"

And Sophie turning, heel swivel as if at bay and to save my life I could not have predicted what she did next: that flushed face pinching, tightening as her eyes went wide and "Shut up," a roar, "shut up shut *up*, don't you *dare* talk that way about him, don't you dare . . ." with her hands before her, still clenching the paper towel, Po in momentary silence and my own dumb-show stare: why such defense, why *now?* Was it that she agreed with Po, that all fault was mine, and was simply enraged as we always are to hear the truth spoken from another's mouth? or was it fury that Po would choose such a spot for her attack, that sore Achilles heart? and storming now to her work station, kicked cabinet doors and slosh of water, shoulders hitched from tears suppressed and the look Po gave me then—dead on, flat stare—was the meanest I had ever had from anyone, dead mean as if she would have liked to kill me, excise me from Sophie's life forever and for good.

Then Lena through the door, right on time: "Hey there," like my guardian angel come to save me from myself and rising grateful from the sofa, hand out as Sophie, jacket in hand, stormed wordless past Po and everyone, stiff-armed out the door and Lena in her wake at once, me at her back and "What's the matter?" to Sophie who would not answer, to my own shrug, hands up because I wouldn't say, it wasn't really my story, was it? and no doubt there was plenty more I didn't know, maybe Po was always at her this way, on and on about me (and Lena?)

until today she finally cracked; maybe anything; and my shrug repeated by Lena who gathered Sophie to her, one-armed big-sister hug and began as we walked to talk determinedly of other things.

Dinner too quick and silent, glance to glance but the play turned out to be funny, a farce set in a hot dog factory (*Dog Pound*, get it?) and the ex-client was terrific, droll slapstick and Sophie laughing in a way she hadn't for so long, long enough for me to see there that other Sophie, bright eyes and clapping hands, dear ghost I used to love and in fact the night entire become a ghost, almost, of the way things used to be: the three of us cab-squashed companionable, rare moment grown to grace to carry us home where the moment held, sustained by careful handling, the most exquisite care: little jokes and courtesies, little smiles and nods and was it all, I wondered, somehow born of that battle with Po, a kind of purging, pressure released at least for now to grant Sophie a kind of ease that by extension rippled out to us: there in the kitchen, pouring nightcap wine and "Go on," Lena's whisper and whisper-light kiss. "Go on, go to her. I'll sleep out here tonight."

And through a moment's strange jealousy (of what? for whom?) I did, two glasses carried to the bedroom, door eased almost to and see Sophie cross-legged, nudge of breasts through her shirt as she reached for the glass and I looked at her, my pause almost theatrical but it was as if she were a stranger, someone seen but all unknown: beautiful, yes, but past the smile so very tired, lines of strain across her forehead, at her lips the faint corners' droop etched by sorrow's gravity, as if she had grown older, grown in the tumble of loss and need, pulled, as I was, far and farther by this orbit of change and dismay but close enough—this time, this moment—for me to touch her, for her to kiss me, lips grazed soft to mine and "You know," she said, "you shouldn't listen to that shit. She doesn't know how it is, no one knows, no one ever has."

Feeling her shoulders, little bones, bird bones and "Po," I said, "oh sure, she never liked me anyway. But it was nice of you to stick up for me," and her wounded mouth to kiss me again, my hands in motion to stroke her, undress her, image of Lena in the other room but *no*, I told myself, *this is for Sophie, be here with Sophie now*, and pressing her gently, gently to lie down, lie beside her as her kisses changed, become as it had been, eager, demanding, hands swift between my legs but even though I tried—and I did try, I swear—still all I could see was Lena, the slope of her breasts, the long angle of her legs and Sophie somehow in comparison less—less what? or simply *less*, no depth there I did not know, no hidden rooms, no twists or secret spots and the more I tried the worse it got, flaccid to her touch, limp to her mouth and her squirm, jerking upright to shriek, "You can't even get hard for me, *you can't even get hard for me!*"

Her reddening face like a fever, like blight and "I'm just not *enough*, right?" crawling wild from the bed, naked and furious, "it has to be *her*, too, right?" and my own fury of innocence spiked with a shiver of half-belief because what if she was right? What if Lena had gone so far inside, become so integral that she *was* my desire, dream and act and what happens if I can't have her? Does the desire go as well, the capacity for heat?—like telling a fish all the water has gone, brutal evaporation, *you'll just have to do the best you can*—but Sophie still shouting, waving arms and out of the room, running to Lena who after long and sibilant whispers like cold wind through ocean grass brought her back into the bedroom and asked me—past Sophie's face averted as if, unseen, I might with great luck disappear—to please leave them alone.

Which I did.

Retreating as always to the fold-out, TV on to shroud their voices, the ribbon of Lena's alto to encircle Sophie's shriek; scent of Lena on the blanket wrapped half around me, half asleep and thinking, wondering if anyone had heard Sophie shouting about my impotence, my vast new lack and with a certain irony I thought of Jim, crouched low and listening and he would have heard an earful, his own drop of kink to soothe a last or lingering loss.

And what if, I thought, clicking aimless through the channels, shoot-outs and earnest faces, ad after ad after ad, what if kink though unnamed was in some strange way universal? What if everyone in the building, in the city had their own habits of attention, of addition, wide eyes and listening ears to gather, glean, and then make, brick to brick, their private wall, map's masterpiece built of little stones and tumors, arguments and bliss unseen but guessed, figured, refigured in a picture to show them not only the lives of others but the meaning of their own, society of heart's voyeurs stretched across the city and the world, watching and learning, amazed by what they knew . . . but thinking this I saw its fallacy, its assumption that looking was seeing and to see was to know because everything around me, the world inside and out told me

165

the opposite was true: the goal was not to think, not to examine, not to look and not to know because sometimes knowing means pain, means you must act or cease from acting, means something has to change, has to give, has to rupture: and it could and would be you.

There on the couch with my blanket and remote, the voices from the bedroom and the TV gone to one, sound without reason and sleep without dreams and when I woke in the morning it was to silence around me, the silent fact of the bedroom door like the wall of kink itself, to show me what I did not know, and that I was not wise.

As if what she perceived as my willful impotence was the last possible straw Sophie seemed now released from the obligation to try, to pretend to pretend she could live with the two of us in any kind of harmony, false or true; and if this release did not bring her pleasure—it never seemed to—still it gave her an advantage, abandonment's upper hand, carte blanche to slam doors and stare past me, to parade her new theme song, crap pop that was big that year in the clubs: " 'I don't want you to be unhappy/But I can't be happy with you' " and she sang it all the time, hum and murmur, murmur and drone as monotonous as a chain-gang prisoner, changing of the guard and at first I tried to ignore it, yes Sophie I hear you but as she kept it going, on and on and on I wanted to shake her, wanted to yell *Stop it, shut up already, if you have something to say why don't you just SAY it?*—yet silenced by the knowledge that I could at any moment have said the same thing to her: I don't want you to be unhappy, but I can't be happy with you. Not this way. Not anymore.

It's amazing how much turmoil the human brain can master, or at least profess as mastery; amazing how we went to work, went out, made plans as if nothing was happening, as if tomorrow was a place the same as today where we might expect in tandem to arrive, still trio, still doing the things we did although with strain like a weight borne in the body, its pull most visible in hindsight because for me at least each day was only treading water, barely breathing in the air of what might be while ostensibly in my cubicle, desk, work station, focused and serious, staring at a screen; or in a coffee shop at lunchtime, in line for the movies, there but not there like an actor in a role, the mask of activity an empty hole inside which I turned and burrowed like a worm in sand, struggling to see that the next step, the real step was instead a series, a complex weave of step to step: *follow the path and you become it*, who had said that? Wear the mask of circumstance long enough and inside the face deforms, curves to fit the shape that binds it, becomes what it seems to be because *pain needs to happen*, don't stand in its way.

But while I could tell myself these things, could even believe that this pain might reward me in ways I could not understand, still it hurt and I didn't want to hurt, didn't want to long helplessly for Lena, there and not there, didn't want to spar with Sophie who seemed unable to accept my presence without some mockery or complaint, all remarks its detonation: such as my mild question, why did she never wear the earrings I had bought her, the ones I gave her for Christmas? to bring her sourest sideways stare: "Oh, earrings, right. You gave *her* a *ring*."

"You *liked* those earrings, you—"

Slamming down the magazine she held like a club truncated: "I don't want to talk about it, all right?"

Sometimes it was my haircut she hated, my choice of entree, even my temping: "That's you all over, isn't it? Surface dweller, you only care about today, right now, this minute—"

"Who fed you that shit?" I said, too weary for anger, for anything but weariness itself. "Your mentor, Po? Or did you read it in some lifestyle magazine?"

Chin down and glaring, the lines of her face carved sharp as if by illness, fever to burn from the outside in and "You think I'm stupid, Jess, but—"

"I do *not* think you're—"

"Wrong, because *Po* doesn't think for me, *Lena* doesn't think for me, I think for myself! I *think* for *myself!*" loud and louder, convincing me, herself, anyone in the vicinity of doubt and my own voice rising, trying to match hers: "Just stop it, Lena, just—"

" 'Lena'? My name is *Sophie*, asshole, *my* name is—"

"I didn't say that," knowing I had, "I didn't—"

"Yes you did," that carved face as if much older, Sophie in ten years staring at me now. "Yes you did and you know why? Because you don't even know who we are, do you? a woman's a woman, right, it's all the same to you," and my own desperate denial, self to self *that's not true, that's not true at all* but did I, somewhere inside, confuse one with the other, or had they to me become two faces of the same feminine monster in that growing sense of dislocation, the inner compass lost, fun-house desolation intercut with my fantasies which as each day passed began to seem remote and bizarre, a promise left unkept to rot and inside me then a voice like Po's saying Well look at you, little Mister Surface Dweller, how's the weather down in the deeps? in the muck and the shit, what's it like? and *this isn't me*, I thought, watching Sophie storm from the room, back straight as some glass rod a scream could shatter, *not me, this really isn't how I am.*

Is it?

Follow the path and you become it.

Coffee-shop and cubicle, deli and club and all I could do was keep going, keep hoping, wring from tension and monotony the nourishment—even if pressured, even if skewed—of time alone with Lena, to kiss her, hold her, try with desperate persuasion to make her see that this continued balance was worse than useless, time lost on the altar of pain and we had to decide, together and soon, what was going to happen, what we were going to do: murmuring my version of what things would be like for us, concrete plans for her approval and we'd have to move, live somewhere else because I couldn't stand to stay here where so much had happened, so much gone wrong—and in our wake Sophie must go as well, move out; but where? Where will she live? afford things? how can she—but why give concern or worry to Sophie who so patently loathed me, Sophie my rival; just stop thinking about her, about her life which she would have to fashion on her own, away from us, apart: *stop thinking* but my thoughts gone circular, flung fragments dissolved, *think straight* but I could not, sometimes felt I could not think at all and "Lena," at last more whine than plea, "Lena, we have to *do* something."

"I know," closed eyes and nuzzling soft against my neck, "I know, I know," but knowing seemed to lead her nowhere, keep her in place and me stranded beside her, watching the strain made manifest, the burden unbearable carried too long: small thumbprint shadows stretched and grown beneath her eyes, the way she never seemed hungry, seemed unable to sleep the night through but must rise, go off alone to sit on the fold-out, look out the window at the cars and the dark but when I tried to join her, silent to share whatever vigil she made, she would send me back—lovingly, but send me back: "I have to think," softly, my head to her breast, mouth in infant reach for her nipple, mindless and wordless, and sometimes, sweet and oh, so rare we would make love, bundled on the fold-out in gasped silence and need, helpless and gorging on her body as if lost in a land of famine, her flesh my talisman to keep me safe from harm.

But there was no safety, our house divided: and Sophie's rage ascendant, expressed now by a cascade of injuries, stumble to fall down a half-flight of stairs, struck dizzy by a cabinet door, palm cuts and dry abrasions and "You have to be more careful," Lena would say, examining the sore spot, the lump or the bruise. "You have to—"

"I *am* careful," woefully, skin ripped to blood and oozing drops; how young she could seem, even now. "I am careful."

Which was a lie, although she seemed not to know it, self-goaded to idiocies large and small: even smoking again, clandestine at first but then the burn holes here and there, saucers for ashtrays, stained fingers and breath—and deeply sullen at my protest, my reminder of how glad she'd been to quit the first time: "Remember how you said you'd never start up again, you said you—"

"Things are different now." her narrowed eyes, smoke smell the smell of anger. "Aren't they? *You* are."

You are too, I could have said, but why say anything at all? and at dinner, Sophie's favorite Italian café but cramped in the tiny smoking section, lighting up as soon as she hit the chair and "You know that's not good for you," said Lena, one gentle hand on Sophie's as she reached again for her lighter, red plastic, Shagg's Ale and scarred at the edge. "You're coughing a lot, and your breath is getting really—"

"Really what?" and without pause to me, small smile of large dislike: "Oh right, get her to do the dirty work."

"What?" from Lena, her gaze swung back and forth and "Sure," I said to Sophie, hiding none of my contempt, "it's all a big conspiracy, me and Lena and the whole world, everybody's against you, everybody wants—"

"I don't give a shit what 'everybody' wants, I'll do what I want." Hand bunched trembling on the lighter, her chin outthrust, cords in her neck like a little girl aged by rage before her time, that clenching hand a handful of bone. "I'll do what *I* want!"

And Lena as quiet, gathered as Sophie was not, all of a piece and that piece a weapon as she leaned close and closer, some special edge I could see but not read and "What *you* want," looking straight into Sophie's eyes, all the way down. "What about us? What about what we—"

"Who's 'us'?" and bitter to shove back from the table,

clumsy yank at her coat as she stood but "Sit down,"
Lena's voice deepening, dark alto like honey in blood,
"I'm not going to chase you, I'm—Sophie *sit down*," so
flat, so cold that Sophie flinched and I did too, brief dread
of having that voice aimed at me, the strictured ordnance
of that stare and "You're embarrassing," Lena said,
"you're acting like a—*stop* it," as she snatched past Sophie's grab at the cigarettes. "You can just listen a minute
without your prop, right, without something to *hold* in
your *hand*," which to me meant nothing but brought to
Sophie instant tears, focus drowned and Lena elbows on
the table, cocked stare and still that deeper, harsher voice,
the voice that tells you exactly what you are and exactly
what you ought to do about it: "You know I've had just
about enough of all this pity shit—pity's an *insult*, Sophie,
pity is *shit* and I won't stand still for it anymore, you hear
me? Answer me. Do you hear—"

"I hear you fine," now crying openly, the people gone
silent in the flanking booths, *all the better to hear, my dear,
fuck you* but I'd do it too, wouldn't I? *wasn't* I? and "I hear
you *fine*," angled forward now so the edge of the table
pressed into her concave belly, she and Lena face-to-face,
seeing only one another as if I did not exist at all, not participant or even voyeur but part of the background, kin to
the void and "Why," that cracked voice rising, "why don't
you say what you really mean? Why don't you say—"

"Sophie—"

"—*exactly* what you mean—"

"*Sophie*": not loud but with such pure ferocity that it
made of her a stranger, stripped opacity of all the masks to

show the final face below: yet calm, dead calm, one hand still on Sophie's cigarettes, faint shine from the line of the clip in her hair and "Sophie," again, still quietly, "get out."

Bell-jar silence, Sophie still weeping but without sound, both hands tight to her mouth as if to catch vomit or screams and then awkwardly, an animal desperate from a trap she half stumbled from the table, tripped on the chair as it toppled, on the grasp of its tangling coat: and to the door, the street where we saw her hunched as if lost in some other landscape, wailing like a child abandoned, but: "Don't," said Lena, wrung stare and very pale now, one cold hand on mine as cold beneath. "Not this time. Just leave her alone."

"Her coat," I said stupidly, watching her cry through the window: oh such pain to see hers, but wasn't that supposed to be over, wasn't it over yet? "She left her—"

"Let's just *go*," the words like a bone in the throat and turning half away from me to cover her face with her hands, the gesture *pietà* as if forced past her own control and my first emotion a kind of empty terror, how can this be happening to *her*, to Lena who never cries, never: and I reached for her, my hands on her arms but gently, gently so as not to move her, dislodge a shelter she needed: and from inside that shelter a word, something, something I didn't hear till she said it again: "Enough," as she opened her hands, as she gave me her gaze, eyes dry but bright as if sealed away behind some living glass.

"Let's go," napkin tossed from her lap to the table, plates still full, the wine undrunk, threading through tables to the door and the street where Sophie was nowhere to be seen and "Do you think," I said, coat on my arm and trying not to scan, not to peer through the crowds, "she went home?"

And Lena's stare: "Do you care?" which was no question at all but all she said, we said till we reached our door, stair climb like the world's last mountain, drifted smell of smoke inside and "Enough," again but only to herself, and then to me: "I want to talk to her," squeezing my hand with both her own. "By myself. All right?"

And like a blow I knew: *She's going to do it:* all the nights and days and hours tunneled down to this, this second, this cold hall and her colder lips to press against mine, dry kiss and I should have said something, done—what? held her, kissed her for courage, something, but instead stood as I had in the restaurant, blank as an empty room: looking, only looking until at last "Shouldn't I," my voice a stranger's, hollow as a bone, "I mean isn't it better if we both talk to her, if we both . . ."

Only her gaze, stare stripped to sheerest need: *I want this* and "All right," I said, stepping back, away: from her, from the door and what would happen there, damp whisper of my own cowardice, my own urge to escape: *get her to do the dirty work* and I almost stopped, almost insisted but instead "I'll come back . . . in, in half an hour, all right? Is that all . . ."

Key in lock, already turning but she gave me one more look—dark and distracted, as if on the threshold of some place I could not see—then was inside, the closing door and my footsteps on the stairs, one and two, down and down and conscious now of how late it was, how tired I was, how much I wanted it all to end, to just *be over:* and all the rest a chaos babble, what will she say, what will Sophie say, what will happen next, step to step in primitive rhythm, *the next step* and had it been half an hour yet? less? more? Should I wait, go in, what?

And finally turning, blind pivot to bump into someone, some older woman who glared then let her face slide into blankness as she saw me because maybe I looked dangerous, crazy, maybe I was crazy because I had walked long enough, *enough:* and down the street, up the stairs, each step like ten to our door and inside: to silence and the feeling of wreckage, cigarette smell like ozone from a storm and on the fold-out, side by side but not touching, Lena whose gaze rose to me as I entered, Sophie slumped, almost curled in place and

oh my God she looks terrible oh God oh Sophie

and "Go on," said Lena, touching Sophie on the arm. "Go on and tell him."

Pain in my side like a stitch, a piercing: *here it is, here it comes* and "Tell me what?" I said, what else was there to say? "Tell me—"

"We're leaving," half a mumble, Sophie's voice choked and broken, without sense: *we're leaving*—but Lena should be saying that, Lena not Sophie, Lena *to* Sophie, right? Right?

Bewildered my stare at Sophie, at Lena who said nothing, sat absolutely still to give me back my stare with one like glass, mirror's gaze to offer nothing but what you should already know and "We're leaving, Jess," said Sophie again, "we're moving out . . ." and then weeping, dry sobs like dry heaves, her whole body hitching and rent and "What do you mean," I said, loud, stupid-loud, "what

175

do you *mean?*" as if I could not hear, ears ringing from the pressure inside, vertigo and my heart a rung bell, louder and louder

we're leaving

what do you mean

"—wouldn't work," Lena's voice, Lena talking, had she been talking like that for long? Moving mouth, mouth I had kissed and "I did everything," to the backdrop of Sophie's sobs, "I did the best I could but I'm not God," and "What the fuck do you *mean?*" my own cry like an animal, a barking dog, *bad dog* and I tried to grab her, take her arm, make her make sense but smooth up then to pass me, out of the room and I stared not at Sophie—sick face, red eyes, crying so I wanted to scream at her, *stop it, shut up* because I couldn't think and I had to think, figure this out, make it make sense

and beyond the bedroom door the sounds of motion, Lena emergent with two bags, black nylon carryon and Sophie's old red overnighter, frayed at the seams and the edges and "What are you doing?" to Lena with her coat on, Lena cold and smooth as an implement, terrible, impersonal and "There's just no other way," she said, not so much to me or Sophie as to herself, calm assessment of a losing situation and "What do you *mean?*" and I wanted to stop her, grab her but I didn't, didn't touch her, stood with my hands hanging dead at my sides as if she knew what I might do and stopped that too, stopped everything surely and at once and the sound of my voice like an echo, without true depth or force: "What about what we . . . Lena, what about us—"

and "Get up," to Sophie now, Sophie who did not move or answer, Sophie whom she yanked upright, rough as an angry parent and "This is us," Lena staring at me, hipshot-tilted beneath the weight of both bags, arm hooked through Sophie's as if Sophie could not stand on her own, might fall without control. "*This* is *us.*"

And my body turning, wheeling from them both in a panic so vast I could not breathe because to look would make it real, this thing that could not happen, the world at end and if I looked I might see, might scream, might *do something* at the heart of this reversal, plunge like death because

we're leaving

and moving now, small sounds, the click of the lock and Sophie's voice: "*Jess,*" with such agony that I almost turned, almost looked straight at her, "oh Jess I can't *help* it, I can't *help it,*" and caught somehow or struggling in the doorway, Lena's curse: "Go *on,*" and from Sophie a sound like a cough, thick sound past speech

and then gone, both of them gone

without me

but *gone* doesn't mean anything I said to myself I said to myself *gone* is *shit* as I turned at last as if compelled, pursued, forced to see nothing and took a step, one and two toward the open door, no sound of descent or escape, no sounds at all as I hit the wall with my open hand, palm flat and stinging and the door was still open because why should I shut it, why should I scream because *nothing's over,* NOTHING'S OVER past the ringing phone and I hit the wall again, both hands this time, hands to fists again and again as something split, something broke, pain inside like a ringing bell but I didn't stop because I had to keep going, keep moving

because nothing's over

NOTHING'S OVER

not for me.

"You live here?"

Eyes blinking dry, on my back in the doorway, half in and half out as a big fat cop stared into my face: warm cigarette breath, "You live here?" again as if he might keep asking all day, all night—was it still night?—and "Yeah," I said, to make him stop and go away. "Yeah, this is, this is our place."

Blood on my shirt, on my hands.

"Had a fight with your girlfriend, right?"

"Two girlfriends," someone said, someone past his shoulder that I couldn't see, why couldn't I see? Dizzy now as though I was drunk, sick-drunk, but that made no sense and I tried to get up, sit up at least from my doorway sprawl but when I pushed my palms against the floor the pain threw me back, toppled me and "Watch it," the cop said, bending to raise me, tilt me to sit with my back to the hallway wall. "Looks like you broke 'em, maybe."

And past his bulk stood neighbor Jim, staring at me, saying nothing, he must have been the one who called: *domestic disturbance*, 911 and the cop saying something, talking to me: "*Two* girlfriends, is that right? And they're not here now?"

No, I said, I thought I said but no one answered so I

shrugged, tiny shrug through the shriek of my hands, *looks like you broke 'em maybe* but the intern in the ER said they weren't broken after all: "Fucked up, though," with his head to one side, "fucked up pretty good in fact. Hope you're not a pianist. What happened to the other guy?"

Balanced on the edge of the gurney, ammonia smell and soap and "I am the other guy," I said as naked past pause or warning came the pain, real pain to dwarf hand-maiden all the others in its path: Lena's face, Sophie's howling tears and every word, every look, every second like a bone snapped in half, two bones, four bones, expo-nential and

we're leaving

this is *us*

"—injection for now," the intern said, his voice soft and slow, "and I'll give you a script, you can get it filled down-stairs. At the pharmacy, okay?" Touching my hands again, knuckles dissolved in bruise-red flesh. "It'll be okay," he said, the needle engaged. "The pills will help too."

Blue pills in an orange bottle, three a day for two weeks and one for good luck, *for severe pain* and "Sign this" but I couldn't, fat hands clumsy but you need your hands, with-out them you can barely get your wallet, pay a cabbie, put your key in the lock but just seeing our building stripped me closer to panic, *run and scream* as if my own death waited within and "Keep going," I said over dispatch sta-tic, "go on," and we drove for twenty blocks before I stopped him, found a way to take money from the wallet, found a coffee bar because I did not want to take the pills on an empty stomach but food being out of the question made coffee the next best thing, black coffee with sugar but I couldn't open the sugar packets, seal paws on the counter but "You need help?" from some woman, woman beside me with a black baseball cap and too much perfume, thick scent a taste in my mouth and she opened the packets, stirred the coffee and "Hurt yourself," she said, pushing the cup to me. "What happened?"

Injection drawl, my head turning slow as if by gears imperfect and "I beat myself up," I said with what I hoped was a smile and she looked at me, one look then moved away, two seats, three seats down and drinking the coffee was not as hard as I had expected, balancing the cup, steam in my face and it was, I found, possible to exist without thinking, thin grayish wash of numbed sensation: my throbbing hands, the taste of the coffee, the woman's perfume like a stain on the cup: late, very late, maybe morning. The pill bottle had a childproof cap; the server opened it for me, shook a pill into my palm.

"Don't put it back on," in troglodyte mumble, something wrong with his mouth or my eyes and so the pocketful of pills like beads unstrung, empty bottle and the people I saw on the streets ignored me, even the beggars, who talks to a dead man? Block after block, a wind mild and warm and I had gotten almost all the way up the stairs before I had to stop, black blossom of panic to bring like bile the coffee into my throat, pill dissolved and *stop it*, I said to myself, maybe out loud, "stop it, stop it," at the door where I fumbled, fat hands, for my keys, painful search of both pockets but only the pills dug free, scatter bright across the floor and I wanted to scream, scream and kick the door, kick the pills so they flew: "*Fuck!*" and shoving, one shoulder and dead hand on the knob but it turned, it opened, the door was open because

they were back

but inside to find nothing, silence, no one: empty. Empty.

"You forgot to lock the door," I said aloud, adrenaline pound in my head, in my hands like two red clubs, "when you went to the hospital you forgot to lock the door," but it was like talking to nothing, words unheard and barely felt past the panic, brute airlessness inside because look around you, look past the sweaty vertigo and see: Sophie's T-shirt, Lena's books, someone's cup of tea left cold on the counter, no outer difference or shift as the dead body resembles the living, same eyes and mouth, arms and legs, nothing's changed except everything and in me now the hunger for wreckage, whirlwind grab and destroy—their clothes, their books, jewelry and knickknacks and maga-zines—force the corpse to look the part but, but: breath hot and slow through the opiate drag, slow as my thoughts past the shielding rage and all these things, I thought, all this *stuff*: they'll need it, won't they, need it and want it and come back to get it

but what if they don't? What if they never come back, all things abandoned, become detritus just like me, just like me because didn't I know, couldn't I feel, hadn't I seen—in Lena's stare, in Sophie's tears—*oh, yes, cry you should cry* because it was over, all over and they had fucked me, tricked me, stabbed me in the back: and how long had they known this, planned this, Lena on the fold-out star-ing out the window, Sophie in the bathroom wiping her nose and a sound from me then, dupe's moan because that meant it was all lies, wasn't it, all along? Planning together, secrets shared like kink gone mad to turn the world a stranger, my own world become weapon against me, emptied as it emptied me, made of me nothing but just another asshole, just a fool deceived because they had taken that too, the feeling of being special, set apart, different from everyone and left me instead just one of the herd, the great unenlightened, just another stupid guy who never saw it coming and "Oh *Christ*," my voice like a mouthful of meat, *oh Christ* and no shield now, no nothing, just the truth and my body bending, folding, knees and elbows and the distant urge to vomit, dry scald in my throat past nausea's curl but nothing came, nothing but a taste like sour blood and hunched that way like an animal tied I started to cry, less tears than a dark wheezing sound, *hunh hunh hunh* from the center of my chest, heart's voice and I wanted to hurt something, break something, pound my swollen hands against the floor but I didn't, did nothing, hunched there instead as if I had finally found my one true posture, the ravaged supplicant, and must stay that way forever because there was nowhere else to go.

Nowhere.

They're not coming back.

Light now, morning and the hallway visible, blue scatter of pills and slowly I moved, crab's crawl to sweep with dust the pills toward me, drag closed the door and rising, slow tremble down my back, the backs of my legs and it took me three tries to get the number right, phone balanced with my wrist against my ear: two rings, four and the message clicked on, Po's voice smooth over no-brand jazz: "This is AmBiAnce, but right now we're closed. If you want to leave a message for one of our stylists . . ."

Sophie: you took her.

Lena: you lied.

You both *lied*.

Eventually the phone clicked to disconnect, recorded voice to tell me to hang up, which I did to call again: the temp agency, another message to say I had been in an accident, I was on medication and "I should be in next week," but next week was another country, a moon in some other sky and in the rise of traffic noise, the day begun for others I lay at last to sleep, stretched wooden on the fold-out heavy with the scent of them, scent of both as if together they had become one creature and this its carapace, split cocoon discarded in the rush to newer life.

And in that sleep I dreamed: fierce stew of images, faces and limbs and I woke once, twice, my hands all pain but I had the cure for half of that: two pills swallowed dry and sleep, sleep in darkness without boundaries, black inside and out and when I woke again I was weeping, crying in sleep and hands above my head as if tied there, rack-tied and the ringing phone, how long had it been ringing? and I grabbed for it, ah my *hands* but "Hello!" with the phone to my face, pressed tight as if this was it, Lena calling to say she was sorry, sorry and it was over, all over, all a hideous mistake: "*Hello*," and even to me I sounded crazy, someone no sane person would ever want to see but a voice on the other end, woman's voice

Sophie's voice

to say my name, say it twice: *Jess Jess* as if I might have forgotten who I was, pause of breath and "*Jess*," again and crying, voice snagged ragged as if on some shoaling bone, bone in her throat and "Where are you?" I said, crawling upright, legs stiff and blanket tangled, a feeling in my heart like the dry edge of the knife, "Sophie *where are you?*" but then silence, the sound of disconnect and "*Fuck!*" my scream itself a broken thing, "fuck fuck fuck" to the empty phone, the empty room but *stop it* from some other voice, darker voice unmoved by pain or panic, *stop it right now* and I did, sat slowly back to think or try to: she had called, why? To see if I was here, if it was safe to come get her stuff, *their* stuff: why else? and so all I had to do was wait, right, wait right here and they would have to come back, one or both, bags and boxes and I could make it easy, I thought, I could pretend to be gone the next time she calls, let the machine pick it up and then when she thinks it's safe, when she thinks I'm gone . . .

and the mind's eye picture, me in spider-crouch behind the door, waiting, waiting . . . but then what? Even if she came, if they both came what would I do? What *could* I do: yell, scream, lock them in? Argue with them, reason with them, shake them to make them tell, *tell me the truth* but what presented truth could negate the fact of their leaving, sisters in kink and me just a discard, fool wrapped in lies and how believe them at all, now, no matter what they told me, no matter what they said because *this is us* was the only truth that mattered: they were *us*, and I was nothing.

Head down and hands hung thick and hideous between my knees, cartoon hands there on the fold-out, Lena's coverlet, the dainty red pillows as soft as her breasts and we had fucked on this fold-out not two weeks ago, her spread legs, her closed eyes, her mouth to mine as if without me she could not breathe, could not live: *Jess, Jess* and her smell all over me, over me now like an animate presence, her smell and Sophie's mingled, all the love in all the world but cold, so cold beneath that coverlet pulled high and rich with their odors as if I had crawled inside their bodies, sleep there, hide there and it was like that for three days: sleep, turn, take a pill and sleep again, three days like dying and each time I woke it seemed again to begin, first time forever like waking to find your legs missing, your arms, find yourself chin-strapped and paralyzed and *what happened?* you cry, *what's this* and they tell you: and after screaming you sleep and sleep and then *what happened? what's this?* and they tell you, and tell you, and tell you again.

But then—if you decide to live at all, live without feeling, live without limbs—comes a final waking, Lazarus cramped and hobbling to the bathroom, brief dizzy piss while surrounded by their unguents and I noticed then that my hands while still sore were human again, fingers like fingers, definable palms and in the shower, scraped crud and three days' beard, three days' tears, scrubbing myself as if of contagion and then drying, dressing, standing by the window, sidewalk stare with wet hair and jeans that felt too big, could I have lost weight? in three days? and below the people passing, women with dark hair, quick-walking women and maybe, I thought, worm's last turn of faintest hope, turning from the window, from the world to the world within, maybe if I talked only to Lena, talked to her alone I could make her see, I could

—but oh remember, worm, remember: *"There's just no other way"* and her face as she said it, that clinical gaze, *this patient is dead* and Sophie sagging and falling beside her, Sophie hauled to the door, lying Sophie to cry over the corpse and *there's just no other way* meant simply that, no alternatives, no way out for me because she had decided, *they* had decided that our triangle was dead, me with it and I didn't get to argue, didn't get a vote because they were *us*, GirlWorld, Tampon Nation, fucking bitches and what do I have to do, I thought, cut off my dick to join your sorority? give you my balls in a box? but that rage was foolish, juvenile, because there was nothing to do: case closed, all the end because they just don't want me, they don't *want me anymore*.

And the thought suffocation in these rooms full of their presence, the two of them everywhere I turned and why— putting on shoes, a coat and what was the weather like? abdicated world, are you warm or cold?—why hadn't they called again, tried to come back? but maybe they knew better, knew I was here waiting, knew that like they seemed to know everything else and so what? as I clumped downstairs, one step and two like the dead re-born, so what if they did know? I had my own plan now, first flickerings but I had to eat before anything else—pale cheese on black rye, black coffee drunk hot enough to scald and I can add my own sugar this time, thank you, neat circling spoon with my functional hands, hands to slip coins in a slot, punch in a number and "AmBiAnce," some voice I didn't know, some guy. "How may I help you?"

"I need to speak," phone tender to my chin, "to Sophie Sprause. Is she available?"

Buzzing pause, then tentative a voice, her voice and

"Hello," but although sad still unsuspecting, no idea and "Sophie?" I said, not quiet, not loud. "Sophie, it's me."

No sound, not even breathing: and "I want you to do something," I said. "For me."

Waiting, all patience now for her to speak, I could wait forever but finally her voice, rough as if through unshed tears: "What? Oh, Jess, what do you—"

"I want you to come and get your stuff. All of it. To-day."

Silence, the pause Marianas and see my smile, bare teeth: not a trap, Sophie, not even an order but some struggle there on the other side, rising squirm and it pleased me, I found, in a dark and distant way, pleased too to hear her say "I can't" as if frightened by her own re-fusal, as if I might jump through the phone at her, leap to straddle her lying mouth, squeeze her lips like a feeding fish, feeding frenzy and "I can't," she said again, "but we . . . but I can come tomorrow. All right? Can it be to-morrow instead?"

"Tomorrow," I said, considering tone but what differ-ence did it make to me? An extra day, extra night in a sea of extras, a world of nights unwanted and "All right," as if granting some unheard-of concession, "all right," and I hung up, heart's leap in promised rage and tomorrow, I thought, I would be ready for them, ready to confront them, all their sins assembled and though it would change nothing, grant nothing but spleen's satisfaction to throw their cruelties in that cold collective face still it put me in the mood to celebrate and I started off, jaunty death-row stroll down to the AmBiAnce district, back and forth past pink-and-black windows, amazing transformations

within and all for the asking, all of them due to you, Sophie, you can make a happy man sad, sad man sadder,
dead man walk the streets; and going uptown, where the
corporate writers might be presumed to be, dart and
scurry, drone and queen, Lena in black and silver and for
one frozen moment I thought I saw her, dark hair, long
legs but when I could breathe I saw I was wrong, the
woman too tall after all, legs too thin, hair too short but
oh that inner clench, desire's other face with teeth,
strange smile and after that near miss I felt I ought to have
a drink, something dark and sour and strong; it's amazing
how much false pleasure a drink can provide and two
drinks even better, third drink sipped slow with gaze
turned purely inward, thinking, thinking, red tally of their
betrayals, ones known or only guessed because even if
there was no truth left still there was rage, the rage to
know, to find out just how stupid, just how deceived I really was: all the way, bit by bit through the enormity, all
the lies now seen as a kind of paradigm for what really
happened, map in retrospect, drawing-room mystery
where the audience can see all the clues but the actors are
footlight-blind, of course, of course because the hand is
quicker than the eye and if you want X to happen you
have to do Y first, and A and B and C and all the steps in
the dance, all the motions one motion to achieve one special end: give one to the other at my expense, heart's cur-
rency paid in blood and that bitter memory, Sophie's first
urging: *why don't you call her?* and of course I had called,
Bluebeard's wife at the door—but that was unfair, wasn't
it? Glass in hand, the inward peer and be fair, tell the truth
if no one else will because the desire was mine as well,

wanting to call as much as Sophie wanted me to; as much as I had wanted to fuck Lena, love her, have her for my own.

Intersection of desires, collisions of need—like that Christmas party, standing in the snow: remember? The pure conviction, the purest love: *I need you:* and seen that way everything suspect, everything and especially the good times, making love, *lust* and was it all bullshit, was I the stupidest man in the world, the greatest fool, the most deceived? Think back—and have another drink, dark tasteless lubricant to help ease down the bones, mouthful of gristle, your own slippery heart and time a hall tableau to show the way, all the way back to—remember?—our first fight as a trio and all in pivot on a secret, secret shared between Sophie and Lena and thus denied to me: because isn't Lena her Deirdre Bacon now? bad girl's giggle, laughing all the way to bed and spread and ready for *the next step*, sure, the largest step of all because *it was all a lie, you lied to me, you never meant any of it: you used me*

but that wasn't true either, was it? The desire had been there, believe in that if nothing else because she *wanted* me, they both did; we all did for awhile.

And if hideous the memory still I could smile, a little smile to think of that first enormous passion, red carousel of misery and desire as I walked the streets, as I nursed my secrecy and thought it was the worst that could happen, unfed heat and I had had no idea, no idea how bad it could be to sit here like this and know she was gone, gone with Sophie, Sophie who used to love me too but who got so greedy, so needy, Sophie who wanted it all for herself

just like you

but "Fuck," I said, surprised to hear my voice aloud, quite clearly drunk but I didn't feel drunk, felt rather good in fact, felt like taking another stroll, man on the town but in the end found it easier to fall into a cab, fumbling for cash with my aching hands and when had I last had a pill, anyway? This morning? yesterday? but I settled for a drink, another drink, the last one for today because I had a lot to do, packing and sorting, mine and yours, the books and the tapes, the fold-out on which I lay now feet up and growing sicker, bread and cheese long drowned by all the drinks, brackish brown and hot as acid and sodden too my brain to give me pictures, flash pageant of betrayal and oh the things I would say to them, the lies reveal, the truth a hammer to drive one from the other and both into the prison of guilt because they should feel guilty, shouldn't they, for what they'd done to me? Shouldn't any sane person feel guilty, feel sorry, feel *bad?*

Tomorrow I would tell them, show them, make them see exactly what they were: tomorrow after I had packed up their crap and detritus, their stupid clothes and shoes and think of all the room left behind, room for my own stuff, my own life in whatever form it would take, formless like the void, voice moving over the waters, sea like blood in my stomach and waking now—had I slept? passed out, what?—to gagging breath, half on and half off the fold-out and much too late for the bathroom so I let it all come out, dark feathery rush like my pain distilled, spit poison and

key click, voices
someone's here
and they were, here too early both of them and Po be-

side, Po and some guy I didn't even know, beefcake blond with an armful of boxes, empty boxes to drop and fill and for a moment they all stared at me, upright cluster and "Jesus God," said Po as if from very far away, "I think he's dying."

Fuck you, I said, wanted to say but only vomit emerged, toxic dribble and lifting my gaze—sweat and stink, staring sideways through my hair and trying to raise myself, awkward on my elbows but instead lost what was left of balance, slid slow off the fold-out into my own puke and "Oh, I can't take this," Po's voice rising, "I'll be in the hall," and then Sophie in tentative approach, close enough, if I could, to grab her ankles, vomit on her shoes: "Jess, what's—oh your hands," alarmed, "Jess what *happened* to your—"

"Sophie," sharp from Lena, "stop it, come *on*." Dark jeans, dark hair tied back but somehow I could not look at her, she and the blond filling boxes, swift and efficient, books and tapes and "Wait a minute," I croaked, crawling upright, "just wait a fucking minute, all right, before you start dividing up the—I said *wait* a minute, motherfucker," up at last and to the blond, one hand on his arm and he was bigger than he looked, much bigger than me but he didn't touch me, only stepped away so my hand fell loose, back to my side like a broken stick and "Don't worry," he said to me. "They're not taking anything of yours."

"Oh yes they are," I said, gaze swimming but still I could not look at her, dark star, black hole eclipse, *I can't, I just can't* so instead my stare to Sophie, as if she were the locus of all my pain; betrayer, sure and worse, successful—

she had done what I had planned, and done it right: she had won, she—"took everything," my mumble, still talking, was I talking? "You want *everything*, that's your *kink*, right? Right?" as Sophie, bags in arms, made for the door, white sleeve protruding like a kidnap victim's from one of the big black sacks, garbage bags, body bags and "Here," shoved past the door presumably to Po, back for another armful and "Don't forget your coffin," I said to her, at her, "your fucking armoire, don't forget . . ."

And then the blond was hoisting boxes, two and four and out the door and "Wait a minute," because I had said nothing, made no speeches, assigned no guilt but my own for being drunk and sick and unprepared, pathetic spectacle and worst of all unready, again, *again* and as she passed me I saw that Sophie was crying, silent sobs to jerk her body, hitching breasts and my own approach, determined sway to plant myself before her, stop without touching and "I just want to know one thing," I said, "one thing, all right, and you can go."

White face, big eyes and sore, swollen as my hands were swollen: garbage bag in her arms half-filled and clutched like a rescued child, hands clenched and— "What's that?" in numb distraction, attention's swerve to the ring on her finger, "what . . ." and looking closer, peering at her hand, left hand and "That's my *ring*," my voice all scourge, "*that's* my *ring*." Braided silver ring, my gift to Lena, Christmas gift, token of love and I reached to take it from her, yank it free of that clenched hand but Lena herself moved to halt me, hands reaching to put me aside, Lena and the blond and "Hey," I said, elbows jerked like a drunk shaking off a bouncer, "hey now, hey—"

And "*Stop it!*" Sophie's shriek, bag dropped like a body and hands pressed to her face, wild as if set upon by thieves, "don't touch me, nobody *touch* me!" her face turned and twisted, tears and tears and *go on and cry you quisling bitch, you'd cry at my funeral wouldn't you, you'd cry at my fucking grave*—and "What do you think you're doing?" my own voice risen, black croak and the ring somehow enormous on her finger, I could not take my gaze away. "You guys are lovers now, you're married, is that it? So what does that make you, Sophie, what are you supposed to be?"

"I'm not 'supposed' to be anything!" Screaming now, face blotched and slick and "You can't tell me what I *am*," as the blond, stoic, stood waiting, Lena gone from beside him, gone from my field of view and "You don't *know* what I am, you never—"

"Of course I don't know," my voice climbing to hers, "how the hell can I *know* when you—" and "Somebody's calling the cops," from Po, head around the door and ever helpful, "they're probably already on the—"

"How can I *know* when all you do is lie? Day after day, week after week it was lies, all your—"

"*You* lied too," and her mouth twisting then, fierce edge not wholly hers but Lena's, Lena's stare overlaid and strange, oh terrible and strange on Sophie's face as if somehow I spoke to both at once, twin selves, one flesh and right in her face now, close enough to kiss and what a cruelty that would be, wet wormwood lips to squirm against hers, rising voice to drown her cries—but "Leave her alone," from Lena, protector's arm to pull Sophie away, toward the door with the bags resumed, the blond standing shotgun and at least she was honest, Lena, honest in her open haste, fleeing the scene of the crime as "Go on," hot nausea in my throat, my curling guts, "go *on*" as if all I wanted of life was their retreat, down and down, huff and puff in caravan and turning slow as they departed, slow tremble in my arms, my painful hands and inside the rooms denuded, swept clean, remarkable how thorough they had been: tape player, silver lamp, tchotchkes and all bundled swift and gone, the armoire doors hung open, empty inside of clothes and shoes, Sophie's hats, they even took the pillows off the bed

our bed

and I wanted to cry, to scream, rip the doors off the armoire, hurl the bed into the street: wanted to run after them, follow them, find out where they were going, *go on*—but trudged instead into the other room, rinsed my mouth then swabbed the vomit from the floor, hands and knees and the ringing phone, two rings, three and the machine picked it up, Sophie sunny and brisk from long ago, old message to say *Hey, we're never home* and my reaching hand, my own voice raw, anything to shut hers up: "*Hello.*"

"Jess?" some guy surprised, "that you?" and after the first dull rage—who's this, some other helpful mover? someone else I never knew?—a muddled back-and-forth at last to recognize Ed, late of *EdVentures*, Ed who was having some kind of a party and wanted to know if we would like to come and "All right," head down like a bull, red eyes and stinking hands: *good thing he can't see me.* "I'll be there."

"What about the Sisters Grimm?"

Silence my answer, silence so long that he had to know but maybe he knew already, maybe everybody knew: bad news travels fast and especially gossip like this, vulture's grin, *have you heard?* The triumvirate dissolved, oh my and "Just bring some booze," said Ed and so I did: slim bottle of iced vodka tucked beneath my arm, Sunday night voyage past another day's desert, the empty rooms with discards scattered, stuff here and there and fighting the urge to fashion either holocaust or shrine instead had forced myself to pick it all up, gather the leavings: discarded scarf and dance-music tape, the little china cups, the earrings—Sophie's earrings, Sophie's gift green and gold abandoned on the dresser because she had the ring instead now, didn't she, Lena's ring, *my* ring—and I took those earrings, shaken like dice in my hand, carried to drop, one two down the bathroom drain: narrowed elegance, little mouth an O of feigned dismay but once consigned to their destiny the earrings refused to fall forever, stuck instead like a bone in a throat, plugged the drain almost entirely and "*Shit,*" full-tap gush of water, crouching to my hands and knees, "shit shit *shit*" as I pounded the pipe but it was no use, faint shower of rust and the feeling that if I struck the ancient iron again it might crack, fall off into my lap like some strange enfossiled organ: so crouched then with flashlight and tweezers, blunt-nosed tweezers to trap the slippery gold and all of this would be pretty funny, I thought, if it were happening to someone else: someone else's earrings, someone else's life—but once retrieved they went into the box, wrapped in toilet paper and dropped onto the dance tape, the paperback *Vidiot's Guide*, the last of the last of the junk and when the movers came—Mutt and Jeff on a Saturday, time and a half but it didn't take them long, just the fold-out, the armoire, the dresser and a couple of chairs as "You need me to sign anything?" trying not to follow them from room to room, not to ask where they were going with all this stuff: *the address, just give me the address.* "You need me to—"

"Nah," from the shorter one, black beard and black T-shirt, "'s okay," although of course it wasn't and when they were gone I realized I hadn't given them the box, last evidence but so what, I thought, I'll just throw it away, toss it in the Dumpster with the rest of the garbage—but instead shoved it into the closet, bedroom closet so empty now, I never realized how much space they filled, how much of all of this was *theirs:* how much still was, how little left of me.

Because if this life lived had been theirs more than mine, if I was a satellite then imagine me now, cut off from gravity and orbit and left to drift through the dark, pure vacuum but *no,* I said to myself, *no stop it* because if I started to think that way, if I let that drift come real then what was there to make me move at all, to make of me more than the sum of my pain, make me walk down this street with my vodka bottle cold beneath my arm, to find Ed's new address as sleazy as the old: one step up from a welfare hotel, fifth-floor climb into screech and clatter, people on the landing dropping beer cans down the stairs, some girl in a red sweater spray-painting circles on the wall and if I had, even subconsciously, worried (or wanted) their presence, my two exes, it was worry and want in vain because "They're not here," from Ed almost as soon as I crossed the threshold; sick-yellow shirt, cabana shades, he looked like he'd lost some weight. "They said they couldn't come."

Don't ask, as I searched for ice and glasses, ancient gnome of a refrigerator plugged with bottles of wine: but traitor from my mouth, "Really?" as Ed nodded past my elbow, cloudy plastic cups in the countertop scatter. "Why not?"

"Busy, she said. Still settling in."

"She who?" Oh don't do this, please don't do this, don't be what you've always mocked: relationship ghost, divorce bore but "It was Sophie," he said, pouring vodka for us both. "I didn't talk to Her Highness."

My silence, no possible response and then his squint, raised brows and "So what's your version?" as people shoved past us, two guys in matching Bongo T-shirts and a woman in a pinstripe suit. "All I got was theirs."

"Then you're one up on me." The vodka cold and tasteless as some rare and frozen gas, colder lips against the cup and "It's the usual spiel," said Ed, drink already drained. "Insensitive man, boo-hoo, and the women are the heroes. You heard that shit before, so there's nothing else you need to know, right?" but of course there was plenty I needed, plenty I wanted to know but it wasn't going to come from him so I shrugged and drank my drink, left the kitchen to loiter by the door, voyeur's reflex, black spasm of—*say it*—kink: like the twitch of a corpse's toe, dead frog jerked Frankenstein, my sad self unable to recreate alone what had no life, no art without them but to deny the hunger is to deny the self and if the next step was the step into negation I would rather be alive: *between grief and nothing I will choose grief,* who said that? Faulkner, right? who also said *Only vegetables are happy* so expect no happiness: instead here the weapons, the setting, the dance and do what you can, little man, crippled man, take a look, look and see because that's what you're best at, isn't it? Voyeur: *see this,* watch: like frieze and puppetry, room-ful of people talking, arguing, dancing to the music as it mutated from air-wreck rhythm to carbonated pop and back again, background TV looping through synced bands of static and "You want to dance?" from somewhere behind me, some guy in black jeans and a knockoff Aster jacket, eyes long and Lena-dark and "No," I said, "no, thanks," as he shrugged, as someone else approached, dead-faced blonde who looked familiar, someone I almost knew and "Hi," she said, slow nasal voice and it was the cowboy artist, what was her name? Edie, right, in a pink Dale Evans dress, galaxy of little pins scattered bright from neck to hem: ten-gallon hat, a bucking bronc, rhine-stone cacti and "Hi," again as if I had not heard, one hand out but not touching, wavering in the air and "Listen," said Edie then something else, gulped sentence and "I can't hear you," I said, impatient: with her, with her pallid mumble, with the fact of my presence here, what did I think I was doing anyway? Drowning my sorrows? Col-lecting clues? but "Come on," and she tugged my arm, clasp so cold I felt it through my clothing and into a little room off the main one, maybe a bedroom although there was no bed or anything like one, just bookcases jammed mostly with knickknacks, wind-up skulls and chattering teeth, a papier-mâché head missing nose and eyes and "I wanted to talk to you," Edie said, arms crossed to hug her elbows, doorway stance like a guard inured to escape. "I heard what happened, with, with Lena? And I wanted to talk to you."

No answer from me: *I heard what happened.* I bet you did and in that posture, that face—her tilted head, those sad, sad eyes—came like an odor the feeling of stasis, as if part of her was still standing in that long-ago gallery, frozen in hungry gaze and from that frozen moment she said nothing, looked at and past me until "It was the same with me," she said, "just the same old thing. I think I fell in love with her the second we met," and *oh no*, I thought, *don't let her tell me, I don't want to hear this at all* but her silence assumed my understanding, comparison unnecessary before the larger fact of pain presumed and "All the time we were together," hands on her elbows, head to one side, "I never thought I was *enough*. No matter what I did, everything, you know?"

My empty shrug no answer but the only one I gave: *why are you telling me this?* and "Who knows what she wants?" said sad Edie, stupid cowboy dress two sizes too big, hands busy at the skirt the way a dying man plucks the coverlet, nervous little fingers on the cusp of the dark. "I did the best I could, I gave her everything she asked for. But in the end she didn't want it. Which wasn't her fault, I guess." Eyes tear-bright, tears after all this time, heartbreaking that self-delusion but was it all delusion? didn't I feel that way too?—but without the tears, no more tears, if I started crying again I might never stop so "I know what you mean," my voice distant, body held as if in some other room, other place—and then all at once her sharp advance, stumble or lunge and those hands on me, squeezing my forearms, hideous with cold and "You talk to me," said Edie, doll's gaze locked to my own and up close so riven, driven, like an old machine unwanted left to run itself to bits: *I gave her everything she asked for: lovers*, I thought, *just like us, just like me* and who knows how many others, how big a club this really was? *I think I fell in love with her the second we met*, and why not? Didn't everyone?

And those cold hands gripping, raptor's clutch on my arms and "You need someone to talk to," Edie's voice lower now, almost gruff, "you talk to me, okay? Okay?"

Stretched pause and in the background still the party, people yelling, chanting to some stupid VoiceBox song and we might stand this way forever, she and I, sculpture as bare as her twists of split wire and "Okay," I said, wanting only for her to stop, to take those hands away. "We'll talk, okay."

And her smile then, strange flicker of content as if to talk to me about Lena was the next best thing to Lena herself: and at once I left the little bedroom, left her there to merge back into the others, VoiceBox turned into badly warped Sinatra and because the vodka was gone I left too, long walk home to march hands in pockets, block by block, step by step to our—to my—building and methodical up the stairs, into a silence emptied now of expectation, a silence bleached and stretched like empty bones in empty rooms and "Fuck it," I said aloud, said to hear something, anything at all beyond the sound of my own passage, my own breathing in that silence and the dark, "fuck it," like an answer as I crawled into my bed.

So: the crippled life not regenerated but resumed, the peculiar balance of the double amputee but adaptation is a blessing when it isn't a curse and anyway what else did I have to do? If I wasn't going to die I had to work, to pay the bills, attempt at least to afford my cozy mausoleum and so I pressed for all the hours I could get, ten-, twelve-, fifteen-hour days and Saturdays too which helped to fill the gap: time and money, money and time and I bought food and ate it, bought a newspaper and sometimes read it, read books too (all the old favorites—Cady Sopowicz, Richard Rysman, Thomas Pynchon—as if to prove by even wan enjoyment that some things still were left un-touched) and watched TV, lights off and windows propped open to the sweeping warmth of spring gone into summer, a beautiful summer that might have been a scrim, dead backdrop for all the pleasure it gave to me.

Few pleasures at all, now, beyond the brute gift of sleep, waking to my monk's circumscription, bedroom to street to cubicle and circling back again, living the out-come of my choice—for I had definitely had one, named or not; even I knew that. One road led to purest nothing, grief's tumor having devoured all flesh and blood and bone and at last in its great hunger itself as well would leave me in that white dissolution the ability, again, to breathe: but that too was illusion, breath become crust thin and bitter over the fury of the wound, the open heart beating and beating, unable to heal or die: and in choos-ing the other road, choosing to feel it all I had chosen I knew the better part, the pain of purpose, the purpose of pain: *Pain is the wage God pays to the devil*, who said that? Cady Sopowicz? Lena, in one of her metaphysical moods? or was it me, soliloquy in my solo dance of kink, most of what I did a lie but at least I was lying to myself this time, a kindly and manageable deceit to be dropped or reassumed when necessary: eat because you need to, wash because you stink, read the paper because the larger world continues to turn and never mind whether any of it means anything, why should it mean anything now? The only real thing, true thing is that pain inside, distilled to purest essence, pain to grant the energy to rebuild the house of kink.

Because it mattered even more now, to watch, to see, to be: to learn not what was or even what might have been but what *is*, what exists: finger the ropes and the scaffolding, peer at the dance, at the way people smiled or did not, touched each other, fled each other, made each other cry, each gesture and word component, brick on brick in the wall of the world and all the world to me was vision, the need to make of what had happened not sense but a pattern, a template to drape upon the face of the darkness, kink's mask to show me still the difference between myself and that larger world.

And if they could hurt me, Lena and Sophie, strike me each day with the fact of their absence, of the death of what the three of us had been still what they could not do, what no one could do was *reduce* me, subtract me, send me howling back to the arms of the great unknowing, the blank eyes whose gaze asks every pain but consciousness:

stripped of love but not anger because I could *still see*, still watch, still force that black bargain with humor and rage and no one—not Sophie, not Lena, not even myself—was going to take that from me now.

Because that would be dying: and I was not going to die.

I expected no contact, no more visits, no more calls, all unfinished business likely to stay so unless I ran them to ground—which would have been easy enough to do, I knew where they both worked, I could have searched them out but no, not now or ever so instead in my daily rounds, to and fro upon the earth I talked to other people: like neighbor Jim in a weekday stairwell, bland almost-smile almost smug at my wrenched and solitary state but his own wound had hurt too much, I saw, understood with my new and specialized vision, for him to really wish that pain on someone else, anyone else, even me: although in that smile at least a grain of satisfaction, he could not have been human without the faintest urge to gloat.

Calm and casual, pausing on the stairs to pass a little chitchat, preliminary bout and at last: "So, that night," gazing pointedly past me. "What happened?"

I knew what he wanted, what I wanted from him: but let him be the one. "Happened with what?"

"With, you know." One darting look, peep show, *get to the good stuff*. "Sophie. And Lena."

"They moved out."

"I know that, but what happened? One day they were here, and the next day they—"

"We had an argument," I said. "I lost."

Judicial sigh, that measured nod and "So you're going to stay?" nodding back at my door. "You're not going to try to find another place?"

"Why would I want to do that?" although it was a question heard before and often, everyone who knew seemed to think I should move; why should I? where else could I go? "No, I'm staying here."

His nod again, as if at some evidence confirmed and then "It's funny, I just ran into them. Last night at Perdita's, you know Perdita's? They were on their way to an opening," and what was I supposed to say to that? How nice? Fuck you? "You know she was staying with me," Jim said, "for awhile. You knew that, right?"

"No," as calm and conversational. "No, I didn't."

"Well, she was. For a few weeks, almost a month on and off, but she always went back to her flat, that crummy little place she had on—"

"I know that place," I said. "We . . . I went there, I helped her move. They were raising her rent—"

His smile, not even the insult of pity overt, just that smile and "Raising her rent," one arm light on the banister, "that's not what she told me. She said she just had to move, get out of there and be somewhere else. Because, you know, of Saul."

Who's Saul? and that rag of memory, Edie in a gallery, *does Saul know?* but I wouldn't ask, not him, not now and "—had to escape, she said, just *go.* And I told her she could stay with me, for as long as she wanted. But then she met Sophie. And you." His shrug. "Things change."

Things change, right; and *I'm sorry,* I could have said but I wasn't and I knew it and he knew it too or would have if I had said a word so I didn't, shrugged in echo, told him I would see him around and kept going, down to the street and who the hell is Saul? Thinking of that flat, so sterile and empty and *You know she was staying with me*: no, Jim, I didn't: did Sophie? Was that another of the secrets kept without sharing, secret heft like weapons to use when the time was right? Was real knowledge contained only in what I did not know?

Down the street, automatic stride as if I had somewhere to go and think back, I told myself, remember and see: that dinner, first definition of kink and: *Jim, right,* Lena's unsmiling shrug, *you know he wants me to move in with him* and oh the crush of my own black envy, lead-heavy, furnace-bright the image of her living there, fucking him, out of reach forever and *Don't do it,* remember? Remember Sophie's squeal of little-girl pleasure, Lena's slow considering smile: how well we engineer our own disposals.

Raising her rent, that's not what she told me.

Who is Saul?

"Edie?"

Her number obtained of course from Ed, my call to his pause bemused: *what the hell?* but no questions asked and "Edie?" when I finally made connection, two days' tries to no avail, no answering machine, who lives without an answering machine? Over the hum and racket, some kind of background groan or growl: "Yes?" in that same parched scramble, down-home vowels strained through chipping bone. "Who's this?"

"It's Jess," loud enough I hoped to cut the noise. "I want to talk to you. You said if I wanted—we were at Ed's party, remember, and you—"

"Oh sure," with great eagerness, "sure we can talk. Do you want to come over now?" and her directions almost completely useless but with an address I can pretty much find anything and I found her too, cruddy walk-up even worse inside: white paint caked thick over walls and floors, dirt and crap and detritus and in its middle Edie in green coveralls, strange mechanic with one of her weird wire sculptures flayed to meltdown on the floor, rising from her mantis crouch to greet me like a hostess at a tea: "Well come on in," one hand out, ice cold as always and "You always leave your door open?" closing it behind me, turning the bolt. "I mean that's not exactly safe, is it, anybody could just—"

"Oh, no, it's okay. Nobody ever comes here," which on consideration was probably true: the whole space almost intruder-repellent, so obviously a lair, cave specific to one species, one strange creature on its own: patchwork mess on every surface, soldering gun plugged crooked on the stove, hammock bed hung low and piled with clothes and shoes and cowboy hats, cowboy crap on all the walls and everywhere the sculptures, wire bent and wound and twisted, figures stretched like shadows impossible and long and "I was just working," she said, pushing aside some cardboard jumble to reach the little cube refrigerator, "I have kind of a show coming up . . . would you like a beer? or I could open a bottle of wine if you'd rather have wine—"

"No, that's okay. Beer's fine."

"It's no trouble," anxious, lifted corkscrew like one of her sculptures, that sad and pale stare and "Lena," I said, magic word to distract her, "I wanted to talk about Lena. Okay?"

"Oh, sure," on an exhalation, two beers retrieved and we sat on the floor because there was nowhere else to sit, more cardboard squared in piles and "I'm really glad you came," with a smile; almost a smile. "It's *good* to talk about it, you know? Because if you don't then—"

"Edie," I said, "how long have you known Lena?"

"Oh, a long time. Years and years, almost."

Almost. "Well apparently there's this guy, this—Saul, do you know who Saul is? Because someone told me—" and my own silence abrupt to see that white face slapped with color, mulberry flush and "*Saul*," with wide eyes wider, "what's Saul got to do with you?"

Take it easy, I told myself. "I don't know, I mean I don't know anything about him. Is he—was he friends with Lena, too? Was he—"

"Friends," the color fading. "We were friends, yeah. . . . She never said anything about him to you?"

"No," dry, almost grim and now see another of the rooms, the annexes disclosed, I had thought myself deep at the heart but there was so much still of Lena that I would never, ever see—and strangely my thought first of Sophie, Sophie did you know? but "No," I said, "she never did. She didn't talk about her past too much, family, stuff like that," which was odd and oddly true: we had said plenty, Sophie and I, all there was to tell, but in the end she never told us anything.

"Well, I don't know about her folks," said Edie, "I

mean I guess she had them, everybody does, but Saul—I knew Saul, we both knew him. We met him at a gallery, and he—see, he was fucking her," that earnest gaze on mine, busy fingers on the beer bottle, the label: pick, pick, pick. With her chewed-up nails. "He was living with her too, kind of, he used to come to her place, you know that place she had? and then stay for a day or two days, a week and then he would go, just pick up his stuff but not all of his stuff, I used to see his shirts there, and papers . . . and his cologne, once I used his cologne and he got *furious*, two drops and he just hit the—"

"Someone told me," my own voice a bell in my head, iron bell, "that she moved out of her place because of him, because they broke up or something. Is that true?"

"I don't know," said Edie, and drank, two swallows, three like elixir and "Would you like," she said, "another one?" Unfolding herself to rise, a strange and skeletal grace and remembering with a kind of vertigo that dismal flat, rooms stripped and dead as a carapace discarded and *What took you so long?* Lena had said to me—but how long had she really waited? and for what?

Back with the beer, uncomfortable repose and Saul, Edie said, was a buyer, an art dealer, something like that: "He used to run the Concrete, do you know that space? Anyway that's where we met him. And they started going out, kind of, he started showing her things, art, you know," and introducing her to his friends, friends who were artists like Edie but whose presence, whose parties, whose galleries were not open to Edie as they were to Lena, Lena welcome everywhere, Lena on Saul's arm but strung between fact and conjecture the slant of Edie's memories, past pageant of loss-to-be still little help to me, no help in fact at all unless I steered her, guided my own course, questions like keys tried one by one in a door and "Were they," careful gaze down at my beer, "you know, seeing each other, when you two were together? Was she—"

"Was she sleeping with us both, you mean? Oh, sure," the long throat working, medicinal swallow, *this hurts me more than it does you.* "Absolutely, no question."

"How do you know?"

"She told me."

My silence, then: "She told you? How?"

Coat-hanger shoulders, up and down and "She just, you know, *told* me. One night she came home and said I had to clear out for the night and when I said why she said Saul's coming over, he's spending the night and we can all meet for breakfast in the morning. It was kind of," her stare and almost smile, soft looping gesture as if to rope me in, "like you guys, right? Like a three-way."

Silence again, the pause between leap and impact, the instant of the fall and in my chest a cold dismay, fist to squeeze from me air, thought, everything but her words: *like a three-way,* like us but how could that be? when we were different, completely different from anything Lena might have done, shared, been or become with anyone anywhere else, we had built our world like art together, we were *us* . . . but Edie still shrugging, still talking, still telling her story which was Lena's story and Saul's, Saul who was older than them both, late forties maybe, "maybe even fifty," said Edie, "but he had money so you couldn't really tell . . . that kind of sleek look, you know? And he's so *smart*, Saul, he really is and you know how much Lena likes that, she *respects* smartness, you know? I guess that's why she got rid of me."

Picking, picking at the bottle, shred shiny curls stuck wet to the tips of her fingers like skin in reverse and "Hey," I said, "come on, don't say that," as strange the twist of anger, alien and pure and *Oh she's suffering all right*, Lena's comment flip at the gallery, remember? and Edie's stray's gaze across the room? but still talking, wistful tears in those wide eyes and "When she broke up with Saul," said Edie, "I thought she might . . . you know, come back. Or at least let me—but she didn't."

"She broke up with Saul?"

"That's what they said."

"Who said?"

"I don't know," the shrug opaque, glass stare into a past remembered acutely but not well, how to tell? "People. The people we knew."

"Like who?"

"Oh, Eddie—you know Eddie, right, you were at his party—and Annemarie and her husband, they were doing some kind of video or something, a film—"

"About Saul?"

"No," and the sudden smile of real amusement, as if I had made a joke on purpose. "About *art*, you know, about the gallery scene. They had a private showing of it, a premiere, like? oh and Lena wore a tux, a real tux that she rented, she looked *so* gorgeous—"

"Why did she break up with him?" and like an echo the question, was someone asking that right now, Lena and Sophie and some earnest third party, *why'd you break up with Jess?* and what would they say? If I asked them myself what would they say? "I mean," grim, empty bottle gone warm in my hand, "if he was so smart, and rich, why would anybody want to—"

"Oh, I don't know," her own mournful smile, "maybe she was just done with him, you know? And people said they fought a lot too so maybe that was it—I don't know," again and all at once she was crying, long clear tears through which her smile continued, hands still picking at the label on the bottle and "Don't," I said because it was not something I could watch, because it could have been me there, old wounds probed to blood by some near stranger and "Don't," again as I knelt to rise, one hand out to pull her standing, pull her upright and "Let's go out," I said, to say something, "let's eat. You eat anything today?"

She had to think about it, wet face blank so "Let's go," insistent till we went, or rather I led and she followed, clumping docile in her coveralls even though it was at least eighty degrees outside, shuffling down the sidewalk and we ate corned beef at some diner, K&J's with its door brick-propped open, counter dulled by scratches and old grease but "This is good," I said, mouth full; and it was. "You come here a lot?"

"No," she said. "I've never had corned beef before."

Strange cargo, Edie, Edie my friend and my role begun as, what? interrogator? good cop to the bad cop of memory, the world, Lena's face like a hidden picture in every picture she ever saw? but there turned out to be more than that, more anyway for me and for Edie, well, who

211

knew? Every third time I looked at her I was convinced she was crazy and glad to be, but the more we met—loose schedule, maybe twice a week, maybe twice in a day when I was feeling particularly low—the more I seemed to need it, to sit across from that hunched construction, pale and twitching face and watch those cold fingers strip crusts from bread, label from bottle and listen to her talk: about Lena, about their time together; about Lena and Saul; about Lena in love, Edie the prophet from a place I had never seen—hours, days of Lena's past, offering to me those sights, glimpses, facets I never knew, what Lena herself had never offered.

Yet *You're using her* said self to self, my rare shame in our times apart, husk hunkered by the dead TV in my museum of silence and loss, but was it necessary, that shame, or only reflex? for wasn't she using me too? Dovetailed obsessions a cozy box while still aware, in some sane but tiny spot in my own black brain, that this was not the road to sunlight and a cure, the fabled post-tragic new life but oh what difference could that make when it felt so *good* to scratch the sore, press pus like a creamy stream and the need to know, to *see* become its own wound that found its twin in hers, both needs the same: to talk about Lena, about what had happened to us, about how we missed her, wanted her, wanted her back: only Edie understood why I would not move from the apartment, last place shared, why I had to work and work to stay there; only Edie knew why my rage was for Sophie (as hers was for Saul) and not for our object of desire, for although whatever had happened between the three of them was nothing like us, still she needed him for ballast, for a place to weep and point while I had Sophie on whom to hang the blame, while portioning to Lena, faithless and perfect, some smaller share as well: thrall has its own judgments, its own exclusions and beliefs and "You know she's not like other people," Edie would say, head to one side as if freighted by memory. "She just doesn't *think* like other people."

Circling spoon, iced coffee cloudy and strong and "How does she think?" I said. "Tell me."

"She thinks by herself." Coffee-shop chatter of a weekend crowd, Edie's cheese sandwich dissected on the plate. "I used to ask her, what's the most important thing in the world? And you know what she said?"

"No. What did she say?"

"The *world*," fingers in conjurer's spread, handful of bones. "She said the world's the most important thing in the world. Isn't that *smart?* And she's right too."

"Like kink," I said, eyes closed in a moment's painful ravishment: Bella Luna, etched crescents on the cups, the pale shine of the wine and *You see the world through each other, you use each other to change the world, make the world* and "Kink," I said again, open eyes like coming to, the coffee shop, Edie's bleached and puzzled gaze. "She said it was her theory of life," as again that inner voice, her voice: *Nobody ever understands what the hell I'm talking about* and for just that instant, that wrenching beat I wanted to cry, just put my head down on the table and cry till tears were gone because I *did* know what she was talking about, knew better than anyone ever had: Sophie, Edie, a cast of thousands, even the mythic and unseen Saul, fuck them all because *I* was the one, the only one who knew or ever had

213

but what rights did that give me, what good had it done me, what place had it carried me to after all? Here: and nowhere: the palace of kink where all the rooms are empty and the walls all glass to show what might have been and "Come on," I said, pushing up from the table, unable to sit there a second longer. "Come on, let's go."

And quiet to rise, to follow me in a display of yet another of her virtues: that great simplicity allowing her to question nothing I did—my sudden urges to move or stop, leave or stay, talk or be silent and it was all the same to her, differing symptoms but still manifest of that disease she shared so well and we walked then, my stride slowed to accommodate, her eyes squeezed almost shut against the light and "You know, it doesn't get better," she said, "it doesn't even start to go away," which should not have cheered me but did because it was what I wanted to hear then, some confirmation, some assessment real as bone of all this pain: not *you'll get over it* or *things will work out* but the brute imprimatur, proof that I was not mistaken: *this is all just as bad as you think it is.*

And her touch on my arm, brief squeeze and turning off at the next corner, walking home alone and my own gait rising, quick step back and into silence, a week's worth of as much work as possible and struggling home one evening to find a message on my machine, voice unknown at first but "We're going to be in town for a couple days, why don't we get together so you can buy us dinner? joke, joke," from my brother the comedian, my brother unchanged when we met at some black-and-gold tourist place, Mexican-Thai cuisine and "Hey," the handshake, dry blue-eyed glance and then away and his wife—Sandy?

Sally? Sally—giving me a hug, her breasts warm against me, asexual and sisterly and soft.

"So what're you drinking?" my brother said. "We ordered wine."

Music in the background, temple bells and mariachi, Sally's smile red and white and they talked about their vacation, about our parents, about their jobs and their plans and it all ran past like water, tepid water down the drain but it was better than sitting home alone, better than a sharp stick in the eye, stake in the heart except it really wasn't, was instead just another reminder that there were chasms and chasms, gulfs and deeps and wherever I might be my brother and his wife along with most of the rest of the world were sure to be on the other side, busy and industrious, untroubled by too much thought—although he was not stupid, my brother or Sally either, they were both very smart, very sharp but very dull, blinkered walk through the maelstrom as if the unseen was dismissed without risk but even while I envied their oblivion still it was no place I could covet or share: *I will choose grief* even if it chooses me first so drink and think and wait a decent interval, think of how they would have enjoyed a dinner like this, Lena and Sophie, cat and mouse but only the tips of the claws because these two before me were relatives after all, *any brother of yours* and I almost smiled to consider their pleasure but how find pleasure in this without them? and the cycle sprung back to vampire life, question to question ouroboros: how could anything good be good to me now? How can they live without me when I can't live without them? How did this *happen?* and the answer unchanged and unchangeable, the only way out was farther in, just keep going, live through it until it was time to—

"—about you?" from Sally, glass raised for the last of the wine. "And your girlfriend, what's new with you two?"

"Well," I said, trying not to sound sad, or angry, trying not to sound like anything at all, "actually I don't have a girlfriend. I used to have two but now I don't have any." Silence. "Supply and demand, you know?" my joke unsuccessful as the silence stretched, their glance for one another and "Oh," at last from Sally, her small unhappy smile. "I'm sorry, I didn't mean to bring up anything unpleasant."

Excuse me for seeing your bleeding stump but that was unfair as well as unkind, how was she to know? and "No harm done," I said and meant it, meant only to forget it, let it all go but Sally then off to the ladies' room—maybe a signal had passed: *I'll go: you talk to him*—and my brother's frown fraternal, gaze gone troubled at the thought of actual talk, the possibility of feelings expressed and "Look," that lowered voice, "you know I don't want to pull rank on you or anything—"

"Then don't," but as usual he wasn't listening to anyone but himself and "I wasn't going to say anything," he said, "but you look like, you know, not so good. What happened, anyway?"

"Nothing," I said, which was quite literally true: *nothing* was happening to me, happening every day but how to explain that to him? and so for the next few minutes it was his version of *Women: the trouble with* braced with a little "pull yourself together," "lots of fish in the sea," and I sat nodding, wondering if he and Sally had agreed as well on a time, *give me five minutes* and toward the end I even smiled, a tiny little smile from a million miles away and "I'm fine," I said to my brother the stranger, "really. I appreciate your concern and everything, but I'm fine."

"Well, listen. It happens to everybody, right?" His pause, but not through yet, not entirely. "Two girlfriends, you said," and looking then straight at me with a kind of hungry puzzlement I recognized at once from a thousand guys, a thousand questions all the same and here it came: "You mean like at the same time?" and I smiled again, a real smile now, *now my hands are empty but oh what they have known* and "Absolutely," I said, from the heart of that smile, "absolutely two at once," because that was what he would understand, my brother, not the passion and grief but the pussy sandwich, not the broken heart but the rising cock and something else there in his eyes, born of my answer, mute glitter deep but gone because here was Sally, Sally back and smiling because it was safe now, because the guys had talked things over and no one else need bring it up again.

And we didn't, kept instead on neutral subjects, kept all subjects neutral until we were shaking hands outside the restaurant, I was waving for a cab and "Take care of yourself," said Sally with another one-armed hug, "don't forget to call," and "Take it easy," said my brother, ducking into the cab and the worm's turn of satisfaction, watching them drive off, memory of that flicker in his eyes, the edge that said *you?*—and the story to Edie at our next day's lunch, my corned beef sandwich, her crumbling saltines and she laughed when I told her, rare sweet bark and "That's *funny*," as if in apology. "That's really funny, Jess."

"They don't get it," I said, "they just don't understand. It's like Lena used to say about kink, about the way we see the world." A pause, half diffident: "You ever talk about all that, with her?"

"What do you mean?" to bring my own clumsy explanation, a theory of living that was living itself, vision and its object, all of it there for the one who sees and "Oh sure," her nodding head, slow motion as if underwater, sealed in liquid glass, "sure, I know what you mean. It's kind of like what we used to say, me and Lena, like how no man is an island? But you *are*, really," dreamy fingers in the crumbs, cracker crumbs stirred and drifting, cold fingertips and salt. "Everyone's all alone because they have to be, right? Because if you aren't, if you get too close you start . . . *rubbing* against each other, rubbing off the skin, *hurting* each other . . . so to protect yourself you have to stay a little bit away from everyone, even the people you love the most, *especially* those people because if you don't you might hurt them, right?" and my own head nodding, dumb-show puppet past the chill of dislocation, as if I had peered past her eyes to see inside no human bones but "Listen," said Edie, "I meant to tell you, there's an opening tomorrow if you feel like going. . . . Jon Bishop? At the Höeg-Hareton?"

"Sure," still nodding; no man is an island, right? "Sure, let's meet," and so we did, planned collision a block away and Edie waving, waving, strangely festive in fringed skirt and pigtails, bright dash of lipstick in that arctic wash of skin; when I got close enough I could smell she had been drinking, red wine and more than a little: "You know, I used to know him," too loud in my ear as we entered, street heat banished in the welcome wash of cool. "He paints dogs."

"Isn't that impractical?" but my little joke lost in the larger crush, elbowing through to the drinks and all the time the usual background crisis, dread and hunger, *will they be here?* my paramours, the animate knives in my back? but no, or at least not glimpsed by me, I could barely see anything through the press of the crowd; what black luck, to see them never, even in places like these . . . and all at once Edie back beside me, cold fingers on mine and "Jess?" with a drink in her other hand. "Annemarie is here, you should talk to her."

Who's Annemarie? but one look brought memory: chic and child-small, that folded dwarf's face first seen at Ed's *EdVentures* party, there with her husband, here alone: "Well, how are you?" because it seemed she remembered me too, motioning me to one side, between the door to the gallery office and a noseless concrete dog splashed thick in clumsy primaries. "Jules and I are just back from San Francisco and we've been rushing around seeing everything, trying to catch up. There's just so much out there, so much assimilation—" and my manufactured frown, simulated interest in her moving mouth when the real prod was that question, one question masking many: *what can you tell me about Lena, what do you know that I don't?* but in the end she saved me the trouble by asking a question herself: "And what about Lena, and that other pretty girl, what was her name? Are they here?"

"Sophie," I said, "her name's Sophie." Wishing I had a drink, something to hold in my hands. "We're not, we don't live together anymore."

Rote murmur, "Mmm, I'm sorry," but then the sudden smile grotesque: "But really, should I be? She's a *handful*, Lena; maybe you're better off?" It was truly a question, she expected an answer so "I don't know," I said; what else could I say? "It's kind of hard to be objective."

"Of course it is." She had strange teeth, this woman, small and sharp as some antique predator's and she showed them again in that strange smile. "But it's something to learn from, isn't it? We did."

We who: she and her half-remembered alligator husband? and learn *what?* but "We put her in peril," said Annemarie, pause at my blank gaze until I reheard her, understood the word instead as a title, *Peril;* some film they made? the film Edie recalled? "It was very unstructured," she said, "nothing at all like the documentaries—really it was Jules's idea, to do it strictly for the experience—and of course Lena had her own ideas, very demanding . . . in some ways she's the most demanding person I've ever known. You know she could have been a professional, there's no doubt about it."

"A professional what?"

"Actor," her glance peculiar. "All her instincts are dead on."

I bet. "So what finally happened with this film? Someone told me there was a premiere, or something?"

"A premiere? It's odd you should say that. There was never really any distribution, we never made a serious attempt—at any rate the film per se no longer exists. We ended up using bits of it elsewhere, in other films. None of the parts with Lena, though. Those we kept." The rim of her glass thick with lipstick, dark Rorschach smear. "We've lost touch, I'll admit, and then of course we were away . . . but that's just history, isn't it, we should concentrate on what's happening today . . . what *is* happening, with you and, who is it—Sophie? What are you and Sophie doing these days?"

"Nothing," I said. "She lives with Lena now."

"Really?" with real interest but no sympathy at all. "Now *that* I wouldn't have predicted, with her it's usually slash and burn, you know, raze the village and move on." Those soft contemptuous eyes, was it contempt? Does everyone hate people who can't see what they see? oh kink, oh irony but she was still talking, talking about Lena and "With us, you know, it was the same way. Close, completely *intimate:* and then nothing. Even with Saul: when it was over it was *over,* no handkerchiefs in the wind, no scenes on the pier—it was something I always admired in her. Not many people know how to cut their losses effectively."

Speaking as one of the losses, fuck you but I didn't say that, shrugged instead past my own inner churn, freshet of questions like what exactly do you mean by *intimate?* but she was still talking, something about *Peril* and "I'd really like to see it," I said. "Is, is Saul in it?"

"Well, yes," and she made a little face I couldn't interpret. "It was certainly a new direction for us, ultimately unsatisfying but still—do you know Saul? No? You really ought to meet him."

"I'd like that. Is he in town?"

"He should be . . . actually I'm not sure, but you know

we're just back in ourselves—Lissa," head turned as her voice rose half an octave, one arm up as if she was trying to flag a cab and then to me, "Lissa will know."

But "I'm not really sure," said Lissa, six feet of ascetic pink and black, "he might be in Sacramento. He has a place there," dismissively to me, as if I should have known better than to ask and then she and Annemarie began talking, exclusive argot to send me edging away but before I had gone completely that gargoyle touch on my elbow, cool and brief and "We'll talk again," said Annemarie.

"Tell Jules I said hello," and one last glance for the room, nodding to Edie who hurried to follow me out, quick and unsteady to match my stride and she was drunk, I saw, and frankly hanging onto me, one leg hooked thigh-high over mine in the cab because she couldn't walk, not really, not the way she was: eyes at half-mast, damp clutch around my neck and if I turned my head just an inch to the left I could see straight down her blouse, ugly cactus-patterned blouse, little white tits with nipples tiny as a girl's but me so prim and placid, flaccid because this was not that nor ever could be: no funny stuff, no groaning into each other's open mouths; even though I had seen no one's tits, had no sex since my last time with Lena, how long ago was that? and here, now, with her it would be easy, I wouldn't have to say please, wouldn't even have to ask, just touch, take—but don't start, don't calculate, just drag limp spurless Edie where she needs to be, home and on the sofa, her groping, fluttering hands and "Lock the door," stern to her slack face and she was really drunk this time, drunker than I'd ever seen her and

222

why tonight when we could have talked things over, this notion of Lena working with Annemarie, with Jules her husband making films (*intimate: like a three-way?*—oh Christ, oh no) and oh, poor Edie as "Lock the door," I said again, "you hear me? Edie? I want to hear it lock," which after long moments I finally did, *click* and *thunk* and then off home in my own darkness, dark and hot in that desert summer to lie naked on the bed, airless smell of dank flesh and my cock half-risen in desire *for* desire: not for Edie, fleeting image of those little Milk-Dud breasts, numb guess at how they might feel in my hands but *be honest, tell the truth* because the truth was that no one, no woman attracted me now, all of them hung on the poles of twin yet differing needs: for Lena's wide thin lips, dark hair wound around my fingers, the strength in her long thighs—and yes, for the ghost of Sophie too, Sophie's little-girl face, pale pout and who out there could match what they had offered, who in this world could ever give me that?

There were women I might have, could have dated, taken out, taken in and fucked but before the process could begin always the *why*, first and last question to quell all impulse—like the woman at, where was it? the bank? the accounting firm? Two weeks ago yet no memory of more than her face, pretty face, very pretty and she came on very strong, *hi this is my department, why don't we get some coffee* and over coffee her questions, how long had I been temping, did I like it? and would I like to join her for dinner at this Italian place she knew? "The food's terrific," she said, "real Sicilian cooking," and I blew on my coffee, head down to look up and "No, thanks," I said, the lie as natural as the smile was not. "I mean, it sounds good, but the thing is I'm seeing someone now."

"Oh," her own smile as pleasant in answer and the next day she asked again: never mind dinner, how about drinks and *how about we fuck in the employees' lounge?* but I didn't say that, didn't say anything because I had nothing but *no* to say: imagining a tryst somewhere, expensive blouse unbuttoned, my cold and hungerless hands: *why?* and something in my face then, some frown to make her voice level and soft, no question at all: "You're not really seeing anyone, Jess, are you?"

"No," I said, *no I lied to you, I'm really married or maybe I'm divorced, I'm gay, I'm a gay divorcé, I'm an excommunicated priest but I can't have sex with you or anyone so how about we just forget it, all right?* "No," wondering why bad must inevitably lead to worse, "but I'm—see, I just went through a very bad experience and I really, I can't—"

One hand brief and gentle on my arm and "Oh, well, that's different," smiling kindly, the smile one gives a menial, a defective. "But you know you shouldn't be too upset, that kind of impotence is almost always temporary," and my wild urge to laugh, donkey's bray as she turned away but what if—the pouncing thought come later, lead in the spine on the long way home—what if she was right? What if this nullity, this hole where the heat had been, was (or would become) somehow permanent? What if I had given over with my love the gift of real desire? but how want anyone who wasn't them? As if, grown ill and thin, still only one food can bring then satisfy the hunger and nothing else will do, starvation or not, death or the maiden and my gaze to seek inevitable as magnetism only the women who resembled them, dark and light in paradigm, in the places we used to go, places they presumably might visit still and for every time I thought I saw them—although I never hunted, never sought (and proud of it too, in my own dreary way)—still I might have seen them once, maybe twice, heads together or maybe not, maybe it was only a trick of vision, double vision, doubled loss and again I thought of Edie, poor drunk Edie who understood as no one else did the pure hunger of obsession, the *kink* of it: Edie in her cowboy clothes, Edie's leg hooked hot around my own, so thin and pale if bare, bare as milk like her little tits but irresistible then—again; forever?—the overriding thought of Lena, here in this very bed and oh what we had done here, washed by a loving greed so great that even now it took my breath away, made me hard, made me want to cry but instead my hand in motion, deliberate to work as it worked my cock the memory, the *lust* and Sophie too, remember? Sophie's open mouth, warm planes of her thighs, head back to give the strong line of her throat—and remember, now, don't turn away, don't hide, don't *hide*—the three of us together, in thrall, entangled, *you mean like at the same time* and as I came a cry, tears in my eyes and "*Fuck!*" to roll and tear at the pillow, the pale pattern of the sheets ripped, stripped free in the strangling urge, the cry internal to *let it go* but go into what? go *where?*

Silence: the echo of my breath; someone moving in the rooms upstairs and when I slept at last it was to the sounds of that motion, old voyeur's dead attention to a dance already done.

"Hey, Jess? you know what?" Edie my good angel, Edie on my answering machine. "I talked to Eddie about that movie, the one with Saul?" and it turned out Ed knew a guy who knew a guy who had a bootleg print that he might be willing to let me see, possibly, maybe and "Go see Eddie," she said and so I did, up those grimy stairs again, new spray paint to cover the old, some bold pronouncements in a language I could not read and Ed shuffling from the door like an old man in a bathrobe, sweatpants bunched in one hand and "Excuse me a second," shuffling back into the bathroom, gurgle and rush and "I think I got botulism," opening beers for us both. "Doesn't that make you go blind or something?"

"No." Cheap beer, but cold. "That's beating off."

"No, that gives you cancer." Oversize T-shirt, sparkle of sweat and his apartment not hot but not cool either, a kind of damp dull warmth, like the inside of a humidifier. "Anyway Edie called me, she said you want to see that dumb movie. Karl used to have a copy of it, Karl Dresner, you know him? No? I could give him a call."

"Thanks."

"I didn't say I would, I said I could. What do you want to see that piece of shit for anyway? You want another beer? Jeez, you drink slow."

"I have to go to work tomorrow, I can't—"

"Don't tell me your problems. Fuck, wait a minute," and off again to the bathroom, detoured back with a new beer and perched to tell me what an idiot I was for wanting to have anything to do with Annemarie and her husband whom he called Jules and Jim. "They think they're *artistes*," he said, "aesthetes, hanging around at openings like it'll rub off or something if they can just get close enough. God, I hate people like that. Good at getting grants, though, you gotta give them that."

"Well, so is Edie."

"*Edie?*" as if I had made a peculiarly unpleasant joke. "Come on, Edie couldn't fill out a rebate form to get back fifty cents, where the hell do you get something like that?"

"I don't know," the lie cool and dry inside, slim finger tickling the back of my brain. "Somebody told me."

"Well, quit listening to bullshitters," and back again, off again on why Annemarie and Jules were essentially er-satz, uptown art fucks with too much free time and from there into a larger riff, rant to circle back to Lena, Lena whose involvement with them had gotten him involved as well—

"Who, you?"

"Yes absolutely me, why should I be any smarter than you? even though I am," which made him smile and me too, another beer after all and it was Lena who had intro-duced him to a whole group of filmmakers, most of them low rent and doomed to stay so "but there were a few," said Ed, "who were really trying to *do* something, you know? so it wasn't a total loss. We used to go to these pre-mieres, actually they called them premieres but it was more like a work-in-progress thing and afterward we would talk about it, me and her, just argue all the way home, all night in bed—"

Oh no and it must have shown on my face, something,

because he laughed, a short unhappy sound and "Sure," he said, "you didn't know? Sure. Hot and heavy too, I mean I thought I was in *love*, man, I thought she was the one."

My voice as flat as I could make it: "And what did she think?"

"Who the hell knows what she thinks? I never did— hey, don't look at me like that, it's not like I meant to break your heart or anything, I thought you already—"

"My heart isn't broken," I said, washed with an anger irrational; why be mad at him? "I'm just surprised, that's all. She never said anything about you."

"Oh hey," wide eyed now with old rancor ever new, "I don't give a red-eyed fuck *what* she says or didn't say, she's a liar and she always will be, she lied to me like you wouldn't believe. Lied to you too, or did you know all along about her and Sophie? was that part of the gig, or—"

Sweat's itch on my back, "Know what?" and his shrug: "What everybody else knew, that they were, you know, a couple, going around holding hands and all that—we figured you had to know or else maybe you were just—"

"We were *together*," stupid-loud; *calm down.* "We were all three together, it was—"

"I guess they were more together than you, though, huh? Like that show—matter of fact it was Karl's show, wasn't it?" and gesturing to the wall behind, wall of postcards and flyers, finger a pointer to black and white, familiar facing profiles and the nude between: "Karl knew too," said Ed and for me past even anger the hollow rush of vertigo to know, see that what had come to me as

228

armageddon, desertion and betrayal was if not exactly common knowledge then common enough, concentric to that network of those who had apparently known Lena and Sophie as a couple complete beyond the trio, before the breakup, our breakup but who was *we* after all, where did it begin? Traced like ripples, flung stone and was it me and Sophie, Sophie and Lena, Lena and me saying *love*, *love* but more than one of us was lying, right? *Right?* and my gaze swung back to that postcard, facile in-joke for those in the know and me so far in I was all the way out, stumbling in a darkness so dense that the more I knew the less I understood

and something cold against my hand, Ed saying, "Hey, take it easy," and without thought the instant backhand, beer can gone to land somewhere in the background, muffled *thunk* and "I said take it *easy*," affronted, half rising and I stared at him, just that, only stared but "I don't want to fuck with you," said Ed, sitting back down. "I'm not *trying* to fuck with you, all right? I'm just telling you stuff you should already know."

"I don't know anything," I said, and it was true: I knew it. "I don't know anything at all."

"Well congratulations, join the club," and in some amalgamation of reward and pacifier he began to tell me his Lena story, his tale of woe which was not at all like mine except that it was: all that heat, all that *passion* and "I thought, This just doesn't happen, right?" his shrug, half-smile which could have been mine. "Not to me, anyway. But it was really happening, I mean it was really real," and stayed so for how long? He didn't say. But "when we started up the video thing," that inward stare, lips pulled down in a frown that made him much older, "that's when things started going to shit."

"Videos," I said and Lena's voice in memory: *the Hot Dog Vendor*, bike messenger porn and "Hey," with a shrug, "I had to eat, right? and nobody was exactly lining up to finance my real work so what the hell. And anyway Lee was never in them, not really—I mean once or twice but not *really*, she—"

"What do you mean, not really?"

"Like not really fucking anybody, right? Just her ass, mostly, never her face or—God, you should see yourself, you look like somebody's granny. Hey, I wasn't twisting her arm, or *exploiting* her or anything like—"

"No, I know," and I meant it: because how could Ed have made Lena do anything she didn't want to do? How could anyone? Lena was Lena, she did what she wanted and if she wanted to show her ass, her body then she would, simple as that, simple as—

"—videos, but when I wanted her to do a film with me, I mean a real film she just seized up, you know, just went off on a tangent and—you want another beer?"

"No."

"I couldn't understand it," the empty can in hand. "I mean if she was willing to do one why not the other, especially when EdVentures was—But then when my brother got involved . . ."

And more memory, Lena's mocking grin: *And the time your little brother came to town—Michael, and he was, what, fifteen, sixteen?* and "I know what you're thinking," Ed's thin and sour smile, "I remember that party too, I re-

230

member what she said but that was really uncalled for because videos or no videos she *fucked* my brother, man, she
fucked him *up*, he had to move back home when she was
done with him but I bet she never told you that part, did
she? No, I didn't think so."

Fifteen, sixteen: that smile, Pandora's box and "When
was this?" I said, trying to keep my voice even. "Was this
when you, when you two were—"

"You mean was it like you guys? Not that I know of,"
brows up and shrugging but still beneath that nugget of
real loss, real pain and "When I found out I threw a fucking *fit*, I told her exactly what I thought of her and exactly
what she could do—" his notion of which was for her to
stop screwing his brother, with which she did not choose
at once to comply, chose instead to stop screwing Ed, seeing Ed, and brother Michael at last spun loose from her
orbit, all the way back home to Pittsburgh and Lena gone
in a new trajectory, linking at last with "Annemarie, who
was a cunt from the get-go, I mean she was always ragging
on Lena to stop working in the videos, to do *art*—like the
shit they do is art, right? Like *Peril*."

"And *Peril* is Saul?"

"No, Saul was later, after the movie; pardon me, the
film—Jules and Jim, you know, with all their staying-true-
to-the-moment garbage, all their *amour verité*—anybody
could see they were poseurs, they don't even *like* movies,
they just like to *talk* about it—like sex, you know, they
were the same way about sex." Looking at me, hard at me
and "Them too?" I said, stupidly, stupid and deceived, deceived in everything and "Sure they were fucking her,"
said Ed. "Both of them. I know it for a fact."

231

"How?"

"I *saw* them, man, I saw them with my own eyes. That Annemarie's an exhibitionist, why do you think they even made those dumb movies in the first place?"

As if from a well, somewhere deep and free of light: "I thought they were medical documentaries."

"Sure they are. Of her twat. That's about as medical as it gets, right? Gross anatomy," as he laughed and I didn't, said other things I did not hear and then kind, kind the offering hand, cold and tasteless the beer and "They come on one way but they're really something else. Like Lena. And *Peril*. At first I couldn't understand it, why she'd do it for them but not for me, but then I figured out she did it like she does everything, for herself. Listen," phone in hand now, "let me give Karl a call, and if he's home we'll head over there. You want to head over there? If I can walk ten blocks without shitting myself?"

"Sure," I said. "Sure, let's go."

In silence then to Karl's place: very big and very dirty, dark walls and carpet peeled in clumps to show the concrete floor beneath, metal shelving everywhere stocked haphazard with magazines, cameras, mat board, cans of spray mount and varnish and supplies more esoteric for which I had no name or reference—and Karl himself past reference too, soft doughnut belly, big hound-dog eyes that were almost pure surface, a dark and shielding glass behind which could have lived anything, anything but light and "It's a piece of shit, I warn you," said Karl, cueing up the machine. "But I think you'll get the general idea."

Settling back in his seat, weight-warped butterfly chair

stained to a sullen off-brown, Ed beside me on the futon slewed to face the TV and it started with music, black screen and humming and a pinhole light grown from the center to make a circle, sphere in the black in which a woman's face appeared, a face pale and thoughtful, no one I knew but then a voiceover from Annemarie, *postfuturist abstractions, expository perspective* and the black hole receding, rim and gone to show a typical gallery space, white walls, glossed floors on which were placed a collection of frames, empty baroque frames in false and heavy gold and the pale woman reappearing nude, curled on a red mat in the center of the floor and she began to flex, this woman, curl and uncurl like a hedgehog as behind her a series of *tableaux* were enacted by a series of nudes, mostly women, most in body paint as mannered and drab as the continued commentary by Annemarie, mocking counterpoint supplied by Ed as from Karl a more technical critique, cutting list of flaw and blunder and all the time my stare, black and avid as an art, the art of seeing, of knowing through vision all there is to see and know: voyeurism stripped to its writhing bones because all I wanted was to see, see *her*

and instant as if summoned there she was, legs and ass and head tipped back, back to the camera as she moved on her own behind the *tableaux*, moved as if to music, faint percussion in the bones and it *hurt*, watching her, hurt in a way I should have predicted: red the memory of our passion resurrected, of how it had been to kiss her, touch her, hold her in my arms and all I wanted then was to close my eyes, make them stop seeing, make it stop hurting but

"—just bad technique, you know?"

"Hey, they don't *care* about technique, man, they never did. What they care about is—wait a minute, hold it, just—yeah. Jess: that guy there," tapping on the screen, the frieze arrested and beyond a tall man far in the background, dark suit, black domino mask perched absurd on an equine face: "That's Saul," said Ed, "the great man himself," and then à la Annemarie, voice of the all-knowing narrator: "Notice how the figure of the masked man appears in the frame as if by magic, the magic of an incredibly clumsy director . . . he is intended to represent the miracle of constipation, having himself been unable to successfully defecate since 1986."

Tall, dark hair thinning, motions stiff to show he knew the camera was there as he crossed the frame, the room to a chair, high-backed black chair where he sat like a mannequin as Lena approached, steps in cadence as if measuring out a distance, here to there, light to heat, her hands gripping one of the empty frames, rising now as if she would strike him with its edge but instead with coronation grace placed it over him to settle binding and aslant, gold frame against dark shoulders, dark suit and the camera closer now, watching as his hands found the seat beneath, as she paused in grace deliberate, theatrical, one long moment—showing herself, *displaying* herself—before reaching for Saul, to part and unzip and reorder his clothing, to lower herself atop him and straddle him there in the chair.

Hair flouncing, fingers gripping his arms, the frame's gold edge pressed hard against her breasts as the camera inched closer still, the camera my vision as I watched her fuck him, my own faint arousal a muttering ghost—and shamed as well to see her this way, in this company, Ed and Karl seeing her naked, watching her hump and writhe like a lapdancer at a strip bar . . . and yet the numb and distant wonder, *is it real?* because the camera, my vision could not be wholly sure: his posture stiff, expensive suit disarranged like a trick's in a cab but like porno backward I never saw his cock, never saw him in her—only his hands, greedy manicured grasp on her hips, her flanks in motion but still it *seemed* real, real enough to make her sweat, damp at her temples, sheen on her breasts, the camera closer than that masked face so close to hers and someone, some man (Saul? Jules?) made a sound, a noise and her eyes, till then half-closed, came open, wide open as she turned her head to look directly into the camera

directly at me

without passion or defiance, no heat at all but only cold, enormous and self-contained yet aimed in that stare like a sting, like her gaze in the club so long ago: wasp's measure, weighing, *I see you*

like the stare of kink itself, bleak past hope or mockery, the secret that everyone knows

and riding harder now, wilder, shoving herself against him, against the wood of the frame and maybe it was real, real sex because she was jostled then by a motion not her own, buck and thrust and a sound from her—gasp, laugh, something—as the camera retreated, hasty pan to the clustered nudes as if shamed by its own avidity, abashed on the viewer's behalf and "Didn't you used to, like, see her?" said Karl: to me? to Ed? to the air? but no one answered, no answer possible from me and he said it again, "Didn't you used to—" and "*Yes* I used to fucking see her,"

Ed's voice harsh and loud, "and so did he, and so did *he*," sharp nod to the screen, to me and no more talk then, the movie ending as the gallery emptied, first Lena gone—demure now, gaze aimed decently down—then Saul rezipped and then the others, finally the uncurled nude who, passing close to the camera, seemed almost at last to smile: and in that empty space the gradual drain of color: to black and white, to white alone and then the gray buzz of empty video, Karl's voice to say "*Fini*," and Ed rising at once, tense and abrupt and "I gotta get home," he said, "my fucking guts are coming out. Thanks for the movie," and he was gone and I was rising, silent as the tape rewound and *hey Karl*, I could have said, *where'd you get this movie, what do you do with it when no one's around?* but instead I said nothing, mute's nod in the hollow of that vision spooling still behind my eyes: naked in the chair, her stare, my stumble down and out and all the way home to sit as if bound at the kitchen table, hands flat on a pile of unread mail and the image of Lena unrelenting, taunt and evidence of all I did not know, had not suspected, could not guess: riding him, fucking him, masked lover the one she could never forget because hadn't he gotten to her, Saul, hadn't he been the one? *She said she just had to move, had to get out of there because of Saul.*

She broke up with him?

That's what they said.

And that stare to the camera her stare in the club, in the dark as she came naked into the room where I lay with Sophie, balance and scales, weight of kink like the marriage of gold and lead: Lena with Saul and with Edie, with Ed and his brother, with Annemarie and Jules and she always

236

at the apex, the shifting axis, the balance of the triangle
heart

maybe she was just done with him

and maybe not.

"No I don't *know* Saul, not like a friend." Ed irritable,
pouring ketchup on matted scrambled eggs. "He doesn't
have any friends—what the fuck do you expect to get
from him anyway? You a necrologist or something, you
like digging in the dirt, digging up graves? What you have
to do is get it through your head, it's over. You, me, Saul,
all of us, it's just over."

Yellow bun before me on a bright blue plate, yellow
crumbs and cranberries and Edie's wise frown, shaking
her head at Ed: "No, Jess is right," pouring syrup, brown
spill thick and oversweet. "You have to follow your heart,
you have to do what you think is—"

"Edie, excuse me but you're full of shit. All this Heath-
cliff crap—" nodding to me, "he should get over it already, go on with his life, right? I mean, *I* went on, it's not
like it was the end of the fucking world or—"

"Everyone's different, Eddie, you can't just—"

"And that goes for you too, Miss Lonelyhearts. You're
like a parrot who only knows one word: Lena, Lena,
Lena."

Silence: and tears at once in Edie's eyes, child's tears on
her cheeks and "Oh fuck, forget it," as he slid out of the
booth, slammed change to tabletop, "just forget I said
anything, I'm an asshole, alright?" and out the door as
Edie wiped her eyes on a napkin already clumped and

sticky, syrup smell in the silence and "What I wanted to tell you," forcing a smile for me, "it's about Saul." Wiping her eyes again. "That Concrete thing, remember? There's this retrospective, the history of the Concrete—I might have a piece in it too. . . . Anyway I was there yesterday and someone told me Saul was definitely coming to the opening."

"When's that?"

"I'm not sure. Pretty soon."

Pretty soon; not soon enough but I could wait, and while waiting decide exactly what to say to him, exactly what to ask, make the most of whatever time I would have—but Edie still talking, head ducked and smiling and apparently she had met some woman, Samantha, there at the Concrete, assembling material for the show and "She's really something," said Edie, drawing lines in the syrup with the tines of her fork; tic tac toe, *X* and *O*. "Just really something else."

"Is she an artist?"

"No, oh no," droll her smile, "she works at the gallery, sometimes, and sometimes she models, life models, you know? She's *so* gorgeous," and something in the way she said it, strange memory uncaught until *oh, and Lena rented a tux, she looked so gorgeous* and the question sprung at once from my own surprise: "Are you two, are you seeing each other?"

Head ducked lower still, and shrugging: "I don't— maybe. Maybe, we'll see."

But I didn't see, not Edie, not for days, a week then two; my messages unanswered or, if returned, her own brief and distracted, she would call me back, we would

238

meet for coffee but right now, today she was very busy, she was getting ready for the show but pretty soon, pretty soon and so I stopped calling, let her be, spent my solo time instead constructing Saul's interrogation, versions made for two minutes, five, fifteen, various distillations of the same blunt cry: why? What did you do to her, what did you mean to her, why you, Mr. Mask, and not me?

And imagining—at work and after, lying sleepless in the earliest morning, vacant slump before the TV news— endless scenarios of connection, his willingness to talk, his unwillingness, what I would do or say in each case: and the sudden vision of the two of us, the stranger Saul in bright gallery light turning upon me to see, what? Half-stalker, the lunatic fringe grasping warm at his sleeve: *hey mister, did you love her? hey mister I have to know*

but what if he knew nothing, or, knowing, would not say? what then?

The sound of steps above me, crossing heavy from the door; traffic outside, the noise of the TV, the noise inside my head like the whisper of secrets, the memories of others given hasty in the dark: *I don't know*, the dry refrain like a second heartbeat: *I don't know, I don't know, I don't know.*

The postcard was Edie's doing: stark white, black sans serif "La Historie Concrete" with some quote from Voltaire, oh brother, and a list of names I did not know but only one name I needed to see: there at the bottom, the very end: Saul Berensen.

Leaving work for once early, home to shower and

change, change my shirt twice to the scald of faint mockery, *well don't you look nice:* like getting ready for a date, dates I never now had but this would help things, change things, wouldn't it? Wouldn't it? in the cab, staring out the window and too quick the swerve to the curb, *here you are* and there it was, storefront in black and faintly soiled white, green-glass doors and inside a crush already, milling queue for the wine and bypassing that I found a friendly corner, right angled to bad sculpture and what looked like a fire door: and waited there, with my stare and my damp hands.

But it was Edie I saw first, pale and garish in lipstick-red, and there with her a woman, dark hair shorn crisp and jagged, dark-circled eyes and oh my God, I thought, it's *Lena:* then saw more clearly that it was not but instead a kind of clone, false Lena draped on Edie like a wrong-size coat and "Hi, hi," Edie gripping my hand with her free one, so cold, so terribly cold. "Jess, I'm so glad you came, I—listen, this is Sam. Samantha. Sam, this is Jess."

"Well hello." Wine breath, flat vowels, something odd about that mouth and up close less like Lena than before but still the resemblance was sharp enough to trouble me: where did you find her, Edie? and "How do you like it?" Samantha said, head to one side and it took me a minute to realize she meant the show.

"I haven't had—I mean I just got here, and—"

"Have you seen Edie's piece yet? *Divine Distortions?* Well it's a killer, it's just a completely killer piece," and "No," again, "I just got here," but no answer was truly required, neither was listening, they were kissing now, wet kiss and Edie's cheeks flushed dry and bright, dilated grin

240

and "Isn't she terrific?" said nominally to me. "Didn't I tell you she was terrific?"

My nod, my smile in tandem: terrific, sure: Lena Lite, just what you needed and "Edie," I said, "just tell me one thing. Is Saul here?"

"Saul Berensen?" and Samantha shrugged. "I heard he wasn't coming, I don't even think he's in town—"

"Oh sure," said Edie, "I mean I thought he was, someone told me—just wait a little bit," to me, that hand again on my arm but she was far away, some other place entirely and "Thanks," I said, last husk of a smile and "Nice to meet you," said Samantha as I moved away, toward the table with the wine, cold and white and the glass drunk empty before I knew it, clutched there in my hand like a weapon; *he's not even in town*, what the fuck did she know, he had to be here, right? Right? and *You're a fool* from that inner voice, calm and conversational, just pointing out something I should have known already. *You're a fool, there's nothing for you here: go home.*

Not now. Not yet.

So what then? Wait: and watch Edie and her swain in orbit, more people out and in and I got more wine but did not drink it, prop in hand and a thin woman in white jeans and a turban clapped her hands and started calling "Attention, I need your attention," *I'm here to announce the death of art* and when it was more or less quiet she started in on a ten-minute spiel on the Concrete and its pioneering history, its unique position as a catalyst of important work and, as if planned for me alone, the sudden fire-door emergence, smooth and practiced as a magic trick as "Saul Berensen," said the woman, leading off the brisk applause.

Impeccable in a lean black suit, hair cut prison-short to hide the march of skin: older, much older than in the video, a looseness to that horse-chinned face tanned caramel-dark, something drained and almost sick beneath but when he spoke it was pure cream, rich as the center of some brandied treat, and the applause as he finished came longer, followed him to the wine where he made some joke I didn't catch, made them laugh, took a glass and that, I thought, is Saul: patron of the arts, public speaker, rich and well traveled gargoyle; Lena's lover, the answer man.

They all wanted to talk to him, queue up, rub shoulders; and me there with my glass and my silence, willing to wait and in the end, past all my plots and complex strategies, plans A and B and Z it was so easy, just as easy as a suicide bomber, assassin's grace to send me walking up to him, there by the wine, one hand out and "Lena Parrish," I said to that face, those dark exhausted eyes. "Lena Parrish told me I should meet you."

No reaction, or nothing I could see; just the faintest smile, like a window to an empty room. "You're a friend of hers?"

Not anymore. "I wonder if I could talk to you for a minute."

"We are talking."

"About Lena. I want to ask you—"

"I haven't seen Lena," no pause past the name, no tremor, nothing, "for quite some time, we've completely lost touch so I don't really think—"

"You two were lovers," and a man and woman, approaching, turned to one another, one glance then away to leave us, the crowd made wall in private confrontation and was it all going to be this easy? Face to face, accusation and reproach, no feeling in my voice; almost a smile. "She moved out of her place, that ugly flat, she said she couldn't live there anymore. Because of you."

And still from him nothing, not even the whiff of anger concealed, not even at my rudeness and "That's a matter of opinion," with the faintest of frowns, less expression than twitch, "and to be honest I can't imagine how any of it is any of your business."

"I helped her pack," as pleasant and calm as he, we might have been mannequins, dummies in a window, puppets on a stage. "She moved in with me and my girlfriend, just the three of us—like you and Lena and Edie, remember? and Annemarie and Jules? And *Peril*—remember *Peril*? Quite a movie, right, a love story, because she was in love with you, and you were in love with—"

"Excuse me," he said, not loud or rudely, without change of posture or pitch but with the air—all at once, like stone—of a closing door, implacable past protest or pursuit, leaving me there where I stood but in that last open moment he looked at me, looked into my eyes and for me the sense not of a wound, not some beating, breathing heart but instead a bone scraped to marrow, something bleached and leached and airlessly alive and "I don't want to talk about these things," he said, but gently, as if I should have known; and turning then away from me, two steps, three to move back at once into conversation, the couple who had tried before to approach now beside him to say how wonderful he was and how glad they were to tell him so.

And I did not follow, said nothing, kept back as he

243

talked and smiled with apparent ease and pleasure and to corner him again here or somewhere else I saw would give me nothing, nothing more than I had already now that I had glimpsed the bone, deep hole, dark house too dark even for disappointment at seeing in Saul no answers at all or not the ones I wanted but instead only a simple map to the place where I might in time begin to go, purged of pain by the absence of feeling, *between grief and nothing* . . . and in some ways his choice worse even than Edie's, Edie with her terrible hunger nurtured and unfed, gorged now on the emptiness of this strange woman, this Samantha who like some other kind of magic was suddenly there in my face, hand on my arm, wine breath and insistent: "So did you see Edie's piece?"

I stared at her, at that fun-house resemblance and "Excuse me," I said, as Saul had said to me, *excuse me* and away, through the crowd and out the door and I saw it had been raining, drab wash and sullen breeze through which I moved, walking without thought or destination, walking as I had before—remember? and the same burn now in my heart like a black machine, the same restless, sweatless stride—that long walk when I had at last decided, or thought I had decided, that our trio was now only struggle, strangle, choked by what I saw as Sophie's overriding need, her greed and my own decision to force a choice once and for all—and that strangle, that choice considered then as a kind of trial, dark twin to the birth of our sweet triangle but really it was just another step, *the next step*, kink dissolved to show beneath the iron bones another kink, another choice: truer because deeper, deep as the pain of its gestation because the real choice had already been made: and not by me, either, odd man out, last one to know—and now see me still as helpless, as foolish, as driven as before

and I stopped there, right where I was, stopped dead in front of a dry cleaner's with both hands at my sides: chaingang felon abruptly loosed, stupored by the smell of liberty and *no*, I thought, *I'm wrong, I've been going the wrong way* because all along there was only one person I needed to talk to, one voice to give the answer I must hear: *why you?* and "Sophie," I said, as if she stood there before me, *Sophie* because she was the one: not Saul made king by rumor but—say it: see it, yes, Saul at last discarded with the rest, left behind with Ed and Edie and Annemarie and all the others whose names I did not know, in whose rooms she had lived, Lena, constructing her own rooms, own house of kink built to raze in an instant and construct again like magic in the rooms of someone else: only Sophie still in residence, the last true expert, witness to the freshest crime of all—and I stood there like a piece of wood, past astonishment at this knowledge and knowing instantly that it was right: Sophie, my Sophie, Lena's Sophie there now in duo, flesh made heart and answer to the question of my pain.

I have to see her, standing there in the street, soft scatter of rain begun anew. *I have to see her now.*

"Fuck off," said Po. "I'm not telling you *anything.*"

Pink and black, deep déjà vu to pass through those doors again to witness no change appreciable in the ambience of AmBiAnce, light jazz on the radio, toxic whiff beneath cosmetic goo: open late on a slow night, only two chairs occupied, my quarry nowhere in sight and "I wouldn't spit on you if you were on fire," said Po, who also had not changed much beyond the addition, or subtraction, of a new haircut, very very short, which made her look if possible more fierce than before and especially now, looking not at me but past as if she could not bring herself to meet my eyes, acknowledge my presence there in her domain, "and I can*not* believe you have the balls to come walking in here like Marley's ghost after all this time and ask me for a *favor.* I always knew you were heedless but this just about takes the cake."

"Po," very careful to be civil, keep my voice even and low although hers was neither and had turned the few heads in the room, "I'm not going to harass her, or anything, I just want to—"

"You *just want.* Well isn't that you all over, Jess, you always *just want* something from somebody, from me, Lee, Sophie, who you *just wanted* to drive right around the bend, you and all your sorry bullshit, you and Lee both but let me tell you something," close to me, closer still and for a moment I expected her to grab me, hit me, something: I could smell it on her, that penny smell of rage and "First it was *you,*" stiff finger to poke me in the chest, "and then it was *Lee,* how much do you think she can take, anyway? Just how much shit do you expect her to take?"

"I don't—"

"Of course you *don't,* that's your whole problem but I'm not here to smarten you up, OK? It's not my *job,* OK?" Cold, recollection and grievance like stones on a grave, her voice a river of bones and my own voice barely heard, risen in that river to say "—that I was in here, all right, just tell her that I'm—"

"Jess." In my face now, all those bones and stones. "Listen to me now, Jess: *I'm not going to do anything for you.* I'm not going to tell anybody anything or pass any messages or tell Sophie you came here and if you come back, if you *try* to come back I'm calling the cops like I would for any other asshole off the street so why don't you just take the hint right now and fuck *off.*"

Silence.

"*Now,*" she said, and I did, out the door and into the street where it was still raining, trickle in the dark, irresolute to walk a block, then two, double back to stop at a coffee shop and sit staring at my cup, thinking, trying to think: now what? How to look for her, where to go?

No answers, no ideas past a scrambled litany, obsessive catalog of where she once had been, had gone, what she had liked to do but what we were isn't what we are, who had said that? Sophie herself, right? Sophie who had known what I didn't, Sophie who could be anywhere, new haunts, new home, anywhere at all . . . and the image of her ghosting through the city, past the reach of all my need made her suddenly exotic, as strange for me as Lena once had been: that vision distant of a whole life built without me, stepping-stone of day to day in a world where I did not exist, spent in places I would never be—or maybe worse still intersecting, both of us in the same places but at different times: what if she was, say, this very minute at the Concrete, sipping wine and staring at the art, at death's-head Saul in his natty black suit? Or step-

ping into AmBiAnce to retrieve some mislaid item, pick
up her paycheck, cool pause to hear about my visit: and
shake her head, a dry little, wry little shake to second Po's
decree: *fuck off, Jess.*

Or she could be in line at a deli, a bookstore, buying a
hat or a tape or tickets to the theater, she could be anywhere and I—a minute late, a cab missed, a corner turned
in maddened haste—would never find her, never know:
and the worm's turn of irony to find myself chasing her
whom I had once tried only to lose: oh yeah, I get it, I get
the whole joke now.

Ragged the rhythm, litany of *Sophie Sophie* as I drank
my coffee, *Sophie Sophie* all the way home, up the stairs
into the dark, no messages, no calls and I could not sit
still, went from kitchen to living room and back again,
looking out the windows as if I expected her to appear,
magic response to the heat of my need, *Sophie where are
you?* and the more I thought the more overwhelmed I be-
came, flung moon in lost trajectory, unhappy orbit farther
through the dark because without help or direction how
would I find her? AmBiAnce my only clue, I could hang
there like a stalker, skulk and sniff like a tracking dog
which is what I ended up doing, the next day and the day
after that, after work to wait a block away, wait and watch
like a freak in a trench coat but I never saw her, coming or
going, saw nothing but a line irregular of transformations
big and small, her specialty: *oh Sophie where are you, oh Sophie, change me now.*

And past those afternoons turned evening back I went
to sit at the kitchen table, try to reason, try to think: calling Edie for help but she was no help, she was never there,

no reason to leave a message because the friend to whom I could tell this trouble, the fond strange guide was guide no more, consumed by her own hungers, Samantha a fresh blind alley leading back to her old pain; and Ed when I called him gave me only ideas I had had already: *did that, went there, thought of that too* and "So forget it," he said sharply, music in the background loud enough to blur his voice. "Take it for a sign. You struck out with Saul, right? and good riddance, the guy's a mummy, he just doesn't know to lie down . . . and what's her name, Po told you to fuck off too which is a double sign so why don't you just fuck off already? And *don't* talk to Edie about it, Edie's back in the box so—"

"I can't even get her on the phone."

"Well, be glad. The last time I went over there she never said two words to me, just sat there and giggled and here's Samantha in my face like a pit bull, from the minute I walked in till the minute I left."

"She looks," I said, "a little like Lena."

"Oh, you noticed. Did it give you a hard-on? You know she sold that piece at the Concrete, Samantha did, don't ask me how but now she's telling everyone she's Edie's rep, she even tried to sell me something but I threw holy water in her face and got out the back way. . . . But listen to me now, I'm serious—are you listening? This is probably your last good chance to forget about all this shit and get on with whatever else you have to do. Because if you don't, Edie's what you're going to turn into, Jess. I hate to say it but I know it's true."

Follow the path long enough and you become it—Edie with her dazzled smile, half there and half with Lena, still with

Lena, fool and martyr, *no man is an island* and "All right," I said, past the jeer and howl of the music, "all right, you're right, I won't do it. I won't chase her, I won't do anything. OK?"

He seemed happy, or if not at least satisfied and so the lie was, I thought, a kind one; no more of my burdens passed to others, I was going to figure this one out alone but alone I garnered no solutions, nothing but more of my dreary stakeout and even if I saw her, going in or coming out, what was I going to do? Leap up and grab her arm, make her talk to me? What if she ignored me, stormed past me, screamed at me, what if anything? yet unacknowledged still I felt a confidence so palpable and strong that, doubt and all, I must believe: if I could only see her, we could talk. Not like with Saul, a prearranged interrogation, questions and answers but like we used to, just the two of us, Sophie and me drinking coffee or walking around and I would turn to her and say, very simply, as I should have long ago, *What happened? Sophie, what happened?*

And as simply she would tell me, explain my hunger and my pain, explain the end I could not accept because in all the world she was the only one who could, the only one who had in any way at all—far more than doomed Edie, dead Saul, Ed whose very anger was a badge of memory— had seen what I had, knew what I knew, lived in that bright cocoon of passionate minutiae, palace and cell of kink constructed of our flesh and breaking hearts, and emerged as I had not, whole and sure and happy on the other side.

It was a Sunday when I saw her.

My one day off, a dedicated fool if nothing else: watching the door of AmBiAnce as people went in and out, rainy day and dumb in my misery, wet hair and water in my shoes, helpless inner conjugation of what even I must acknowledge soon as a red queen's chase, all the effort I could make to stand there, Lena's *Peril* stare a loop to bind past to endless present as I stood waiting for something to happen, for Sophie at last to come.

Go home.

No.

And absurd the gift of circumstance, of grace because look now, look up right *now:* and let vision seize your heart for there she is, that walk unmistakable, wrapped like a child in a too-long raincoat, gone like a genie behind the AmBiAnce door and "*Shit,*" my voice more breath than word, hands clenched in my pockets, staring—as I had once before, remember? on the steps of her college porch, wet wicker and empty hands, watching her go where I could not follow and now look, look to see time passed and gone in circles but me still waiting, stupid and yearning, heart in my mouth and trying at last to work up the balls to approach, *balls, guts, nerve,* as if only in the brute strength of the body could we ever find courage enough to enforce the heart's demands, to gird ourselves internally—for more pain? or only to feel again, really feel? and as if that thought was a door, *the next step* there she was again, quick outside and crossing now the street toward me

and my jittering hands, my panic and vast relief because here she was, already at the curb, clear view through the rain and I saw her face: changed, not thinner but somehow sharpened, refined to a new maturity, no more the perpetual child—but still Sophie, my own lost Sophie to come before me now and "I saw you," she said, voice calm and level, utterly composed. "Standing there in the rain like a jerk. I know you've been looking for me."

Struck back to nothing by her courage to see and then approach me, as if it was or ever could be as simple as that: and as simply I asked, "How do you know?"

"Po told me: She said you wanted to talk."

"Well, I do," and strange my voice atremble, so strange to see her again, time compressed and stretched to bring us back together, face-to-face and "I want," I said, "I want to—"

and without warning or volition began to cry, my hands curled open, tears hot then cold on my face: stranded and empty, broken, *broken* and "Please, can we go somewhere?" Sick with my own weakness, hating myself as she must for the tears yet unable to stop. "Can we just go somewhere *inside?*"

Nothing, just her gaze: clear eyes, pure vision as the rain in rising touched her, mist washed across her skin as around and between us people kept passing, jostle of umbrellas, clandestine stares as rain ran down my neck, as I stood there weeping, waiting on her answer as if it held the rest of my life until at last "Okay," she said, nodding back down the street the way she had come. "Okay then, let's go."

"All right," wiping one-handed at my face, foolish and wretched as she turned and began to walk, hands in pockets, head down and in three steps I was beside her, the old rhythms at once resumed: not touching, unspeaking as strangers, yet how easy it was, how natural for us to be this way together, me and Sophie walking down the street: detritus of puddles, wind on my wet face and "I'm hungry," said Sophie, "are you hungry?" so we stopped at the next place we saw: Skippy's Mex with a scatter of empty tables, dull overheads no match for the gray afternoon and she ordered chili, chili and Irish coffee, a hideous combination new to me; new tastes, new habits and finally when her food came she raised her gaze to me and said, "I thought about you, you know. A lot."

My own drink before me, blond Scotch in a cloudy glass. "I thought about you too."

Silence, then: "So what are you doing now?" Spooning up the chili, little brown lumps. "Are you—are you seeing someone? Do you go out?"

All those hours spent with Edie, talking, talking, talking about Lena and "No," I said, "no, not really."

"Then what do you do?"

What do I do. I tried to think, tried to tell her something of how it was and had been—the silence of the apartment, the rage and the exhaustion, certainty of loss unhealed made more intense by time—but every word, every fumbling image an indictment, exposed not only to Sophie but to myself as if the act of explanation, of putting my life into words showed me exactly what I was, what I had become: already Edie, dull husk, straw man gathered to one axis marrow-close, shard in the heart to prove by pain the fact of living, to keep myself alive because without it, without that defining core what was I? What am I now? A walking cipher, a voice crying out in the dark and "I just want it to stop," I said, staring into my empty glass. "I just want to stop thinking about it."

"No you don't." Dry and calm as the doctor who tells you where the tumor is. "That's not what you want at all."

"You . . . Sophie, I need to understand what *happened*, what—"

"You already know what happened. It just didn't work out." Long swallow of her coffee, eyes briefly closed against the heat. "Po said you were pretty upset."

"I was. I *am*," and a breath to steady me, trying to match her calm, trying not to shame myself. "I just, I think we should talk."

"Why?"

Because you're the one, the only one who really knows; and I need to know because I can't stand it, trapped beast to chew myself bloody, I just can't take it anymore and "Sophie," my hands palms up upon the table, supplicant, mendicant, fool, "I really have to know—"

"Know *what*?" with a first real anger, anger at me but then "Wait a minute," she said, in another voice. "Didn't Po—don't you know?"

"Know what?"

"About me and Lena," the name like a mouthful of glass. "We broke up, Jess. We're not together anymore."

The silence like a bomb, black aftermath and "*What?*" my cry as stunned past thought I reached for her, covered her hands with mine: "Oh, *Sophie*" as if learning she was ill, struck by a killing sickness, the same illness killing me but she did not weep as I had, did nothing but disengage her hands, cool hands from my damp grip and "No," she said, "no, really, it's okay."

"Sophie—"

"No, really. It was . . . not good, at first, but I'm okay. But if you want to know about Lena, what she's doing now, I'm not the one you should—"

"No, I'm—that's not what—" A long breath as if airless, caught in some vacuum of surprise and "*Jesus*, Sophie," at last my simple shock. "What *happened?*"

"I told you. It just didn't work out, that's all."

" 'It just didn't work out.' That's your assessment, that's all you have to—"

"Yes. Yes, it—"

" 'It just didn't *work out*,' what the fuck does that mean? How can you even—"

"Stop yelling."

"I'm not yelling," although I was; the taste of the Scotch like turpentine, sour and strong and "Come on, Sophie," forcing myself to quiet. "When you two, when you left it was—I mean maybe not for you but for you to sit there and say 'It just didn't work out,' come on, that's not all there is to it, that's not—"

"Well that's all there is to it for me." Warm with a new authority, stern as something grown by force and "What was I supposed to do? Kill myself? Curl up in a ball?"— *like you did?* but she didn't say it; head to one side in avian tilt unchanged and "You know what she is?" said Sophie. "She's a quick-change artist, she shows you just what you want to see, but it's a lie. It's just always a lie, and I got tired of lies because you can't live in them, they're like a fun house where the walls are always moving, you never really know where you are and it's *exhausting*, Jess, it's just completely fucking exhausting trying to keep it all straight and figured out, so one day I woke up and said to hell with this, with her, all of it, and I put my stuff in a bag and walked out."

"You *left* her?"

"That's right."

Mouth open, dumbstruck and yet in another way how be surprised at all because at heart's end that was Sophie, the Sophie I had always known: at once more foolhardy, more generous, more courageous than I was or had ever been, headfirst into the maelstrom, no risk too great and "Then what?" I said, my voice gone small with wonder. "What happened then?"

Bright eyes; tears? or not? and "I keep telling you," she said. "Nothing. I found a place to stay, I went to work, I lived. What was supposed to happen?"

What was supposed to happen? I don't know, a lot of things: you could have fallen apart like I did, tumbled to decline, become an obsessive and "You know," she said, "how we used to watch people, on the streets? and listen to the neighbors? Like it was a show they were putting on for us?" *Kink:* but I didn't say it, kept silence with a nod and "Sometimes," she said, "when everything was going wrong—with us, the three of us—it started to seem like it *was* a show, like it wasn't real, or it was happening to somebody else. Like my life, our lives, was part of it all, that show, and if I just stopped watching then maybe it would stop. Just *stop*, just—Because I was so *unhappy*," with great simplicity, "every day, all the time. I couldn't sleep, I used to lie awake at night and think *What's going to happen? what am I going to do?* . . . but she said that it would be okay in the end, that everything would work itself out. And I believed her." The tiniest of smiles. "*That* seems like a dream, now. To think that I could ever be so dumb. But I was."

And effortless as a granted wish she began then to explain, to tell me things: many things, kink turned inside out as if in flashback I watched their lives and the corresponding, telescopic lurch of mine, mad collision dance sure to fail yet linear and dense as that mirrored room, fun house I had once tried to penetrate become if not clear then exposed to me, real in a way it had not been while inside: fumbling for the answers, crying for the light but this gift of vision granted solely it seemed by distance, purchased by the mingled coin of her pain and mine and "I used to think, *he must know*," another drink now before her, fingers loose against the heated glass. "He must know, why doesn't he say something? Because *I* knew, I knew you were in love with her like you used to be with me, more than me—you just *wanted* her so much, I could smell it on you—"

"Did it—"

"Did it what?"

Look at her: do that, at least. "Hurt you."

"That you wanted her? Sure it did, some, I mean it was like you were crazy for her, or—But as long as we were still together, the three of us, I figured we could handle it, because I thought we could handle anything. We were—"

"Different," from far away, stranded in the mirrored house, staring at the image of my face revealed. "We were different."

"Right. Except we weren't. But didn't you," earnestly, "didn't you know how it was, with Lena and me? I mean somewhere in the back of your head, didn't you *know?*"

How it was: what did that mean? Did I know that they were fucking, were lovers in a way that had not, had never included me? Yes, more or less. Did I know they were *in love*, in a way that my own affair with Lena could not begin to overcome, imbued with their own velocity, gathering speed and force and "No," I said, the closest answer to the truth. "No, I didn't know anything."

Which was almost funny in a way: the blind voyeur, crown prince of kink defeated by lack of sight and Sophie's sigh, brief and sharp through her teeth and "I wanted," she said, "just to *say* it, get it out in the open, I fought with her for *months* but she said you weren't ready, that you would disintegrate if I said anything, just fall completely apart. 'I'm not responsible,' she kept telling me, 'you do what you want but I'm not going to be responsible.' And then when we—it seemed like she was right, the way you—I was so worried about you, the way you looked, your *face* . . ." and her face now in her hands, not crying but concealed in some private cove of memory, sorrow's room and "I called you," muffled behind those hands. "The next day, do you remember?"

Jess Jess her voice on the phone, disaster's echo and "You can't imagine," Sophie said, hands flat now on the table, eyes creased half closed as if she stared into the wind, bitter wind, "you can't *believe* what it turned into, without you there. At first I tried to give her what she wanted, make her happy—I wanted to *be* happy, I felt like I earned it, paid for it in advance—but she never was. Never. No matter what I did.

"And I—I thought about you, I wondered how you were but I could never say it, never even mention your name because if I did she would just start in again, bring everything up, throw it all in my face—because she was mad, and disappointed—"

"In what? Me?"

"You, me, everything; everything but herself—but mostly me because I was the one who was there, day in and day out, just trying to *measure up*," and see her mouth twist then in a smile I had never seen, caustic and alien, thin on her lips and "No matter what I did," she said, "no matter what, it was never enough."

And déjà vu an old wound's cry: *All the time we were together I never thought I was enough:* in the shout of Ed's party, frozen hands and frozen hunger, Edie's voice and Ed's too: *She's a liar and she always will be, she lied to me like you wouldn't believe*—and Jim in the hallway, *you know she was staying with me, you knew that, right?*

You knew that, right?

And like strung beads, chain links the stories now from Sophie, my own world and all I thought I knew turned not upside down but inside out, the mirror reflecting its own dull silver heart cracked to pieces and each piece to interlock, puzzle but not the picture I thought to see: how Lena had "explained" Jim to Sophie, Jim and Ed and Edie too although Annemarie and Jules went barely mentioned—"Those filmmaker people?" brows arched, "what

about them?"—and even Saul now made, in this kaleido-
scope telling, just a minor player, blip on the screen, a rich
guy who had cared for her and for whom she had cared
a little, for a little while and "She said he was like a tutor, that he taught her a lot about art and that they
were friends, close, you know, but not like lovers or
anything—"

"Did she ever mention *Peril?*" Breasts thrust against an
empty frame; that heatless, endless stare. "Did she ever
say anything about it to you?"

"No," with half a shrug, "I don't think so. Why? what's
Peril?"

"A movie," I said. In the chair, masked face and Edie's
chirp, *a three-way, like you guys:* all truth? or not? or something in between? and "She told me," said Sophie, "that
she needed help with you, that you were getting too pos-
sessive and she wanted to, to push you back a little, keep
the balance; and so I did what she said, I—"

*sat between us on the sofa in restaurants cabs the movies
everywhere in the way always there*

"—but by then I had, I was starting to want her more,
for myself; all for myself," and her hands again to her face,
fingers pressing, pressing and "Everything was changing," said to self as much as to me, "nothing was like it was
before—like at the lingerie place, that stupid Amateur's
Night," Sweet Illusions, oh boy and where was I? Working, stumbling home to the TV and the dark, always in
the dark and they had, said Sophie, signed up to model
lingerie, able afterward to keep what they wore: and Lena
down the catwalk in palest ivory lace "like she was naked,"

said Sophie, "so beautiful. And the way she walked, like a queen, you know, with those long legs—she was just so *perfect*, Jess, not self-conscious, or stupid, like some of the women were doing bump and grind, wiggling their asses . . . but not her. She just walked out and stood there, just stood there," head down, "and was perfect."

Silence: and the stab of those pressing fingers, pressed nearly white at the tips. "Do you remember about Deirdre Bacon? She was a—"

"I remember." The fight about the dance class, Lena taking Sophie's side: all there in miniature, arc and *denouement; If you want to know something, why don't you just ask?*

"That was Lena," said Sophie. "My grown-up Deirdre Bacon. My best friend."

Dull inside the dart, like the ache of a limb long gone: "I was," I said, "your best friend too."

"Oh but that was different, you and I were like partners. Lena was the way I wanted to be."

And now beneath the shading hands I saw her tears, two slow lines to strike me back to silence, past the clamored echo of my voice, idiot-sure of my right to ask of anyone anything at all: Edie and Ed and Saul and Sophie, *tell me, tell me, I have to know* but how could I imagine that Sophie of all people would *want* to talk or answer, why should she tell me anything at all? and knowing now that she and Lena were apart made of me something even worse, something more selfish still bent on examining that wound, agony more immediate, insisting on a document of the steps that had carried her here—dingy little restaurant, ex-lover querulous and grim and "Sophie," said helpless and too late, "oh Sophie don't, don't talk about it if it hurts you—"

Napkin up bright as a banner, bright as her wet eyes but "No," she said, "no, it's okay, it's just—Anyway I was wrong about everything so what does it matter now? It was just that I thought, you know, if I tried *really hard*, if I kept trying maybe I could keep the balance, keep us all together—but then she said she was tired of pretending, that she didn't think she could ever really *love* a man, not like with a woman, with me—she said we were so close we were like the same person, that no man could ever be that close to her, not even you, so she couldn't keep on like we were anymore. Because it would be a lie."

"A lie," as if mocked from a distance, the inverted funnel of time. "That's not what she said to me."

"No, I bet it wasn't," and the briefest twist of smile, of the old mocking Sophie, "I bet you got *two* from Column B. . . . But you told her some secrets too, right? Like—what was it, Bimbos? Some topless bar you wanted to take her to?"

"Chicks," my shrug, tiny motion half-abashed and "She said you guys went to a porno shop once?" the fabled tour of my past, Sophie's past too but Sophie somehow not invited, somehow beside the point because the point had been the locus of our heat, dark magnet shock there in that booth, that first driving kiss that drove me oh, so far and "It really wasn't anything," I said, "it was just a—"

"She told me you kissed her," said Sophie, "that you got all horny and sentimental, that you started to—she knew I *hated* that, when she made fun of—" Her gaze then high and past me; a kindness, I think, in my shame. "But that's Lena; she likes to push buttons. Find them and push them till they break."

And nothing my answer, I had nothing to say or do beyond listening, hearing it through to the end: "Then she told me you were pressuring her, she said you were forcing her to make a choice but she told me she couldn't be without me, we had to break away—"

"When was this?"

"After New Year's it got worse, but then after Kelsey's party—that birthday party, remember?" Sophie weeping in the cab with me hunched next to Lena, hunched and hating those tears; and the next day's dreadful lunch, command performance meant to make an end but instead the spiral continued, down and down and *you want her for yourself*, the cry of inverted hunger, cry of my own heart—

"Now or never," said Sophie, "that's what she said. Time to take the next step. And so we did."

The next step: and for me now the urge to laugh, long red laugh like coughing blood because on some level, kink's level, vision observed from a safer place it was all so purely absurd, farce tragedy danced by puppets, responses born in that fun-house mirror, caught and framed by so much squandered agony, incredible the waste of tears and time . . . and Sophie and I like drowning victims, fierce the gasp and struggle as we pulled each other down, panting to a shore of pure illusion with nothing there to save us but our own sad empty hands.

And what would have happened if we had talked, truly talked there at that lunch, or any lunch, sullen nights and angry mornings yet if we had turned to one another, offering all the truth we knew, then gone together back to Lena with that truth in hand—but I could not think of this, the hope of pain averted, glimpsed cliff of possibility from which one did not fall; nothing ever hurts so much as what never had to be.

The waiter returning, did we want another drink? and Sophie's slow head shake, back and forth as if exhausted: "No, thank you. Just the check." When he had gone I looked not at her but at my hands, cold hands on the table beside an empty glass and "Do you ever," I said, "see her? I mean like just walking around, or—"

"Well, I passed her on line at the movies, she was with some people, some guys—And Po said she made an appointment for next week. To get her hair done."

Anger then, for Sophie's sake, the pain this must cause; *she likes to push buttons.* "But how can you stand to—how can you see her, and not—"

"Not what?" with almost a smile, driven by nothing but the heart of her will and that will driven only outward, toward what was yet to be: no chewing the stump for Sophie, no pinching the edge of the wound and "It hurts," she said, "if that's what you mean, but it gets better too. All the time, it gets better. Because I don't want her anymore. What I want is dead, and maybe that's good." Last sip of her cold Irish coffee, the dregs of the dregs. "You know, I used to lie there at night and wonder, Does she love me? Did she ever?"

My pause the echo of hers, then: "Did she?"

"I don't know. Did she love you?"

Silence: *between grief and nothing* and now in me a presence, certainty like pressure building, rising like heat in the tube of the heart and as surely as *Peril* drove me to Sophie I knew what next to do, the last and final step of all and "Will you tell me," I said, "where she is?"

Silence; a line between her eyes.

"Why?"

"Because I want to talk to her."

"Like you talked to me?" but waiting for no answer she gave what I asked, number and address scratched on the back of a party flyer fished from the depths of her purse and "Put yours there too," I said, "OK? Your number."

Pen pause, as if my request had brought a proof she needed; then more scratching, the paper folded closed and set aside, solemn as ceremony and "Could I call you?" as she rose, hands in too-deep pockets, raincoat a cloak to fall almost to her feet. "After I—can I call?"

"Sure," in that same dry voice, "why not," and bending swift to kiss me, lips warm on my cheek, my hand out to touch her but she was already gone, door closing on her passage as unfolding the flyer I saw in her child's handwriting only one set of numbers: phone and address for Lena, but nothing of Sophie's at all.

For some reason—there at the payphone, hunched in the rain—my thoughts gave me the image of Edie: twisting the skirt of her cowboy dress, dreary little, endless little smile and all those hours consumed by dissection, talking and wondering, wondering and sad and *I gave her every-*

thing she asked for, but in the end she didn't want it. Which wasn't her fault I guess but oh Edie, oh poor Edie yes it was, yes it really—

"Hello?"

And still prepared yet I was startled, her voice after all this time and "Hello, Lena," past the thick red rhythm of my heart; fight or flight, or neither. "It's Jess."

"Jess," calmly, as if she herself had given me the number, as if this call was prearranged: and beneath the calm no emotion or sense of same, not subdued, not amused, not happy or unhappy or anything at all, as if she would withhold all feeling or expression until she could see what would best serve the situation: like talking to a wire monkey, a picture on a wall. "How are you?"

"Fine," I said. "I want to see you."

A pause: honest, or theater? "Well," as if debating an appointment for a minor service, when can one find the time, "I have to go out in a little while—"

"It won't take long."

Another pause, to let me hang, wait on the crumbs of her plenty; then at last, "All right. Where are you now? at home?"

"No," through the rush of rain renewed. "I'm down at the end of your block."

Alone in the elevator, empty in ascent and the building was pure faux Gothic, black marble floors and lily bouquets, whoever she was living with must have money: like Saul? Or maybe more than I knew had changed; I never had been sure what it was she did for a living, maybe doing it had finally made her rich. A corporate writer; sure.

My hands were trembling.

Still rising as if through pressure, up from the heart of the deep; as if each floor were sectioned time, a year's worth in a day and flashing through my mind the jumble exponential, every situation possible or not: we would scream, we would smile, we would stare till someone cracked; she would call me names, I would list her crimes, she would weep and say she missed me, wanted nothing but me back . . . and half a smile for that one, trickled sweat beneath my arms, no end to the self-delusion but no time for that because I had to be ready, prepared for anything: eyes closed, the inner screen to bring me memory, show me dark eyes shadowed with faint bruising, face conjured not from my last true sight (*this* is *us*) or even from *Peril*'s stare but from the last time I had touched her, kissed her, held her in my arms

and at once and unbidden, like some sly outlandish cripple came the ghost of our heat, moist whisper of imbecile lust bearing with it the weight, compound and compressed, of every breathing instance, calm seduction, frenzied fuck: quick and slow, in and out, bed and floor and against the door, braced in the shower gripping tight at her slippery thighs, hands up her skirt in the dark of a bar and what if—head back against the wall and breathing, deep breath and what if in this red minute I walked into her place and grabbed her, just grabbed her and fucked her right there where she was? like dogs in the street, beasts in the dark to stink and cry like that very first time, so long ago, harsh and driven and running hot, boiling hot, boiling over and "*Ah,*" that voice in memory, a groan as if I had hurt her, sucking breath and "*ah*" again, her hair in my hands, scratching nails and I had squeezed her shoulders, squeezed her breasts, flesh in my fists like honey

and the silent slide of the elevator door, empty hall and there her door, grail and path and my slow approach, one step and two and what would Edie think, if she was here? angry Ed or empty Saul and only Sophie did not seem to want this, need this, only Sophie was—

opening now to me, open door to show me Lena, waiting: and beautiful, oh my God so beautiful, all in white *like a queen* and she had done something to her hair, not shorter but sheared somehow back so the bones of her face lay promontory, bones like sculpture, like secret art and "Jess," she said as she smiled at me, a smile less mask than vessel that might have held anything, heat or promise, truth or lie or anything at all and

"Come in," with the door held open, bare the open heart of dream

between grief and nothing

and I went inside.

All black-on-black on black and white, staggered line of lyre-backed chairs, long slab of sofa pale as an altar; more lilies, maybe they came with the lease. Black bookcases, black vitrines crowded with fussy little boxes, yellow and deepest turquoise, red and cinnamon-brown; a collection of something, maybe it was hers.

Standing now before me in her long white skirt, man's

white shirt through which I could see the shadow of her nipples and "Just look at you," she said, still faintly smiling. "You're all wet."

"It's raining out," my dull and troubled voice, shadows still beneath her eyes and on her hands three rings, none of them mine: heavy gold and set with stones like the chipped bones of the earth, big and black and cracked on the surface, sharp edges to spear the wondering touch. "It's been raining all day."

"I know," nodding briefly at the view: six windows, square and bare, ceiling to floor like doors but no balcony there, one step and you would fall like a stone, small black stone to grow as it reached the ground.

"Nice," I said. "It's a nice place."

"Isn't it?" The undertow smile. "His name is David; he's a doctor. Internal medicine. Isn't that what you were really asking?"

David: testing the name like the point of a knife, how much does this hurt? but no true wound at all, nothing to pierce that strange and empty expectation, the waking dream of being here and "Lena," I said, blunt with dreamer's courage, "what happened with Sophie?"

Crossing the room, white mug retrieved but she offered me nothing, waiting it seemed for a crack in my silence, sliver of question like a human bone but when I did not speak she shrugged, put down the mug, came to sit not beside but near enough for me to catch her scent, complicated florals and beneath the smell of her own skin, warm and infinite, infinitely hers and "Did you really," leaning closer, "come here to talk about all of that? After all this time?"

All this time: how many nights, hours spent longing, wishing only for this, the grace of the granted instant in which I could see her, talk to her, touch her by simply reaching out a hand, one hand, one finger on the landscape of that skin, flesh I had worshiped, mouth unsmiling but ready to smile, smile only for me but

behind it like a chasm, that *Peril* stare, last step off the edge unseen and

I don't want to touch her

the answer of instinct, final as gravity and in the shadow of that answer my face changed, must have because hers changed in its own answer and "So, you finally saw her," calm, without inflection; she might have been asking a stranger the time. "When? Today?"

"We had lunch."

"Fun. Did you talk about me?"

"I asked her for your number."

Line of teeth between her lips; a smile. "What a cavalier. Did you know that Sophie used to call you Mr. Concrete?"

Pain in the dream, in her aim; and anger. "Sure," I said. "Thick head, that's me. But compared to you—"

"You know, I'm not really interested in calling names."

"Well, I am. How about Jim? Remember Jim? Our upstairs neighbor? And Ed and his little brother, and Jules and Annemarie, and Saul Berensen. What about those names?"

Unperturbed: "What about them? You weren't exactly shrink wrapped when I met you, either."

"What about Sophie?"

"What *about* her? Did you come here to complain because I stole your girlfriend?" Methane voice like the feeling of vacuum, white sofa, white walls, windows washed by falling gray and in my chest a slow ignition, room in a house on fire, fire in the house of dream and "Lena," I said, "why did you take her? Why did—"

"Because she wanted to go. At least at the time. But so what? We're even now; she left me too, took her stuff and walked out—I'm sure she told you all about it—and now she's downtown, living with a—but you saw her place, right? No? Just lunch? Well take my word for it then, it's a *nice* place. A nice place for a nice girl. If all you want is nice."

"You used to want her."

"I used to want you too."

"But then," my voice kept level, straight line to follow through the fire, "then you stopped. You stopped, and you lied. To both of us. Why?"

Silence: nothing: no expression on that beautiful face, mouth I had kissed, eyes I had watched, slow as clouds at night beneath her lids; like a stranger's face, a picture in a book and "What about *Peril?*" when she still would not answer, "what about fucking Saul on screen?"

"Oh," and incredibly a smile, a real smile of real amusement as if reminded of some madcap fling. "Well, it's not Oscar material, but still. . . . Who showed you? Saul?—no, it was Ed, wasn't it? Oh don't look like that, be honest, you know you like to watch; that's your *kink.*"

Voice from the furnace, the heart of the heat and "That's not what it means," I said, "you know that's not what it—"

"No?"

"Transcending the world, remaking ourselves—you said we were special, we were—"

"Oh Jess, come on. It was just a word. You wanted a name for it and I gave you a name you liked, that's all."

"No it's not," as if I could not breathe, locked in dark imploding pressure, collision of heat with dream: burning, burning. "It's the world, you said it was the—"

"*This* is the world. My world, your world, everybody's world, it's all the same thing. Nobody's special, nobody's any different than anybody else. You get what you want or you don't, that's the only difference there is," and that stare now shifting and turning to iron, iron like mirrors, endless replication like strata in ice and "Oh, Christ, it's always the same," she said, ice to my fire, numb to my pain, "the same thing every time. You, and Sophie, and Edie and Saul, all those names you throw around and there are even more names, Jess, names you don't even *know, people* you don't know and guess what?" Head tilted like the plundered ghost of Sophie, profile sharp as sculpture made to last a thousand years. "They look different and they dress different and they fuck different, but in the end they're all the same person and they all want the same thing."

My trembling hands, sick with heat so I could not hold them, instead let them jitter, strung beasts at my side and "What," I said, "what do they want?"

She made me wait for it: then: "Just *more*. More of what they already have." Little crease of her lips, bare and sere; her real smile maybe, the one I had never seen and "Think about it," through that smile. "Think about, oh let's say Edie, poor sad Edie lost on the moors, the moors of the *soul* but she *likes* to be lost, it's what she does best. Look at what she's up to now, that little witch she goes around with, what do you think that's all about? If she really wanted to be happy she'd spend all her time making art but she doesn't seem to do much of it, does she? No. No, she doesn't.

"And Saul, poor old Saul with his poor old money—he tried to buy me but he couldn't, he tried and he tried and he *tried* but it didn't work and in the end he took his money and went away to find something else that wasn't for sale. Why do you think he collects art, anyway? Why do you think he collects *artists?*

"But you two, you and Sophie—you know I envied you, I don't believe in envy but I envied you, because you had *everything.* All those stories you told me, and Sophie sniveling about her family, she always *had* a family, she had you. And you had her." Mockery, the faintest sneer. "You don't even know what it means to be alone, you were *never* alone, either of you, *so close* but it wasn't enough: you wanted more, you wanted to be Siamese twins and when you couldn't be twins you decided to be *triplets* but that wasn't enough either. So now you're split in half and you're miserable and I'm glad you're miserable; I'm glad.

"Because you deserve it, both of you. You're so greedy you make me *sick.*"

Dry mouth, the mouth of the volcano: my pounding heart. "What about you?" my drier voice, "all the lying, you lied all the time—didn't you love us, *any* of us? Ever?"

Face turned toward me like a compass needle, the cold

north star but nothing there, *nothing*, she was gone: past my question and back to the tablelands, wastelands, self upon self in lunar ice, even the *Peril* gaze, first stare, last look subsumed by that withdrawal, the mirror closed like wings about its own cold heart

and we sat that way for what might have been a minute, sixty long seconds until at last she smiled, muscular reflex of command and control and "It's about time," she said, "for you to go. Unless you want to meet David. Do you want to meet David? Maybe you'd like him. Not to talk to—he doesn't like to talk, much—but we could find something else to do. Maybe we could go to bed together, the three of us. Maybe we could *fuck*."

Wide thin lips, that insect's gaze but "No," I said, "I'll leave you alone. All alone, that's what you want, right? More of what you already have?"

And her smile then altered, fast-glimpsed corrosion like black ice, cold rot in an empty place and I rose from the slab of the sofa, hand outstretched for the deep mahogany of the door—and on the wall beside it a grouping of strange little pictures, little Renaissance men and women fighting, cutting, hurting each other, pictures of murder in detail amazing, grotesque the knives and halberds, fingers and tiny teeth and "Lena," I said, half turning, how could anyone want to look at pictures like these? "What does David want?"

White on white on the sofa; chameleon on a plain of perfect glass.

"I told you," she said, no longer smiling. "Everybody's the same.

"Give my love to Sophie."

Outside the rain had worsened, thick blowing sheets, no chance of a cab but I didn't care, didn't try; I wanted to walk. Long, long strides, wet to the skin and shaking, skeleton ache stumbling home like a drunk to climb at once into the shower, into steam like the breath of a geyser, friendly fog to blur my gaze and yawning I could hardly stop, yawning into the towel and covers, bed a burrow where I curled and slept, still as Lazarus past any dreams at all.

I could have slept for a month, I was so tired.

It took a while just to find them: digging in drawers, shoeboxes filled with junk but there at last in a sandwich bag the rediscovered glint of green and gold: the Christmas earrings, my gift to Sophie discarded; oh, irony, we always play the best jokes on ourselves. Small there in my pocket, hard against my fingers rolling them like stones, like dice as I walked and walked: and stopped, now, in momentary frieze, there on the corner with the rest of the world: two guys in blue suits, a skinny man with a braided beard, two women, baseball cap and blonde and "—such an asshole," one of them with rolling eyes, "I mean he laughed through the whole damn *thing*—" and my own smile brief and pleased because that voice, that tone of light dissection could have been Sophie's, Sophie in the old days dishing to Lena or me and why—as the light changed, as momentum took them somewhere I would never see, river of kink in ceaseless glide—why had Lena talked to me, there at the last, why had she bothered with me at all? One final turn of the knife, parting scar to show I was not unique, to her or to the world? *She likes to push buttons*, sure, buttons that used to be mine, peculiarly mine that nameless, anxious fear of being less than special, unable even to watch that world without distance proclaimed, disclaimer from me to me but in the end, this end my difference no real difference at all: did it take such pain to teach me what at heart I should have known?

Because believing once she was our tutor, kink as art and constant the gift of self yet all she had truly given was illusion, endless gaze into the hole that—unfed except by shadows, endlessly indulged—is only and coldly the self, empty self shown emptier by each new lover, each passion like the passion before and all at last become—it had to— the dry and wizened passion of the mirror: Eros and Narcissus, me times me is me, is no one, is nothing but a mirror after all and if kink at its heart was vision, then the mirror was the symbol of waste: glass wed sullen to silver to show only what is seen before and between that sight and vision, caul and masking shine lives the question, the equation balanced tender between desire and greed: who is it for now, all that passion, to whom is it given at last? The self or the other? the mirror or the gazing eye?

Quick change artist: not what we were, but longed to be.

They all want the same thing.

I knew where I was going, now.

Long streets, blown flyers and Dumpster junk and then the turn familiar, the familiar pink and black: busy, nearly all the chairs filled with clients, radio loud with jazz lite and past its buzz the echo, voice in memories conflating

I found a place

now she's downtown, living with a—a what? roommate, lover, friend? best friend? yet that was not my question either, not what I had come at last to ask: instead a deep breath, tasting that cosmetic air, chemicals and goo and look at her, there at her station, up to her elbows in frizzy curls: gray smock and high heels, wounded and healed and "If you wear these up," brisk to the client before her, "you know it's *really* going to look like a horse's—"

and half her glance to the figure by the door, the offhand look we give a stranger clicking swift to recognition, caught gaze held full and clear and "Hi, Sophie," my smile, I couldn't help it: a smile felt in my body, felt like my beating heart and "You got a minute?" holding out my tight-closed hand, the earrings caught like gilded bones. "I want to show you—I brought you something."

No answer but her gaze on mine, Siamese dream and "Is it something good?" she asked unsmiling, hands still tangled in the seaweed curls. "Something I want?"

"I think so." Oh, Sophie. "I hope so."

Looking at her as she looked at me, in the light of the past demolished, all we had been with Lena as gone as the palace of kink, false rooms peopled with all we did not need and "Okay," said slow on an exhalation, "okay, but

277

I'm busy, it's going to be awhile. Sit down, read a magazine or something," and turning back again to the client in the chair, tuck and pin of the bundled waves, struggle with patience to transformation as on the stained terrain of the sofa I sat with my gift and my silence, vision made window, content to simply watch her and to wait.